MABBY THE SQUIRREL'S GUIDE TO FLYING:

A Modern(ish) Fable

By: Matthew G. Claybrook

Cover art:

- Dorma at Work, Mabby's First Flight and Deela's Battle Gear logo: Matthew Claybrook, all rights reserved.
- https://www.freepik.com/free-photos-vectors/background rear Background image created by Aopsan - Freepik.com
- Front twig border Fromoldbooks.com

Mabby the Squirrel's Guide to Flying:/Matthew G. Claybrook
ISBN:9781973335498

http://MatthewClaybrook.com

Dedicated to:

Teachers everywhere. In particular, the one who has taught me more than anyone; my wife, Laura.

A Brief History of Hesperia.

Welcome little ones. Are we all paying attention? No? Good.

There is something not everyone knows, but should know, about squirrels.

Incidentally, what most of the animal kingdom thinks is interesting about squirrels isn't really true at all, but what is true is even better. Squirrels are ornery. They are bombastic, audacious, and snarkier than the snarkiest of ground-dwelling hogs, or pretentious prairie digging dogs, or the floorlings who clamber about like rodents (but never call a squirrel a rodent or a rat). Such are beasts of the forest some poor souls even mistake for things wanting to be pet. It should, however, always be the rule: if you see a squirrel and want to pet it, try don't first. Squirrels, even of the type familiar to the rest of the outside world, don't like it. Even much less craving of wanton adorey-borey cuddly-wuddles are the type of squirrels in the faraway forest herein.

Fun fact: though nuts are far preferred, and though it is taboo to admit, we do eat meat, as you must know, and bite, as some find out.

In Scurridean legend, this small realm is talked about as myth among many squirrels of the world. The old Rodentian philosopher Riddian wrote the epic The Xerad, a gripping tale of two warring squirrel civilizations, and its sequel, The Hesperiana, in which a lonely, aging general seeks a path home to his beloved land where his wife, son, and pet pygmy jerboa await his intrepid return. It is believed the ancient thinker Spazzicus, who wrote On the Avoidance of Jacknuts, was from here himself.

Hesperia continued in legend when a later scholar, Flyingus Marmoter, wrote of his travels to "...a raised city, completely closed off from the world," in which a race of squirrels so intellectually and physically advanced that they could actually fly had welcomed him, shown him about, and told of many secret and nutty-buttery things. They had invited him into the inner chambers, the secret to their greatness and seclusion, the Chamber of the Great Nut, from which all squirrel life and knowledge flowed. He penned the famous quote, "For if such a nut could have been from a tree of this earthly creation, I should have to be glad to be from it, and think much more highly of my being."

From that statement, the search for the Great Nut of Knowledge has descended into our time, and some still search for it. In his tale, the trees consumed the ancient city in an epic calamity as he departed, though some argue that part of the story could have been a metaphor. Later, the Scurridean historian Toothiana Bones, often pictured with some strange tribal artifact (also known for his penchant for hat-and-whippery), wrote of such a place, but as far as what can be known, the place known to Squirreldom as Hesperia, the city in the trees, has simply always existed. Or not. All of this can be found and read as freely as you like in the Library of the Great Commons Hollow.

There is even legend that this great aeriform *res publica* was once protected by a clandestine band of warrior monks once thought to be called the Cult of Wards, or Protectorate of Aeloron, brought together when the king of Hesperia, a bloke by the name of Floemus (an otherwise unhandsome brute, divorced forty-seven and a half times) sought to banish the darkness of baseless ancient myth and oppression. They fought bravely to protect us, as it is told, with their incredible abilities and ancient arts, the source of which has faded into obscurity, like our realm.

However, you and I know this place does exist and is as real as you and me. For here we are, learning how to fly, aren't we?

We don't want to be bothered by the outside world too much. We just want to be free from the conventions of things-not-being-squirrels. Of course, who can blame us? We are so often misunderstood as lovable creatures. Here in Hesperia all is free, no one to say no to, no other kinds of beasts around to not throw nuts at. Deep in the heart of Nockshin Wood, all are guaranteed certain inalienable rights to life, liberty, and the pursuit of major airtime assuming, of course, they are squirrels.

And there, little ones, is your history. Did you get all that?

Prologue: A Day in Nockshin Wood.
Or should I say, the most mundane and ordinary of events to ever be overblown in all of the recorded history of Hesperia.

Nockshin Wood, where Hesperia lies, is an expansive forest, no smelly fog, no glass mountains or, as some mythical beasts of strange and unforestly origin refer to them, skyscrapers. None of those are to be seen anywhere. And unlike many of the forests of the world, as described by sojourning squirrels of Terrarian Mercantile, there is only one great stone river, (such as we hear of oft there are many as the bands of the horizon in other parts), the one we call Flatrock Way. It winds along parallel to the far side of the Acheron River. The river flows around the base of Nearly Mountain, upon which our lovely town resides, at the very heart of the wood, making us quite intolerable to get to. And that's just the way we like it.

Speaking of those who like to be alone, take the elders of the squirrel town way off in the woods of Nockshin Forest, who live in the 177th tree from town. They were the half-crazy Nock and blowhard Shin, who happened to be exceptional squirrels in their own peculiar right, notwithstanding many, many faults. They spent all their days watching us from above, if not from concern, I assure you for entertainment.

They overlook the town from high above, in a tree some ways away, chomping away on those delicious roasted walnuts from Ballo's farm. Nock and Shin were yorey old dogs. It is thought they don't learn new tricks nor dig new holes, nor do they really ever retire or fly. So they just look silly most of the time, sitting around chewing on walnuts. Occasionally they throw one down, just to see what it hit from their squashed flat, swaying in the not quite whipping wind of Nearly Mountain's somewhat northern countenance. It was from this quaint and rickety loft the two of them watched, waiting for some new thing, or some old thing to pick back up. They would certainly have whatever to do about it when it showed.

One day, long ago, and before any of us were born, there was a shadow beneath the overbrush, at the edge of town, in a completely normal place very few noticed at all.

Nock most often just sat on a rope swing on the side porch, holding his arms up and grumbling, just as he had done that very day. He sat bowlegged and his bushy tail flopped from side to side, making the shape of a curly-q. A squirrely-q, if you will. His straw hat and stringy beard complemented a once fine houndstooth topcoat that had been worn to what I'll just call… twangy. Many of his teeth had been knocked out in the rigors of youth, perhaps in the throes of some flight school chase. So he often spoke in short sentences and had to close his shriveled lips in an "o" fashion around his remaining huge teeth. It has never been pretty.

Shin sat inside on his keister and patiently pondered the walls, and differed little in his demeanor from day to day, as it is often said minds of some sort think alike. He wore a long brown duster and chewed constantly on his own maxilla. He sat inside because Nock, incidentally, was outside.

On the day in question, Nock happened to be in a particular state of bunk. So he decided to test his aim on bees, and peering out far below, the search for a fresh victim took his eyes to the distance.

"Look, Shin, Morgart! One o'clock!" Down far below, Nock spotted the great black cat lurking about, looking for a chance to hop on some poor unsuspecting squirrel who happened to be so unfortunate as enough to get caught on the ground too far away from home. But she didn't dare venture too close to the old great redwoods of proprietary Hesperia, not back then, lest she suffer the pain of a knock or two on the head from a crisply toasted walnut traveling at terminal velocity. They really hurt after falling from that sort of distance. "Lemme git her!" He laughed. "He-he, watch, now!" Nock wound up his overly skinny arm for a pitch.

"Naw!" Shin pushed him out of the way. Nock dropped his walnut on the floor of the old rickety squirrel shack, which rocked and teetered with nearly every movement. "Let me git 'er! You can't hit nothin' no more!"

"I sure got better aim than you, y' old nutball! Gimme here!" The two scuffled, and the walnut was knocked and bobbed about in the air above the old squirrel-squall, till finally Nock flicked Shin on the eye socket. "Aaayow!" Shin cried out, and Nock seized the moment to deftly snatch the walnut in mid-tumble and flick it down. They both stopped stock-still and watched.

The walnut whistled down unceremoniously, wavering in turbulence as it ventured closer to its unsuspecting target. Then, against all odds, it blew open. Walnut bits and cat-limbs flew wildly about, and the bewildered feline slumped in pain with its head under its paws.

"MeowwwWWW!" The visibly dottied confused cat looked about, stupefied, into the trees and spotted the two mad squirrels struggling to maintain their innards as they rolled about in laughter.

"Yihoo! Good one. Ha!" Nock exclaimed.

"I'll teach ya tuh come 'round here!"

"Yeah, you know better, girlie!" They laughed at the cat slinking off, still shaking its throbbing head, "Git out! You oughta know better by now! Be gone! Bye!" They motioned for her to scurry off.

Up on top, Nock turned away, still laughing to himself. "Now you mess with the bull, he-he, you get the horn. Guh!" Suddenly he caught a hard old right to the gut from Shin.

"That's for flickin' mah eyeball." Shin shook his finger once and placed it back into the crook of his folded arm.

"You little..." Nock said, in mid-grumble, giving way to various and sundry mumbly-expletives fraught with fisticuffs.

They meant no real harm, but good intentions, unlike Nock's walnuts, often miss their mark. Not even the surliest of the aged could have fully divined from the ether what was to transpire that day, heralded by the presence of aforementioned strange and evil black cat, Morgart Wingless. They are often considered bad luck to have around, after all. Bad things just tend to happen when they appear.

However, omens are often translated into general misfortune in the course of events. The most unfortunate things occur when the most evil of us are also the most readily dismissed, as is too often true. Nock and Shin could perhaps have done more than act like idiots at this most serious omen, but who would raise an unnecessary ruckus about town, scaring others without sufficient cause? One would have to be crazy. Probably the type to go about with signs, crying cat, preaching the end of things, or to go off to sit in a tree all day and arbitrarily throw things and stare at the sun, against all the advice of modern wisdom. For now, let us simply mark here this moment was when something dark began to stir and for all their smacking around, they paid absolutely no attention to it.

What was paid no attention to, mind you, was but a shadow in the woods, not the cat out in the open. Cats, after all, are thought to be diabolical because they are mean, not because they are clever. The shadow disappeared into the woods and the day slinked slowly off, and all but the harvest moon lazed about sleepily, unawares, drifting into the breaking night.

Part 1. Bolly's Folly

The Winglier's Chant:

The bough approaches. Walk don't run. Fear and love are often one.

Wait for goodness, wait for light, see the one within take flight.

Find the place where Heaven lies; Heaven is your passion's prize.

Top of your head, tip of your toe, around the corner and away we go!

Chapter 1: On the Importance of Not Getting Sidetracked on the Way to School

Long before the unnoticed incident in the dark, a peppy pup named Dorma Dabby became the greatest squirrel ever to wield… a thimble. As it is said, there were and still are no other tailors in Hesperia. Well, we all end up finding our own unique destiny, right? But before he was a great tailor, he was a flying ace. Absolutely top-class.

Dorma lived in a modest but fine home as a child at 102 3rd Ct. Bucktooth Branch, by the Bramblery, which was the kind of street many would say was either "close enough," or "hopefully not." His father never paid for new things, as he believed it to be a waste, so they had just enough, and the Dabby home was filled with homespuns and paw-me-downs. Still he was happy.

He had spent most of his pre-flight days pulling on his flaps to get them to grow, and jumping off of undesirably high things. He, like all others meaning to be at the tops of their classes, had not been able to wait for instruction to get to work on his dream. There was a new teacher there the year Dorma entered. Someone had heard out and about the old marm had gone off to service, whatever that meant. The new teacher was the world's first female flight instructor, and she had quite a presence. She was as tall and as stocky as any male squirrel, and had a meaty face. Her name was Ms. Alfreda Elena Schmelena Gersteinbach Padduck, and round town it was circulated that she was unequivocally single. An unmarried squirrelette? What was happening to the world? The parents were quite worried. Perhaps she was a dowager. Or a spinster even! How terrible. Still others said, before schooling began that year, she was descended from a primitive tribe of giant red-haired squirrels from the deepest delves and squirrel-digs of the Amazon, her name being distinctly South American, of course. Also, according to the rumors, which are always true, much of her red hair had fallen out when she was exiled from her clan (for aggravated aerial assault, obviously), due to the sudden lack of Brazil nuts. Those things cause red hair, you know.

Dorma's parents warned him before they departed from their home that the character of this new marm was definitely still in question. He should stay away from the influences of this "Kitter," a term often used to describe female squirrels who seemed to believe that the faculties of the female squirrel, particularly the young female squirrel, should for some odd affect be proposed to be of comparable contribution to that of the stronger gender. "It's a great deal of work for them," they said. "Why not just let the natural order of things be so. Now, go to school and learn to fly right and proper." Dorma was not to make waves. "Do not demand attention, but only focus on what this deviant sort of lady has to say about flying. She was clearly quite good at that, at least enough to instruct a child." He had heard his father say such things before. 'A rich mayor is bad for morale, poor squirrels make bad decisions.' 'Boys should chase girls; girls should run from boys.' His father seemed to be firm that there was a single way to do everything, but Dorma never could get it straight out of him. He wondered about all this, and came to the conclusion that he would learn what they meant in school.

Dorma was given this speech as he stood outside his home being adjusted and prepped by his mother and father for the journey off to school and to life. He hitched his belt, which had been handed down from his brother Derry. Derry had also given him material, which he had been able to fashion into pants with pins and yarn. His appearance was that of an odd pile of walking sticks stuffed into a sack of flour, with several other sacks inside, and a pair of eyes and ears on top. In the middle was the meandering sash that would have been a belt if it weren't five or six times the size of Dorma's waist.

He considered his home as his parents chattered back and forth about teachers and other squirrels' children.

Someday, I'll get to the other side of town, he thought. *I'm going to get out of here and become the best.*

He left, still chewing on the unassailable doctrine of his parents and some tough pankeybread. It was a meal indigenous to the poor, made of the cheapest things, "pignuts, and whatever." The kits he knew treated it like a delicacy, (but we all know it's "bread for stealing.") He was lighthearted despite the best efforts of his parents. They waved goodbye long after he had gone round the corner, and his father petted his mother to comfort the empty nest in her heart. "There, there, sweetie-pumpkin."

"My little Dormydore-puppypoo!" she wailed. "Leaving me, and what am I supposed to do?"

"It's all right, honeysticks. We've still got each other." He forced a laugh, trying to choke a tiny log down his throat. "Haven't we? And hey, a little more so now, right? Know what I mean?" He jabbed her in her ticklish spot.

She looked at him and broke into sobs. He looked out at the empty, coldening morning.

It was the first day of school. Dorma, looking like a wad of clothing, walked from the Bramblery, where it was said that children cannot adequately stretch their wings due to cramped living conditions. His family didn't talk about it, but Dorma knew everyone else did. Parents of the Bramble-kits often did not accompany their children. Mothers and fathers in poor families were often at work too soon for that. Work, a practice the wealthy were sure would be cured by a little sense, nonetheless continued. Those from the Bramblery had to walk past the upper district, if they were walking and, of course, no one expected them not to be. Dorma padded along Rammerie Way, a main bough leading directly from paths to most of the neighborhoods, but not so close to the center of town that one could not see the Hundred Trees.

The sight was majestic. There were rows upon rows of the most complex and exquisitely conceived structures—majestic spires and rotundas. They no doubt concealed the most beautiful topiaries, reading rooms, and gymnasiums for those who could afford to learn to fly from private tutors. Many of the houses had enough space for outside living areas, for this was the part of Hesperia where the well- to- do lived. The Hundred Trees were an equal inverse in wealth per household to the Brambleries, as it was in size and population density, every other house possessing possessed its own expansive bough, with a bath or private park. Dorma, who slept upon his siblings, or was slept upon, did not know it, but that day was the first of many he would spend lavishing his mind upon the fantasies of the rich and famous.

Dorma knew only of a life in which all must be shared, including the gravity drip-dew bath for instance, which some stench-ridden squirrel had hurriedly assembled to get some form of hygiene from the dew outside the Tanglewall, affixing a branch that drained into the center of the communal area. This had been done years ago, and the shoddy construction had been maintained, so that more got hurt than wet, and no one got clean. Not in the Bramblery. Nevertheless, there was an even poorer part of town; a place they called Promise's End, and so Dorma could still think himself lucky in his childhood. He walked contentedly, dreaming of his future life in the well-plumbed and squeaky life of the top-class squirrel he dreamt he would make of himself one day.

Hesperia was a massive realm. Those neighborhoods, the Brambleries, made up most of the povertized areas, and the Collig, Hillsworth, and Tadwick Boughs, an area they called the Hundred Trees, comprised the rich side of town life. The Hundred Trees had been named after rich squirrels who were thus obviously worth naming boughs after. Though great, it only made up a small portion of the realm, which was constructed like a great wooden bowl. From the outside it looked like an impermeable mass of canopy that extended below to some degree, and the greater branches that could not be made to twist and sprout into the wall were trimmed and/or hollowed and named after heroes and finely built upon.

There were several districts of town, the military, business, and middle class residential districts, places for meetings and sporting events, worship and study, romance and civic functions. It was home. Dorma looked about that morning, contemplating what life had in store, and watched the hurry of life begin around him, with all the dimensions in the round world he knew from far below and far above.

It was all about to change.

At that moment he spied a strange thing indeed. It was a kit leaving her home. Isn't that how things usually change up, yes? But it was the way in which she left her home that bothered him, for she did not exit through the front door like an honest squirrel, nor did she glide squirrelishly as one should, but she shimmied out of a window from the second floor, scrambled, and then fell, toppling clumsily to the deck of her bough, nearly falling off entirely. She managed to struggle to her feet, stayed still for a moment, and looked around as if to see if anyone had seen that happen. Then she sprang up and darted off toward the path Dorma was traveling. Dorma saw all this from afar, and she didn't seem to notice him in her hurry, or at least did not act like it.

As this transpired, Dorma noticed three things. One, she was most exceedingly pretty, from the top of her head to the tips of her toes. She had gorgeous, deep, brown eyes and teeth as white as snow. She greeted an unexpected passerby with a, "Hello sir, very well, how do you do today? Oh no, I haven't seen my parents yet this morning, I'm just out for a walk...Well, thank you. I will tell them, goodbye. Oh no, I'm fine, I just love to be outside in the mornings, with nature and all." Dorma realized he had stopped to watch, stunned by her amicableness, as she rolled her eyes and laughed with the apparent neighbor. "It's nice this time of day." She said, oddly to be saying so while she quietly pulled at her coat. She laughed the fakest laugh he had ever heard in his short life. Dorma however, thought it was awfully cold. "Thank you, you too. Have a good day, sir. Bye."

The second thing he noticed was that she could not use her wings to save her own life. She plodded carefully from bough to bough, staying on the safest path. She yet seemed to be altogether curious acting about it, not to mention having almost died from falling from an easily negotiable height. Number three, he surmised from her timing and trajectory that she was on her way to school. He found himself sneaking like she was, but not to get to school. He wanted to see why she was sneaking. Then, as he rounded a tree trunk known to adults as the Lesser Glimmer Commons Hollow, about halfway on his journey, he lost sight of her. He looked around momentarily.

Just as he was about to give up and go on his way, something clapped him about the ears, bopped him on the head, stunned his shoulders to the nerves with two surgically placed pinches, tactically disabling him, and dragged him blindly, deafly, and helplessly into a darkened nook. The dark, obviously dangerous, and incredibly powerful figure clapped a paw over his mouth just as he was about to protest with, "No, no, please don't kill me! It's not even the first day of school. I've got to be rich—" which came out much like, "Mumm. Mummummum, MumMUM mmm mumuh mumumum. Muhumuhumuhum—" with his voice breaking here and there.

His assailant seemed curious about what this mildly attractive weakling, wearing an arrangement of drapery, must be trying to say in his total inability to defend himself. It removed the paw from Dorma's mouth to hear him pitifully cry, "—Before I die."

As the ringing in his head began to clear, and he started to be able make sense with his head, he realized it was her! He flapped his brain about for a bit to try to think of something eloquent to say, but all that came out was a rather idiotic-sounding, "I'm, Do...Dorma."

She didn't know what to make of that. "Dodorma," she blankly repeated.

He took a breath, trying to smile.

"Shush. I'm not going to kill you, that's illegal. Dorma is a girl's name and a terrible one."

He began to protest, but she shoved him into the wall harder, so he winced in fear.

He kept trying to make a good first impression. He tried to straighten up. “Well, wh- uh. What’s—” he replied nervously. He meant to ask her name, but only offended her more it seemed. She shoved him into the wall again and held him there.

“I’ll do the asking of questions,” she said.

“That was forceful,” he thought. Okay. But she’s so pretty. A piece of bark dug hard into the part of his back that no one can reach and makes one very nervous to have it dug into. He winced as if he were joyful, dying, and losing his intelligence all at the same time.

“Why are you following me?” she demanded.

“Why, I mean, I wasn’t, well, not exact— Well, I guess… I was. I don’t know. You know, no reason, really…Shouldn’t you be with your...”

“Shut up!”

“Okay.”

“What do you know about me?”

“That your eyes are like the finest summer day, that your hair shimmers like fairies in the moonlight, that your smile is like a breeze after the rain, and your soft breath on my heart is like the gentlest stirring of the dust of dreams,” he thought. But instead he said, “Wh-ah. N-Nothing.”

“Nothing?” she pried. “Nothing at all? Do you even know my name?”

He shook his head. He would have shaken anything if she’d asked and stopped stabbing him with a tree. She picked up on something or other and un-pawed him, still staring him directly in the eye with that “fire from below” type of gaze that girls used to convey the imminence of suffering. It was a skill.

“Well. Of course you don’t. Do you know anything?” she asked.

He thought for a moment and, just to be safe, he shook his head again.

“So, you’re just following me around because you think I’m pretty.”

“No, it’s … I just,” he stammered.

"So I'm not pretty? I'm ugly to you? Are you sick? Are you fascinated by those who aren't as good as you and feel like you have to stalk them to make them feel better? Sicko?"

"No, I don't think that." He halfheartedly laughed. He felt the heat in his chest as the dust of dreams caught to the burning flames of failure. "Of course you're pretty," he said. "Who would ever think you're no... no good?"

"Questions!" she reminded him with a gritted jaw and a growl that was actually more adorable than terrifying. "You never saw me. You don't know me. I don't know you. Understand? Or do I have to gut you?" Her words seemed to crack at the register of his question.

He nodded. Then he thought about it and shook his head. Then he thought about it again and just held his head down.

"From now on, you just leave me alone. I have to go to class," she growled.

Wow.

He saw something in her eyes when she got in his face, like pure hate. She was so angry, but not at him against all odds; rather at something else, it seemed. Or someone.

Then two things rang through his mind as she bounded off, leaving him still glued by an invisible force to the tree she no longer held him to. As his glands kindly informed his brain that he could move again, he thought excitedly, "She could be in my class!" of all things. And then fearfully, and then excitedly again. Yes, very exciting.

Then, to the strain of a sudden rapid influx of daydreams of sitting behind her, flying in front of her, and falling directly for her, he remembered that he was going to have to go to class.

Then immediately before broke into a dead bolt to catch up, and he realized class was something she was running to, if he had deduced everything correctly. Running very prettily, but running… because squirrels who hurry are late.

Rammerie's Flight School, the beginning place of squirrelly dreams, the school for elementary flying excellence, founded by someone or other who had done some great thing he was sure he would learn all about bounced into view. That was about the time he finally started to catch up, and saw the violent but precious tail of his assailant disappear into the only open door of the large structure. Several seconds later, the door slammed shut. “Oh no,” Dorma thought. That meant classes had started. He slowed briefly to a canter, considering turning around. Then he ran even faster to the door after the image of his father flashed into his mind.

Chapter 2: Identity Crisis

He walked in timidly. But his hopes of remaining unseen were dashed to dust by a booming voice. All the chattering voices beneath it fell dread silent. "What is your name, spiny, insular cave rat?"

Dorma was very much thrown off by this. He felt the back of his brain tingle at the inescapable force of this embarrassment.

"I. H-H-uh." Everyone he had not met yet laughed. He stared into the furious face of Ms. Alfreda Elena Gersteinbach, something-or-other, Padduck. Her face was red. She resembled the Devil, whatever the Devil looked like.

"Just the response expected of a flightless, mammalian rodent that cannot fly. Are you indeed a *jawed* vertebrate, o' nameless one who comes from the bottom of the world, and enters when the Great Nut alone devises, to grace us with his loquacity and not his name?"

He paused.

"Name!"

"Dorma."

"Sit!" and at that he sprinted to a seat, sorry he had ever met a girl. It had not even been the start of class and he was losing focus on his dream of top-classness. For sham and for shame.

"However! For the rest of you! You had better learn your place! And listen to what I have to teach you! If you obey and study! You! Will!

Be! Successful!... In LIFE!" And at this she shot a glance at Dorma. "But! If you slag off and come to class like it matters not! You will fail!" She had walked over to the door of the schoolhouse and, with the last word, she slammed it shut, sending a ripple of fright through the class, and bringing the structural integrity of the schoolhouse into question.

Great. Dorma groaned to himself. I've come here to sharpen my sense of flying and lose my sense of hearing, and I'm at the *bottom* of the class.

'But just wait, you all,' thought Dorma. 'Just wait till you see me fly.'

Then the red-faced teacher started to call the roll. She must have already introduced herself. No matter, he knew who she was.

She called the names out one by one. "All right now, raise your paws when I call your name! Lora!" As she called the roll, each student stood up, on her orders, and answered some "get to know me" question. "Bora! Harry! Bary!" the process continued. "Burly! I won't have you coming to class with that hair. Get it proper. That is all. Sit." Burly was one of only two that did not get a question. The class snickered as he was not sure of his sin. A classmate pointed to the top of his head, upon which an obnoxious leaf of hair was poking up, so that Ms. Padduck must have thought it was a joke. The poor soul kept his paw on his head for the remainder of the day. "Wurly! Bolly!" The teacher asked Bolly nothing and said nothing—she only nodded, and Bolly seemed to have no objection to that.

"Dolly!" The bright-eyed, very skinny young kit stood up and looked very nervous indeed. She had very light-colored hair that had been extensively powdered, and her face was covered with talc. Hers was clearly the only spanking new dress in the room, bought just for the occasion of the first day of school. Rich folk celebrate anything if you let them. "I understand you are Dolly of the Tadwick family, of Tadwick Angle," Ms. Padduck said.

"Oh, how did you know?" replied the little one, suddenly forgetting her place. "Have you met them?"

"I do believe your father is one of the few in this realm to have traveled beyond the borders of this forest," Ms. Padduck replied. The class bristled for reasons Dorma knew not.

"Oh, so like, did you meet him in, um, like, Brazil, or something?" she said, too excited to think clearly.

At that Ms. Padduck stood still and glared into the skinny one's skull. Dolly slowly sat down, and the class relaxed its quiet angst. She played no further role in the story.

There was silence for a moment.

"Young lady!" Ms. Padduck eyed the girl who had tried to kill Dorma up and down. "I don't see a name for you, young lady! Here on this roll!" she said in her normal voice, which was yelling.

The violent girl of his dreams stood up.

"What's your name?" asked Ms Padduck.

"My name is Debby."

"Debby, Debby what?"

"I'm Debby Quarles."

"Quarles. Well, I've never heard of you." Ms. Padduck said. "Lovely. Miss, you're not on the roll."

"I'm sorry, it must have been an oversight." She used that stupefied tone that Dorma had heard her use with strangers. "My parents couldn't make it to registration, but we talked and you told me to have the papers ready when I got here, remember? You told me to bring the enrollment papers?" She produced a roll of documents.

Ms. Padduck was unnervingly silent, which was for her to be silent at all.

"Don't you remember talking to me?" Debby said. "I have the papers."

Ms. Padduck suddenly snapped to. "I would never have said such a thing! Give me those! These are important papers, not for your eyes to see! Why, what kind of place do you think this is, little one!?" She rudely jerked the papers out of Debby's paw, yelling. Then she took half a look at the documents and slammed them on her desk. "I'll not have such mischief and disturbance in my classroom! Now sit down right there and think about what you've done, and don't cause me any trouble again!" She huffed.

Debby plopped in her seat promptly.

"Now…" Ms. Padduck continued. "Dorma!"

He froze. She knew who he was. She was surely about to reveal to everyone where he was from. Ms. Padduck paused for a moment, then asked the worst thing imaginable. "Why were you late?"

Dorma gulped. 'Nope. Worse.'

"I don't suppose it had anything to do with the fact that this youngling over here came bounding and panting into this classroom only moments before you did?"

Panting. The agenda was clear. The class ooed, then there was a shudder of giggles.

Debby turned her head slowly, and he felt a kind of heat across his forehead.

"Well, not really, I was just…" he started. He never got anywhere.

Ms. Padduck turned abruptly to Debby and asked, "I don't suppose you two know each other?"

"No, Ms. Padduck, not at all. We're fine. I'm fine," Debby said, attempting to deflect attention from herself.

"Fine? I didn't ask you if you were dandy up top, I asked you if you two knew each other." She looked at both of them and, at this point, the class was at the brims. "What's going on here? Do we need to go to my office?" she asked.

"Really, everything is fine. There's nothing to worry about, Ms. Padduck. Nothing at all."

She looked surprised. "There isn't anything you want to tell me?" She looked at Debby.

Debby just shook her head and looked at her desk.

"All right," Ms. Padduck said, "Dorma, my office, now."

He got up grudgingly and followed her, trying to think of anything else but that very moment. He could hear the class snickering as he walked behind her.

As soon as the door banged shut, she was on him. "Well, what do you have to say for yourself?"

Dorma was, at this moment, about as confused as a whirligig in a stationery shop.

"I know exactly what you're up to. I know you're one of those terrible little boys from the bad side of town, and I won't have you spoiling my classroom with your antics!" She held her finger up to his nose and said, "You leave that poor girl alone. I'd better not catch you bullying her, or I will see to it you will never make it out of this classroom alive, much less graduated."

"But you don't understand." Dorma was nearly crying.

"Am I clear?"

He slumped. "Yes, Ms. Padduck." He returned to his desk quietly.

She returned to the front of the class and calmed herself back to her normal state of hysteria.

"Which brings me to my next point. There is to be! No! Fraternization! Whatsoever! Between classmates, hear?" She went to her desk and pulled out a stick about arm's length, then explained that it was called a date stick, to be used in the manner described in the student handbook, which all were encouraged to take home and read. "But suffice to say, for the sake of all within hearing, the date stick is to be kept between persons of mutual interest, with one holding one end like so and the other person holding the other end. At! All! Times! No...er...*Conjugation!...(shudder)*...No exceptions!" She closed the visual demonstration by leaving the stick with Debby. Wonderful.

So between his classmates' struggle to stifle their laughter and Dorma's embarrassment, if there was ever a time a squirrel wished to melt into the floor, this was that time.

Then she finally took her attention off Dorma, to his relief, and continued calling the roll. "Now, where was I?" She tried hard to remember who was next. "Hal? Is it?"

Hal, or Hallo Ballo, stood up straight and raised his paw in a gung-ho salute.

"Yesiree-ma'am-my-name-is-Hallo-and-I's-a-hallo-va-good-student-and-I'm-gon'-be-the-best-y'ev'r-seen-tha's-right-just-yew-wait-ma'am…"

Ms. Padduck sat down mid-run-on sentence, appearing weary. "Yes. Well, whatever you're saying I'm sure it's wonderful, I'm sure. Thank you, sit down. Down. *Down,* down. Yes."

Hal sat down.

The rest of the class was boring and uneventful except when, toward the end of the day, Dorma quietly raised his paw, thinking perhaps Ms. Padduck needed a reminder that they had come to school to fly, which would be done outside.

Ms. Padduck impatiently reminded him that today was orientation day. "One does not go about soaring through the clouds without learning first where the ground is, and it is quite unfortunate when a subgrade winglier forgets how to avoid it." Thus, orientation was the most important day of all, she explained, and he would do perfectly well to be quiet and listen.

Someone, whom Dorma did not look to see, had raised a paw. Ms Padduck nodded, annoyed. "Mizz Padduck, ma'am, my daddy told me that girls aren't supposed to be teaching all this crazy, super-soaring stuff. I mean, what's all these old dead guys got to do with me running my daddy's bakery? It just seems like a bit much, especially learning from someone who's… you know… not as…"

"Yew wrong. YEW WRONG!!" The whole class turned around as Hal jumped up unexpectedly.

Ms. Padduck looked down at the floor, and said very quietly, "This is neither the time nor place for that discussion. Sit down."

Not long after that, the bell dinged and school was out. The dream was over, and Dorma didn't want to go back. He was one of the few students not laughing on the way out the door. Ms. Padduck, who failed to reach the door in time to have a word with Debby, was not laughing either. Nor was Debby, who was out in a flash. Only one other student was not laughing and piping up with comments like "See you tomorrow, lovernuts," "Just wait, Dorma and Debby Dabby's drabby babbies," "Ooh, I love you, baby, wanna go kissy, and marry me, and dress up like a couch together?"

"Chitter-chatter," and "Hee hee, he's going to be alone forever," and making out noises and kissy faces and what not. That was the squirrel apparently named Bolly. He, who never said a thing, hadn't laughed or looked at anyone or anything but Debby all day, as Dorma had just realized. Dorma suddenly felt very agitated. He waited until everyone was gone, so no one could unexpectedly kill him. Then he slowly got up in a black haze, and slumped homeward.

On the way home he spied something. He happened to look wistfully toward Debby's house, and there she was. For all the hurrying she had done, she was standing still, looking up at the window she had crawled—well, dangled and fallen—out of. Then she hopped up. She seemed to be attempting to go back the way she had come out. The frill on her dress was caught on the picket fence. Squirrels don't do well going over fences. The Great Wise Nut just didn't want those things climbed; who knew why.

Dorma called out to Debby as she was attempting to lift herself off the boughway, unable to pull herself up with the strength of her arms. Her feet were slipping and scratching against the slats. She was clearly not as put together as she had been in the morning.

"Hello?" Dorma said, approaching warily.

She paused for a moment but did not look back.

After trying again and failing to climb the high fence, she put her head down.

Dorma approached softly. "Are you all right? Can I help you? Debby—"

The beautiful devil whirled around, with a strange color in her eyes, and screamed. "Gaaaah!" The date stick was hauled back, in strike position, and Dorma dodged backward, toppling over. "I told you, you don't *know me.*"

"Oh! No, please I don't want to die!" he whimpered. "Please, not the stick..."

"Thanks a lot." She turned back around.

"Thanks?!" He was now completely lost. "Well, you're welcome, I suppose, but for what? What did I do?" He continued to question her as it gave him an excuse to keep looking at her.

"You completely humiliated me, made me almost late to class! Now I'm going to be the center of attention, and everyone will make fun of me forever because of your little crush on me! You ruined my life in only one single day! Now everyone will know!"

"I mean, I would hardly call it a crush and even, well, okay," Dorma thought.

"What? I don't know what you mean," he said. He hardly felt he had done all that.

Then she looked at him with a desperation he had thus far missed. "Can't you figure anything out on your own? Look at me. Do I have to spell it out for you?"

He felt he could guess, but he didn't want to risk being wrong at this moment. He had deduced she may be having trouble learning to fly, but that was what school was for, wasn't it? She tried to climb again, to get away from Dorma, and fell angrily to the ground. Dorma was shocked to see her sideclasps come unbuttoned, upon impact, and her wings fall out of her dress. They were stupendously, magnificently huge. There was no way she could fly. He tried to help her up.

She threw off his arm. "Well." She gestured. "Does that help? Have you figured it out, then?"

"You're…" He stopped.

"Yes, I'm an infirm. A helpless invalid. Now will you leave me alone?" She glared at him and rolled to help herself to her feet.

That hadn't been what he was going to say at all. In fact, he had stopped because it didn't seem appropriate to say, "You're even more beautiful than I had ever imagined, my beautiful-as-the-morning, lovey peaches mum mum mum mum smoochy smack..."

"Look, I'd like to help you—" he said instead.

"No, you can't!" she interrupted.

"Awfully negative, this one," Dorma thought. "Look," he said. "You've got to learn how to fly right and proper, everyone does. It might take a little extra work but…"

"What do you know?! No one can help me. I don't want your help anyway. I just want…" At this she began to sob. "I just want you to leave me alone."

"I…" he stammered. "I can think of something…"

"Just go! Please." She was completely crying now. Dorma turned to leave, broken.

"Goodbye, you most likely won't ever see me again."

Dorma said nothing and left. Alone.

On the way, as he headed out of the neighborhood, he saw a movement out of the corner of his eye. It was that squirrel named Bolly. He darted out of view. Dorma wondered how much he had seen.

Dorma walked into his home to find a surprise party to celebrate surviving (if that's what one would call it) his first day of flight school. He felt ashamed after all the times he had told his family he was going to be the best. There were all kinds of questions, like "Did you show them what you're made of out there?" He had to answer, "No, we didn't fly today, but tomorrow we will, maybe. No, I didn't do very well at all. Well, it was basically every possible nightmare, actually. I'm so sorry, but I was late to school, and I had hoped you wouldn't be too disappointed in me. I love you too, Dad. No, I actually…I met a girl. No, she... No. Stop it. It just wasn't like that. She didn't like me. Stop it. We just met on the way to school. That's all. That's why I was late. I'm sorry, but may I go to bed now? Stop it." And he slumped as he walked up to his room, hiding the bitterness in his face, but his tail drooped and told all. When he could no longer contain it, he screamed into his pillow, where no one could hear it. And he lay awake that night, pacing back and forth in his mind. How could he get the sadness out of that poor kit's eyes? How could he give her hope, show her that he cared?

It should be noted that, that first day, Dorma had sat behind Debby, being late and last to class, because students actually sit in the front row first. Something having to do with flying being exciting or some such excuse. He had been able to see what Debby had showed Ms. Padduck. She may have shown no outward sign of distress, like any marm worth her salt, but for your own knowledge, my dears, she had been truly shaken. There really wasn't anything on those papers, not anything official anyway. It was only a pile of blank scraps with a scrawled note in hurried letters.

Ms. Padduck hadn't understood Debby's plight. All she knew was that poor Debby was terribly embarrassed. Everything she had done to humiliate her scary pursuer had only made the poor kit worse off. Still the desperate words, "Please help me. You are the only one who can," and the sight of those quiet tears hanging for dear life, to fall or to fly from her eyes on Ms. Padduck's next words, haunted her. She knew *why* she had become a flight instructor, but this didn't seem to fit with the prescribed way of things. She considered herself well trained. This wasn't what it was supposed to look like. What was that little girl's painful secret? Was it worse than she had thought?

Late that night, Dorma came out of the kids' room to Mother and Father, who were reading. "Mum?" he asked timidly, "do you know how to sew?"

"Why, yes dear, why do you ask?"

"Like can you do it really well?"

"Well, I suppose I'm all right. After all, those paw-me-downs seem to be holding up. Why, do you have a tear somewhere?"

"No." He felt odd but energized. "Could you show me how? I would like to learn to sew."

And you can imagine how they must have felt about *that*.

Chapter 3: Infirm

There is a wide and diverse array of gentlesquirrels for one to meet in life. Dorma had been introduced to many of them in the classroom. There was Bolly, who had been conspicuously quiet during the incident on the first day of school and hadn't had a chance to say anything to Dorma since. Dorma had always left extra early for school. Bolly didn't know he did that to be sure he didn't get surprise-attacked from behind again.

He had already met Debby.

There was poor Hal. They called him poor Hal because he was really poor. He was a farmer's kid. Dorma didn't talk much to him. His physique, however, was clearly well suited and Dorma had thought it best to make friends with him early as he would be the competition. Hal was very genial and high fived anyone who put up a paw. So far Dorma had been the only one to high-five Hal.

The class bell rang. Another boring day of not flying. So far, they had been discussing the history of flying, the mechanics of squirrel anatomy, and the theory of aerodynamics. No one knew how long ago the squirrels of Hesperia had taken to the air. He learned there were believers in the religion of "Hesperianity." They thought that squirrels were eventually supposed to become like birds and that the first flying squirrel in recorded Scurridean history, Scurristus, after whom the art is named, taught his followers that the world was waiting for the Age of Scurriea, when various unmentionable things would happen to anyone who couldn't fly, or something like that. There were even those who had adopted the notion that the world was being set up to witness the rise of the Over-Squirrel, and that squirrels had descended from lower rodentia. This was the reason for the obvious disgust adults had for all those lesser. This was called Squirrelism and it is taught that, if one is to remain rational and objective, one must first assume these things to be true. Of that camp, there were those who believed either that squirrels were destined to transcend even the skies themselves, and there were others who idealized that such things required acceleration. They believed for some reason that was bad, but not the other thing, and still further the things before that were good, and the thing before that was even better, even though some said for good reason it was worse. Dorma believed things get better with time, for time makes silly things make sense. It was most amazing to Dorma that there were squirrels who sat around thinking about this type of thing, and they still found nuts to eat. Second most amazing was how powerful fear could be in keeping a kid awake and in his seat. He wanted to show what he had been practicing.

The time between the first day of school and today had been interesting to say the least. Poor Hal had fallen completely out of social favor, and Debby had skyrocketed upward. She knew all the right answers, while Dorma knew all the wrong ones. This pecking order came to be a way of speculating about who would do well on First Practicum and who would go home a failure. Despite Debby's warning to Dorma, he had continued to see her, and he wondered why she would have said such a thing, but he never asked. However, since she did show up at school, he thought he would drop by her window, after dark, and show her what he had learned from his mother. She didn't seem to mind much not telling her parents where she was going off to late at night. With much coaxing the experiment had presumably worked. He and Debby were both optimistic.

Thus, things had slowly become much better between him and Debby. She treated him normally outside of school, and today she had actually forgotten to give him the Red Stare of Dying Inside, which she gave him each day during roll call. Whenever she gave him The Stare, he knew. It was not necessary to see it, only to know that, whenever it was being administered, it had the effect of a sort of needing to go to the bathroom, only so much worse.

This morning there was the roll call. He answered, and everyone snickered just as they had on the first day.

Ms. Padduck had arranged the class names so she could remember them. "Lora! Bora! Harry! Bary! Burly! Wurly! Bolly! Dolly! Debby! Dorma!...unh...Hal!"

It was just that fast. And if students failed to raise their paws at the appropriate time, they received demerits for attendance that day, which they took home with their normal daily grades. No one was allowed to do homework. There was an obligatory crying room located outside. No one was allowed outside.

Every squirrel quickly discovered that he or she was naturally skilled at some parts of the daily activities and others were harder. Students quickly learned where they would need help and what they could handle alone. Dorma had not realized there would be schoolwork and had spent all his spare moments fantasizing foolishly about flying, rather than dreaming about studying about flying. "Fool," he thought.

He spent most of his hours dreaming about the moment he would be led, with his classmates, to the first physical test, in which all would be revealed. For he was sucking rotten lemons at everything else.

The day had come.

"All right class," Ms. Padduck said in a perky voice. She was making her way to the door. "You have understood our format so far. Today we will finish our initial class time, and we are going to begin our standard process. Henceforth and ergo, you shall all begin to be evaluated. From this point forward you must pay careful attention to my every word. Do not make a move outside, do not breathe unless I say how, do not jump until I say how high, and do not even dare leave a ledge unauthorized unless you want to end up on the ground floor, food for cockspurs and wild-cats. Understand?"

Outside!

Debby and Dorma shot one another a nervous look. Their secret project was about to be put to the test. Dorma had worked quite hard for the past few nights, despite his parents' wondering where he was. They had not overtly objected, since he was obviously seeing the girl he had met, except about his safety. Dorma had been, up to this point, still in the dark about the meaning of Debby's form of saying goodbye, for every night she waited until he was on his way out and said, "Goodbye, I'll most likely never see you again."

The class resounded with a "yes, Mizz Padduck" that clattered about the ceiling of the lecture room. She eyed the class suspiciously for some reason. Despite his racing heart at the sound of these words, Dorma could never be sure, but it seemed like she held a special kind of annoyance with the class. It just didn't seem like she could possibly be so irritable all the time as she was whenever he ever saw her.

It was time.

"All right, class, stand.... UP!" she commanded. "Get into a single-file line!"

They scurried out of their desks.

"Now, up, up, up, kits and pups! All in a line, low to high. Shortest to tallest, leave your notebooks, numpet snacks, feathers, and lucky charms. You will only need yourselves, and any extra weight can only work against you, and you do not need to be carried by the wiles of fortune, any more than excessive inertia!" Ms. Padduck said.

"But Missus, ma'am," Hal gently protested, "my Paw asked me to carry this so's he could see me real easy when I'm flyin'." He held up a little piece of cloth with a strange crest on it. "'S my grandpaw's. 'S a soldier in the ranks, he always said."

"For the purposes of your safety! You shall carry no stick or banner, no charm or prize in this school! I am aware how things were done before. But listen to me, all of you." They all went from shuffling to quiet. "I am not a facilitator of tradition! You are here—"

"But Missus Ma'am!" Hal interrupted. "This protects our family! Daddy said so!"

"The only thing..." Ms. Padduck calmed herself. "The only thing protecting anyone here is a few good squirrels! Who learned to fly right, not with one arm dragging behind for Daddy's sake! Your father is a farmer and will pass it on if you do not listen to me! And I! Have no time for backwoods superstition!"

A look came over Hallo Ballo's face as he stood in line to do what everyone had spent their entire little years preparing for. She had crossed the line.

A quiver came over his lips and a shortness of breath, and his eyes grew thin. "You… gon' make me break a promise to my Paw," he more stated than asked.

"If you wish to continue, then yes."

"It's truh-dition!"

"Tradition divorced from context is idolatry!" she bellowed.

He straightened up. "I love farmin' and I love my daddy, Missus Ma'am. I don't love you." And with that he walked out. The class drew a breath and Lora and Bora, at the front of the line, for some reason began to cry. A look of confusion and relief crept over the line of faces.

"Does anyone else wish to fail?" Ms. Padduck asked loudly before Hal had even left the schoolhouse. He stopped for a moment, and as he looked at the doorway a look came over his face as if he had been clawed in the back. Then he ran off and was not seen again in that place.

In the weight of the silence, someone leaned over and whispered, "I wish Ekkhorn was still here."

"Who! Said! That?!" Ms. Padduck shouted, at a level which was loud for even her. "Anyone who says that name in my presence will be immediately expelled. Never mention that name. Ever! Clear?!" Dorma guessed Ekkhorn had to be the last marm, and whatever bad blood was between them, he would have to wait to hear about it when grownups chose to speak of it.

"Yes Mizz Padduck!" the class resounded.

"Let's go!"

The platform for First Practicum was hidden just outside the classroom, between the Tanglewall and the schoolhouse. The two raised platforms were identical opposites, with stairs leading up to each one from the same side. At the far right and left sides was a wall, preventing anyone from getting a running start or proceeding with any inertia beyond a simple, full contact, full-stop landing. Anyone doing anything other than a dead start and a dead stop, the shortest of flights and the simplest of landings, would find much difficulty. There was a height of about two squirrels from the takeoff edge to the floor, and the same with the landing square. It was about fourteen pads from the takeoff to landing platform, and even though an adult squirrel was about five to six pads tall from nub to nib, this was as simple as a hop for anyone with gliders. But for a rat or ground squirrel, it was impossible.

"Now," said Ms. Padduck, "this is Phase One. Unless you complete Phase One, you cannot move any further in the Practicum. The good news is! It is one, little...hop." She instructed Lora to perform the jump and, before anyone could gasp in doubt, she was across. "Very soon," Ms. Padduck continued, "you will think nothing of this sort of thing, any more than walking or eating. There you are. This, children, is why our fine race cannot be spoken of like pigs, if you understand." Whatever that meant caused her a great deal of internal chuckling.

The rest of the class hurried in line to the platform, with their newfound confidence in themselves, and enthusiastically made the simple hop. Then they jostled down to hop again, and all were soon laughing and squealing in glee, while Ms. Padduck resumed frowning near the back.

Then there were three. Dorma, Debby, and Bolly had waited at the bottom. Ms. Padduck ordered Dorma to the stand.

Though he didn't appear, at first, to be very useful in his manner of gliding, Dorma did well. Since there was no one better practiced, he knew this was his chance, and he took it with all he had. He sprinted up to the line. And so it was that he was noticed as the best at something by the most beautiful young kit that he had ever seen. He never felt totally put together, and she was always completely flawless in appearance. Her hair was gloriously luminescent, and his was uncombed. Her dress was always stylish and of fine make; he often appeared to be wearing a set of drapes belted to a feedbag. She was always ready for a portrait, and he was barefoot. She had never seen him fly in the times he had come to see her and work on her wings. So he didn't understand what made him so attractive to her but, when he stepped off the platform, his eyes drifted over the class and locked onto hers, and she smiled. As she would often describe it to fellows in later seasons, it was as though one were watching a flower fly out of the mouth of a toad. He could fly with such poise that, to him, it seemed only a natural thing. He landed with an "ahh" as gentle as a breath.

He stepped off the last step and sauntered over to Debby, who had just picked her jaw off the floor and was definitely not good at hiding it. She crossed her arms.

"So. Crazy about me much?" he said.

"No," she said flatly.

"No?"

"No, your underwear was showing." She clicked her tongue.

"But, what…" He almost moved to look. He had thought he felt a draft.

"Yeah, like the whole time...And you fly like a girl."

Speechless.

It was Bolly's turn. He approached the stand quietly, yet with a scowl and the posture of the determined conqueror. He grunted as he leapt, performed a double-derriaire, triple-split somersault with a 540 twist. This got him halfway across, and he opened his wings and clapped them together, sending him into a sextuple gainer at twice the altitude he had reached the first time. Of course he landed, feet together, with such force that it shook the boards.

"Thank you Mr. Beeley, that was physically impossible, and we shall all try very hard to be impressed." He smiled.

Somebody whispered, "show off" as he descended with the same countenance he'd had before takeoff.

"Last one. Debby, let's go."

Then Debby gingerly stepped up to the stairs and started to go. Then she stopped and looked back. She began to shake.

"You'll be fine," Dorma said under his breath. He hadn't noticed that Bolly was standing next to him. Bolly stared at him with confusion, then looked at Debby with intensity, but said nothing.

Debby turned away from the stairs and unbuttoned the clasps, revealing her perfectly shaped, absolutely normal-looking wings.

"What?" Bolly whispered. "No!" He bounded over to Debby, tackled her, dragged her away from the platform, and wrestled her down. Ms. Padduck screamed, as did half of the children. Dorma, stunned, saw that he was about to remove the stitches. Then everyone would know the secret! He charged hard and checked Bolly in the ribs, but Bolly's plowing physique was sturdier than Dorma's. He resorted to using his long arms as leverage to pry Bolly's paws away from Debby, who was out of her wits. "Get off of me! Stop!" she shouted. Bolly got a finger in one stitch and yanked, causing Debby to yelp in pain, and she began to bleed.

"The truth!" Bolly yelled.

"Enough!" The booming voice of Ms. Padduck had been said to frighten bears. Everyone stopped just as Ms. Padduck plucked up Bolly and Dorma, like crickets, and carried them outside.

Dorma was completely bewildered and watched as Bolly and Ms. Padduck argued. "What do you think you're doing!?" she screamed.

"It's wrong, you've got to tell her, it can't be this way!" he said,

"Youngrel, what is wrong with anything going on here except beating up classmates?"

He pointed to Debby. "Her wings! Look at them, they're all wrong."

"I am looking and I can see that they are just fine."

"No! She's…" He paused. "You've got to tell her."

Just at that moment, a voice interrupted. "Tell her what?"

Everyone stopped and, while no one was looking, Debby's expression at the sight of her parents had changed from surprise and pain to absolute terror.

"Ms. Padduck, I'll have a word with you," said the lanky, yet authoritative, male squirrel with an even angrier wife at his shoulder.

Only mumblings were heard between the two of them. The action had completely died, and no one was looking at the children anymore. They were all wondering what was going on between the adults. Not even Dorma had noticed that Debby, bleeding as she was, had slipped away and stepped up onto the platform, where she called out, “Father!” and everyone’s gaze traveled to her voice. “I can, Father.”

“Young kitty, you come down this instant. Come down right now, come down. Come *down. Now!”* He pointed toward the ground.

“All right, Father, I will,” Debby said.

Dorma could now understand where she had learned to smile as she sometimes did. She quietly turned, closed her eyes, and opened her arms, and she buckled slightly and winced. The bloody spot where the stitching had come loose was exposed. “She can’t open her wings,” Dorma thought, and he instantly moved to catch her if she fell.

“I’ll be here, don’t worry, just go,” Dorma said. He realized he had exposed himself as an accomplice to whatever game she was playing with her parents.

“What are you doing?” her father yelled. He began to fight his way to the front, through the entryway crowded with children. “How do you know her? You’re that little rat stalker kid, aren’t you? Stay away from my daught—”

Ms. Padduck said, “Forgive me but I thought you were having a private word with me. Now if you have a problem with one of my students, I will handle it appropriately, but you will not accuse anyone here without cause or proof.”

“Fine, that boy there, that little…he has been luring my daughter to this place, filling her head with thoughts of…of whatever, I don’t know, but against my wishes she has been led to lie to me and steal away from our home. Look, she is going to get hurt!” Mr. Corles said.

“So let me get this in order, you are angry at this youngster here because you say he has influenced her to learn to fly?” Ms. Padduck asked. “And that’s wrong?”

“No, it’s not like that, she...” He could no longer hold back the family secret. “She can’t fly, she’s… She’s an infirm.” Everyone gasped.

"I'm sorry, what?" Ms. Padduck was completely taken aback, for Dorma's disguise had worked well enough. "Infirm? In what way?"

Debby held up her arms and winced until the pain was no longer a shock, and tears gathered.

"What have you done to her? Move out of my way!" He was almost through the crowd, and she could just outstretch her wings, though she was fully weeping now from the pain. "Daddy, watch me." Just as her father reached the base of the platform to grab her, she leapt into the air with a yelp.

The children could hear the tearing of flesh. She went fine at first, then she wobbled and teetered. "Come on," Dorma said. Apparently, although of all the children knew what kind of trouble she was going to be in, no one understood what was going on at all. They had kept the secret well.

Her hind legs began to dip, and pretty soon she was no longer gliding but falling at an angle, and then just falling. Dorma shouted, "Reach!" and she reached, despite her yelps of pain. She busted nearly all of the stitches grasping the edge of the platform, and she dug her nails in as her body swung downward, slamming hard against the understructure. Nearly all of the remaining stitches burst. They held the excess flesh, folded underneath where none would see it under normal circumstances due to Dorma's newly found skill with a needle. Debby dangled from the edge, unable to pull herself up, weeping.

"Infirm," said someone unidentifiable. Ms. Padduck looked around, but to no avail. Very soon everyone was saying, "Infirm. Infirm! She's an infirm!" Debby watched as her life crumbled before her at the sound of her most familiar nickname.

"Get her down!" Mr. Quarles shoved Dorma out of the way.

"No!" she cried. "No! I can do it again." Mr. Quarles snatched her down from her death grip. "I can make it, please! Please!"

Mr. Quarles set his daughter on the ground and put his heavy paw on the back of her neck, as if she might try to fly away any moment and someone might see. "This is an outrage. You brought my daughter here to make a mockery of my family. And you nearly got her killed. I will see to it that you never teach here again."

Just then Debby threw off her father's paw and ran to Dorma. "Thank you. Thank you for trying." She wiped one more tear.

Dorma didn't know what to say.

"Goodbye, I'll most likely never see you again."

"Debby! Come!"

She turned to go home, never again to be acknowledged by society.

Then Ms. Padduck spoke up. "Mr. Quarles, do calm yourself." Her voice was louder than her normal pitch, which the rest of us would consider at the top of our lungs. "I'm not sure if you're aware, but according to paragraphs B-15 through B-17 of the Rammerie Flight Training Instructor's Rubric, it is stated that one absolutely must come to a full stop and make contact with the specified platform in order to pass First Practicum and that there is, under no circumstance concerning this standard, to be circumstance. Are you familiar with this rule, Mr. Quarles?"

"Yes, it, what?" he said. "What does that mean?"

"Precisely," she answered. "According to the context of grammar, and if you had paid attention in school you would perhaps have remembered for the sake of interpreting this rule, that a negative followed by a positive remains a negative. Correct?" She waited. "Correct, now, then, it were not as if one were to say that there is absolutely under no chestnuts to be chestnuts, for instance. This is to say, obviously, that given the state of the prescribed condition of chestnut-ness, nothing merely arguably chestnuttey can be allowed, so clearly it is to be interpreted that if a thing is arguably allowable, then it cannot be argued that its allowableness is allowed to be argued, and therefore it must be allowed. So this begs the question, dear Mr. Quarles. Is it arguable that Debby here came to a full stop and made contact with the platform, yes or no?" She waited again.

"Chest...nuts?" He raised an eyebrow.

"The answer is yes," she said. "And if it is arguable, then it is arguably so, and if it is arguably so then it is so. Therefore, your daughter may or may not be arguably an infirm, sir, but if she is she's quite a fine one, for no infirm passes this test!" A cheer went up from the crowd. "Not *this* one!"

"You are seriously going to allow this?" Mr. Quarles replied, frustrated for some reason we still don't know.

"Would you like me to assign you a tutor?" All the kits and pups yelped in laughter at this one, and Mr. Quarles and his wife stormed out, struggling to keep their noses up.

From that point on Debby and Dorma were inseparable. They studied principles of aerodynamics and made dresses together for Debby. Which was quite an accomplishment, since the poor kit's parents rather disapproved. "He's not fit for you," they said. "You'll grow out of him." But she didn't; in fact, he saved her, at least according to her. And he eventually grew into his clothes.

Chapter 4: On the Value of Being Late

Months later…

He met with her briefly, before the race, where no one could see them.

"Hi." His eyes lit up when he saw her.

"Hi," she said and just looked at him and smiled quietly.

"I brought you something." He pulled a rose out of his vest.

"A rose for me?" she exclaimed. "Really?" She grabbed and smelled it. "Wait," she said. "Did you just pluck this? Like, from the wild?"

"Umm, well," he stuttered.

"Dorma, there are still thorns on this." She began plucking them off and started giggling as he tried to explain.

"I, well, I was running a little late. I'm sorry."

"You're sorry? I mean, I was about to ask if you were okay. It's beautiful." She loved gifts. She smiled and hugged him, much to the dismay of his perforated chest. He wondered if he had not punctured a lung. Love is pain, he told himself. She kissed him on the lips.

He nearly doubled back in surprise, but ultimately remained still, for elation and a strange fear overtook him.

"Our first kiss," she said as she let go of his lips and wrapped her arms around him.

"I've wanted to say for some time…" Dorma started, and Debby looked up into his eyes. "I love you. Always have—agh!" She fell into his chest and hugged him tightly, and he found there were a few thorns still in his pocket.

"(Gasp) Are you okay? What happened?"

"Oh, he he, it's nothing, no matter," he said as he found the remaining culprits. She laughed at him, clapping a paw over her mouth. Her tail shook with the sadistic humor he had come to expect from her, and he began to laugh, genuinely this time.

"I meant it though." He got serious again. "I love you."

She was still chuckling.

"Look, can a guy just have his moment?" he said.

"I'm sorry," she said, stifling herself, and pulled him in again. "I love you too." The sensation of her nestling into his chest made his heart beat ever so fast.

"We had better go," she without lifting her head. "We'll be late."

"Hey," he called to her as she turned to go. "Good luck."

"I don't need luck, I've got you." And with that she was off, with him not far behind.

"You're my dream," he sighed to himself.

They made their way to the starting line, and everyone was already there.

"You two. Late again," Ms. Padduck said. "This…pattern." She waved her paw in their general direction. "Everything here is wrong. Am I to be worried about this?" She leaned in close to Dorma. "Am I going to have to come...*find you?"*

They both shook their heads.

"Welcome all to the 451st Annual Racing Extravaganza! Here at Munger's Top Raceway, the most treacherous course in Rammerie's School of Flying, we shall see the best of the best, flying and trying! No worries, it's all in good fun as our contestants compete for top of class. Let's cheer them on!"

This was the announcement heard at the grandstand. Big Race Day. Graduation from Rammerie's. No one had been late. Dorma looked around the starting point of Munger's Raceway, used only for the day of graduation. Up in the sky, it was a beautiful almond morning. On days like this the birds above the designated squirrel airspace could be heard calling happily with their magnanimous good-day chatter. Only today it would be overpowered by the distant cheering in the grandstands by the finish tower, much higher than the starting line. It was not too cold to stretch. They were all in a line. Dorma looked at his competition on either side, all classmates he had come to know. "Sorry," he thought, "no holding back today." Today is mine.

While the spokes-squirrel informed the audience, Ms. Padduck turned to the class. "Class, your attention please. This is your final evaluation. You have heard what the announcer has said, and I have to inform you, do not listen to any of it. He is not your instructor and more importantly he is an idiot." The class erupted with laughter. "Listen to me. Now that we have all come to know each other, for the next few minutes of your lives, you need to forget everything, and... EVERYONE that you have learned in our time together. What has become ingrained in you will carry you, and what you have not mastered will work against you. And so will everyone here."

She looked over at the distant grandstands, which had just erupted in laughter at something the announcer had said. Then she ushered everyone in closer. "You will hear in life, rat eat rat, gerbil eat gerbil, vole eat vole, every rodent for himself. The problem with rats is, they're all stupid. You, all of you, need each other, and the world needs you. But for right now..." They leaned in. "Right now you better get out there and make me look very, very good. Or I will kill you!" She was speaking in an unusually low tone, which was the most frightening of all possible things.

"As you all know; the rules are simple." The announcer's words wafted over as Ms. Padduck got them all in line and ready to start. "No time limit, no biting or fighting, no leaving the arena until you cross the line or forfeit! All you have to do to graduate is cross the line." He made it sound so simple to the classmates looking toward the voice, but they knew no one could just glide to the finish line. They would have to use their surroundings and conserve all the momentum they could. Dorma quickly realized this course was not the same as the other courses. This one was about finding a hero. They could make their way from the low branches to the high ones and coast down, but if one wanted, nay, needed to win absolutely, it would require the impossible: literal, sustained flight. That's fine. I can just beat these kids at their own game.

As they waited in position for the signal, he took Debby's paw. She was shaking fiercely, though her face reflected more determination than fear. She felt his paw on hers and immediately shot him a smile. "A smile," Dorma thought. "She smiles at me now." His heart was already flying.

"All right, feet straight. Form, no matter what. Hear?" Dorma said, smiling.

"Okay, don't worry about me," Debby said.

"Just feel the wind. Imagine it carrying you, okay? Did you check your, uh, you know? Things?" he said below the noise. He had learned to do more than a simple baste stitch since the incident at First Practicum, and her wings now inconspicuously sported a cased bind. He had incorporated the fur into a fusible interface, giving her more control with less effort. He had quietly wondered if he should patent the design, but when he tried it on himself the improvement was marginal and the itch was murder. It was the best he could come up with and, although she still could not take off, once she was in the air she could make her way now that there were no extra folds to ruin the necessary unity. "It'll have to do," he thought.

"Okay, I got it. *Okay.*"

"And just yell if you need anything and I'll be right here, don't worry."

"Dorma, stop," she said. "I'm fine, okay?"

"Just..." He gazed into her eyes, which were glowing with that old familiar magic.

Ms. Padduck seemed to be waiting for something. She held the flag into the air. She closed her eyes and let it down.

"There they go," the announcer cried into the sunrise, through a cone that amplified his voice.

The little ones started pouring from the ledge. No one knew how Dorma's paw could have provided support to Debby's takeoff. That was to be left to speculation by the judges. No rules, after all.

Dorma and Debby made sure to stay close to the middle at first. Their eyes locked. "I'm stable, go." She smiled gratefully. "Go, silly!" And he was off.

He closed his eyes for a moment. "Concentrate, Dorma," he heard himself say, and he felt the wind on his cheeks, felt every sensation of turbulence, cocked his paws, and shifted his feet. An obstacle wooshed by, and Dorma had the presence of mind to avoid it. A few others were still worried about themselves, and they were hindered by obstacles. "Form," he thought, "that's the mistake, but everyone else thinks you keep one thing going and you can beat the wind. There is no race, except against oneself."

On he went, checking himself inch by inch, darting through trees, conserving every bit, and letting instinct carry him past one opponent, past Lora, then Burly. Each one glanced at him in surprise, losing more time because of their concern. While everyone had been taught, for the sake of posterity, techniques for fighting or coping with wind velocity, he had realized wind was fuel, not an obstacle. So he had pointed his nose toward pockets or eddies, rather than a stable, predictable trajectory. Fluidity allowed him to take a longer route and yet come to his destination more quickly than the most practiced winglier.

Down went Barry and Dolly. Dorma just needed to pass Bolly and he would be in first. He looked around, the wind combing back his cheeks. He was strangely absent. Dorma knew then that it was over, and he listened to the ever-growing cheers from the grandstands. "Too easy," he thought, "but I suppose it's lonely at the top." He drove ahead like lightning, barely touching off of each obstacle and precipice, and the crowd cheered more and more loudly till he could hear them above the roar in his ears. They were in an uproar when Dorma, having come from behind, won by a wind-slide. His father clapped him on the back at the finish platform. It *was* too easy. Everyone else started to arrive some time later, as Dorma watched and regained his breath.

"Congratulations, son!" his father said. "I'm so proud of you."

"I won." Dorma smiled. "I won, and it seemed like nothing at all."

"No, son, that's what it feels like to struggle before the race. It's like I told you, the only one you have to beat is yourself." His father laughed.

"I don't know, Dad. Something's not right." They walked away from the ledge where Dorma was waiting. He had thought perhaps he had just missed Debby, but then he saw something sway, far out, in the midst of the course, and his fur went up in terror.

And now all would be known. Dorma realized at once that two completely horrific things were happening in his absence from Debby's side. Debby had fallen tragically behind, which the announcer had taken the liberty of telling the audience. Just ahead of Debby, there was a groaning sound and a flock of birds rushed upward in the sunshine, darting this way and that. Someone screamed. Something snapped, and the groan became louder. Dorma realized helplessly that a bough, nay, a tree was coming down where Debby needed to go. Everyone else was far ahead. Simple, just get her. He glanced upward to see if anything was going to fall as he planned his course. Dark things were zipping out of sight high above. "No time, just go," he thought.

He jumped and everyone gasped, and he realized this was not a test or a course run. This was real.

"Oh no, folks, it looks like someone is still on the course!" said the impeccably observant announcer.

Debby looked around to see where the sound was coming from. She'd had to let Dorma go even though, with one look at the course, she knew she could not make it. He had believed in her too much. She had to stick to the outer wall, curving around the track in a great French curve, the longest possible route, reserved for those utilizing the no-time-limit rule in order to just pass.

How she wished he were here, holding her up and taking her away from that frightful noise. She gambled and scrambled from branch to branch, hopping and nearly toppling as she went with her stiff, well-meant wings, kicking herself for every mean thing she had said about him. "I've got to get through, one way or another, for him," she thought. She didn't know how she was going to negotiate it, but she had to see him win instead of holding him back like she always did.

She was about halfway through now, and no doubt everyone was waiting on her. She jumped and caught the next branch, sighed, and shimmied, and she felt an odd lurch in her stomach. She saw a gap in the Tanglewall and was frightened to hear a voice, nearby, in the dark shadows beyond that border. “Take them out.”

“What?” She was busily climbing up one tangle in the outer wall so that she could glide down to the next. “Who’s there?”

“Take out the binds,” a voice said. “You can *fly.”*

How could anyone know about the binds? She worried she had not kept it secret and climbed on.

Something wobbled. Then she realized the tree, or whatever was talking to her, was getting farther away. She nearly lost her grip and her stomach sank with the terrifying realization that the world was not off its hinges; the very tree she clung to was unstable. She scrambled about for a bit. There was nowhere to jump with her disability. She froze, ready to scream, and prepared to helplessly watch herself plunge into oblivion.

Then something blurry whirled around from the other side. “Come on!” it shouted.

“Dorma!”

He came down hard on the surface of the tree. How did he get there so fast?

He jerked her out of harm’s way. Just as she latched onto the bough ahead, Dorma felt a rush of wind pulling him down. The tree, which was a city block, hammered downward and crashed through the bottom level, taking out countless homes before it left a gaping hole below, revealing the forest floor. The city was exposed. Who knew what intruders could come crashing through that gaping hole at any moment? They gazed at the destruction and held each other, Debby shaking in his arms. Everything had fallen quiet. Then Dorma looked at the grandstand and saw everyone looking at them. He took Debby's paw and guided her to the next precipice and stayed with her until she reached the finish line to the sound of cheers, screams, and bells.

They were met immediately with a few guffaws and congratulations, while others went to deal with the destruction.

"I don't believe it," Debby's father said, emerging from the hubbub. "So was this your little plan all along? You use my daughter to make yourself look so great, and keep her down, just so you can win a race? You cost my daughter everything, and now she's last place because of your little antics out there. I bet anything this was all you!" Dorma had hoped, for a second, that this would help Debby's parents see him in a new light, but the old dog stared at him with narrow eyes. How had he not just seen all of that? "I'll get to the bottom of this," Mr. Quarles said, "but I already know, when I do, I'll find you there. And I'll make sure you never touch my daughter again. Mr. Hero. Sure. A lowlife cheat." He took Debby by the shoulders to lead her home. "Once a lowlife, always a lowlife," he said into Debby's ear as they walked away.

Just as they disappeared into the crowd, Dorma's father found him and hoisted him onto his shoulders. Dorma was paraded about the grandstands, with much ado and celebration, as the 450th year's champion of Rammerie's Race Day. He was given the gold-plated trophy with a silly looking squirrel on the top, and slowly the crowd began to disperse. His heart was several stories below.

When things had settled down, so that Dorma could think again, he noticed out of the corner of his eye that Debby had returned. She looked at him and smiled. He tried not to faint with joy and relief. Dorma sheepishly held up his new trophy. She met him and looked into his eyes and touched his paw. "This is what happiness must feel like," he thought.

"You're late," she joked and chuckled, and she immediately put her paws to her face and thrust herself onto Dorma's shoulder. "This poor thing has all the luck," he thought.

She pulled her head out of the crook of his neck and looked at him dreamily. "I thought I was going to die." She sobbed. "I didn't know what to do, and I thought, I felt so helpless and alone, and then…" She let out a heave of sobs. "I thought… I thought I was never going to see you again. That you would never be there for me, and help me up…"

"Shh, don't say that, it's okay," He wrapped his arms tightly around her. "It's okay. I'll always be here."

"Always..."

Chapter 5: The Wedding

The day had come entirely too soon. They met behind Brimbole Branch, some ways off from the busy parts, at the Hightower Chapel.

Dorma sat outside on a white bench, swimming in his head. He thought about the days and years to come, doubting that such dreams could come true. His coat shone, and no one knew he had made it himself, having learned a great deal of skill from the nearly constant work of patching up his bride-to-be. He thought about all the relationships of youth, and how they seemed to so often fail. It's really just because we stop paying attention and forget—the simple things, he thought. The simple things.

And he rose when he saw her, the waning rays of afternoon light shining on her face, and his heart flew as her blond cheeks plumped and sparkled in a smile. A smile at him.

"I'm glad you came." He stumbled over his words.

"Of course I came." She bopped him on the head.

It was the eve of the Honeycomb Festival, when the first junepies would be in town, and when the billybubs and lantern bugs were all around at dusk, and gold was the mum.

Likewise, her gown reflected the old Hesperian tradition of fashioning one's nuptials after the seasons. Naturally the time of the year at which pups start their adult lives is the best time for a shindig, there being plenty of young cadets with time on their paws for a ball. Thus, many young kits' dresses were gold, with lockets and jewels to make them look like the very sun, and at this particular dusk, under the rising honeycomb harvest moon, this was particularly true.

"You look so beautiful, just radiant," he said. "I'm sorry. I was so worried you might not show, you know me." He took her paw and smiled.

"I've managed to hang around this long haven't I?" Her excitement was decanting.

"That's fair,." he said, though she hated it when he said it., but his heart was unstilled. "How are they holding up?" He stooped to make sure her new bindings wouldn't make problems for the ritual, and to change the subject.

"They're all right, I think," she said. "Okay. Okay, they're fine, don't worry." She laughed as he chased her around in a cute little circle then spun her around and caught her in a hug. He had figured out early on she loved to be worried over and, as it happened, this was his special skill. She fake protested once more and he gave her a long, unexpected kiss, and they stared into each other's eyes.

"Are you sad?" she asked as he broke the moment.

"No. Pensive." He paused.

"What's wrong?"

He took a deep breath, revealing the tremble in his heart. "Well, you know, I think I might just miss this. I mean, I got to really know you this way. Through our little secret. And now I'm going to lose that. I don't know if I'm ready."

"Hey. You got me." She took his face in her paws, grabbed his tie, and pulled him down to whisper in his ear.

"Yes? What? Got you… Oh. And… Oh! What was that again?" The points of his ears were making circles. "Oh! That's disgusting!"

She let go with a cheesy grin.

"Debby, I'm offended," he said.

"No you're not," she said.

And to that he had no response.

With that they went off, and they arrived separately and at different times, to be sure no one suspected them of having met. For in those days that kind of thing was often grounds for retraction of blessing. But to them and the world, that day it was their eyes that shone as if they had never been apart.

At the ceremony, everyone gathered without many objections. It was presided over by Squire Walley, chaplain of the Great Nut, an exceptionally pretty blonde who, thankfully, spent more time in his rectory than hearing of secret meetings and was happy to invite them into his "well-bred flock" of matrimony.

When squirrels get married, it takes everyone. There is a movable stage upon which the couple stands and, when they say "I Do," they are hoisted up and the whole town joins paws. Slowly at first they move till the wind takes wing, and up, up, up they go to the sky, embracing in a circular, windborne dance of golden rapture.

She stared at him, tearing up. "Everyone said you were no good for me. They said you would need a lot of fixing. But you and I know I needed a lot of fixing, and when I thought no one could, or no one would ever care to, you saw me. You fixed me, and I love you so much for it. I always will."

"I know what everyone is thinking. I am a skinny nub, I am a stick, light as a feather, but the truth is I may not look it, but I am actually quite arrogant, you know, on the inside." Everyone groaned. "You put me in my place. Everyone thinks of you and me so differently than how we know each other." He choked up. "I want you to know that you know the real me, and I don't want that to ever change. I don't want to know anyone like I know you and like you know me. Only you know where my heart belongs." Dorma's voice dropped, and he fought to pick it back up again. "And it belongs with you."

"By the power vested in me by the Great Wise Nut of Nuts, Giver of Life and Aid, by whom all things are possible, the one who shows us the way to fly, up to the sky, whose great spherical nature, and that is to say without beginning and end, whose deliciousness goes far beyond the physical perception, far beyond its salty golden shell. Its dry roasted goodness, with a little bit of honey, goes *infinitely beyond...* "

"Get on with it, old boy! You're heavy!" said someone in the crowd. Everyone moaned in agreement.

"Er, uh...I now pronounce you squirrel and wife."

Everyone cheered, even Ms. Padduck. Even the extraordinarily good-looking, blond Squire Walley cheered momentarily, but he was met with the oddest, most unexplainable, despotic devil glare from Ms. Padduck, and he immediately swallowed and stared at the deck. There were the rumors. And at that, the slow procession in the sky began to release its outermost formation, and with a "ready all, one, two, three," began to descend in a single file post spiral, sending the very center spinning faster and faster until the last one broke free and the couple were sent soaring into the clouds above, sending up cheers from the forest below. It is said that if a newlywed couple does not break the clouds and get their once-in-a-lifetime glimpse of the great white heavenly forest realm above, they can be broken. But they must never forget the moment of absolute joy they are meant to give to one another, like that moment in the sky.

In that moment it occurred to him that perhaps there was something to that old legend about a Great Wise Nut up in the sky somewhere, with all understanding. Heaven is to be understood, and understand.

And in that moment, after looking together at destiny, she looked at him and kissed him in the gliding rays of the setting sun.

Chapter 6: Birth Pains

Flight school was not for the faint of heart. In fact, some young pups trained for it vigorously before they even began, some as early as the crib. Perhaps some parents are more eager than their children.

So it's true that parents and children alike live for the opportunities for life and prosperity provided by success in flight school. Some parents have even been known to brag, "My little kit is the fastest flier I've ever seen. Why, we were trying to get him to bed last night, and I tell you we just could not catch him! It was the darndest thing!" and "My little Doree was such a bother last night, why, I went to give her a kiss goodnight, and just as I was about to close my eyes, she shot out of the bed and started flying around the room so fast I could hardly see her! It was like lightning! Well, I think I'm just going to have to enter her into the Great Races even though she hasn't seen a day in school, just to calm my nerves." And all that sort of "woe is me, whatever shall I do with my excellent, excellent child" kind of silliness parents always do.

But woe it is when some poor unfortunate is found to have a "defect." Despair is cast. Grief and sorrow abound if a pup has a mangled foot or a wing that is too short or too big. The future of that poor young one can be all but decided then and there. It is an increasing debate among some Scurridaean historians whether entire squirrel societies have crumbled under the burden that these types of souls effect. Some have even embraced rather unfortunate and final solutions to the "inferiority question." If the Great Nut were so good, wouldn't it give everyone the same kind of fortune? How can we go on as a competitive race in a dangerous world while allowing these kinds of "defects?"

Being right and proper, after all, started at the beginning.

Sad to say, such was the case the day little Mabby was born.

"Dorma, what are you doing?" It was someone from his lovely wife's side of the family. Dorma sat furiously stitching a corset and fighting off a sweat.

"What? If you're here for a stitch, get in line please," he shouted from the back, not hearing who it was.

"Dorma!" It was Aunt Lemmy, poking her head out from behind a curtain. She was rosy. There is a class of squirrel that lives as if to say, "Well, *I am* rich, but that's okay." The poor lad whose casing was blown out the sides shuddered in fear of those who would soon know he was actually quite fat. He took the occasional break from holding his arms up to reach for his cake, which if one doesn't know is entirely improper in a clothing shop. "You've got to close up!" she said. She looked at the poor helpless furry-limpet type of creature Dorma was throwing a coat over.

"I should think so! Get out of here, can't you see I'm working!" he exclaimed.

"I guess I did come for a stitch!" she said, laughing.

"You're being obnoxious. This is a place of business, more importantly *my* business, so will you please stop ruining my good name...*dear boy would you please put the pastry down, you're getting crumbs everywhere.*"

"Nonsense, old boy, it's all right."

"Well, no, it's not all right, all right?" His voice went up an octave. "It's not your—"

"Oh for goodness *sakes,* boy, you're having a baby."

Dorma stabbed himself with the needle. "No, I'm fine. And no, he's not. He's a customer. Look, would you just *get out?"*

"You are, aren't you?"

"Aren't I."

"Aren't you."

"*You* are?"

"I'm not?"

"*You're* not."

"Your wife is having a baby."

"I *don't* have a baby."

"Your wife is *having* one."

"One...baby."

"She is."

"Right."

"Isn't she, yes. The one she's been pregnant with."

"Pregnant."

"Pregnant, yes for some time now."

"Isn't she?"

"Yes, she is, no? Almost like it's time she was done soon."

"Done. With. A baby."

Lemmy was, at this point, dearly exasperated. "Dorma, you need to go to the hospital."

"B-because m-my baby."

"Right."

"Is having a wife."

"Go! Hurry."

Dorma stood up. He was starting to understand.

"Baby. My baby is having a wife. I mean...my baby is having a wife. I mean my baby is having a wife. I mean…" She slapped him. He ran out of the room. The poor pup groaned, for the needle he was still holding was attached to a string, which was still attached to the girdle, which was still attached to the poor thing's ribs, and Larkspur's yarn is very strong. Dorma popped back and looked about for a place to put the needle. He said he was sorry and put it in the pup's shoulder.

"I've got to go, dear youngrel, I'm very sorry to inconvenience you but my *baby is having a wife!*" He darted out.

Lemmy and the small pup both sighed and shook their tails, for different reasons. "His baby is having a wife." The pup reached for his cake.

The next second Dorma was running madly through town, awkwardly stopping for a moment to buy flowers. Wiping his forehead and shaking, he fumbled with some other things. He darted off and then immediately returned.

Dorma's mind was in a whirlwind at the harvester's market to purchase a few wares, such as an odd number of towels. He snatched up a few things he found that rattle and squeak. He passed the dairy aisle, where he normally stopped to taste the pungent morsels of fresh fromage. He was a mess, darting about in midair, changing his mind and going back again, muttering to himself. It became apparent to all, on that particular day, what had Dorma so befuddled, what with his shabby hair, beads of sweat running down his face, and shortness of breath. "I'll tell you, it's coming soon," they whispered to one another, staring openly as squirrels do. Dorma looked at no one. "What did she say? Oh, dear, one percent, two percent, oh I'll just get what I like and I suppose I'll hear about it. How can she possibly expect me to remember all of this, oh dear, oh dear, so little time," he thought as beads of sweat dripped down his vest, which had been buttoned up wrong by his shaking paws. In his rush, he had forgotten all about keeping kept and impressing all with his dapperness, which was always good for business, and his wife, little Debby, sure loved it when he put on his best ties for work. All that was a thousand redwoods from where he was on the dairy aisle at the harvester's market, forgetting quite effectively how not to get yelled at by the missus because his baby was having a wife.

"Hey there, sweet chunks!" The younger swooners accosted him by the storefront. They should have been better paying attention to the streets. "How are ya?"

"Oh, uh, fine thanks. I... Oh." And he darted off, suddenly remembering what apparently held the gravity of the discovery of a national treasure. They giggled gleefully as he vanished into the bottles.

"When's the big day, big guy?" One of the elders, who knew Dorma was married because old folks can tell that, spoke to Dorma over his paper as he passed without even stopping to greet anyone in his normal pleasant way.

"Nuts!" he exclaimed, and a few young kits gasped. "I should get her nuts." He began searching. "No nuts *anywhere!"*

A grocer piped up, "Yeah, sorry bud, no new shipments. Bolly's Farm is always late."

Drat that character.

"Oh, it's, uh..." he said. Everything was a blur. "It's... *today!"* he shouted unexpectedly. His head popped around the corner and vanished again. "Big day's today. Today, having a wife. I mean my baby's having one. Got to go, excuse me please, my wife is very much in a hurry and I am in labor."

The business quadrant of the squirrel town erupted. "What news! What a great thing to talk about!" they all exclaimed without knowing the onus of Dabby's rush that day. The hour was not speculative any more, but was upon him presently. He had just received the greatest of news, that his wife was in labor, as he spun his morning Larkspurs yarn and poked a needle into someone. He had stammered and streaked out the door of his nockhole-shop, forgetting to flip his open sign, and all had turned to see a wild blur vanishing into the open day. And now he was being held up by gossipers and mongrels.

The big day for the dapperest squirrel in all Hesperia! "Is it a boy?" they asked, "Do you think it's a girl, maybe twins, what will be the name? Have you got all your bundles, don't forget the bath stones, and pick up *Badger Rockering's Handbook to Diaperage*. Oh, and have you got *Scrammy Dillow's Quarto on the Snivels*? It's gold, just gold." They began to press him for information, and he looked for a way out the door. He thought, for a moment, he might have seen fangs.

"I know it's going to be an ace, right?"

"Just like Dad."

"Why did he become a tailor again? Anybody know?" Shrugs went around the crowd.

"I hope he grows up strong. Or she," they said, waving their fingers. They began some talk about shadows at the edge of the forest, someone being seen. "Enough with that superstitious stuff. But that is always old news. We're safe, and nothing ever happens. They make sure of that."

"They who?"

"You know!" someone shrieked. "Them! The ones. That do that sort of thing."

"Anyhow, don't be rude."

"What's the little thing going to be, Dorma, when he grows up, I wonder?" they all shrieked. "Is he going to become a fire squirrel? (And at that someone flexed his biceps.)

"No, silly, it's going to be a girl and take up sewing like her father."

Giggles. "Hmph. Well, I think she'll be a *model* for the family clothing line, wouldn't that be fantastic?!"

"Oh, even better!" Someone perked up. "A *male model!"*

He was suddenly overtaken by visions of his progeny standing in front of a painter in some nonsensical pose, saying some awful thing like "Och, don't hate me because I hate you," or "My clothing is muscles." He dropped everything he had unintelligibly gathered and declared, "My child shall be..." He looked at them over his nose. "A squirrel." They were speechless. "Good day." He strode out the door and toward the hospital and, in a moment, resumed his confused form of sprinting.

He was shown to her room when he got to the birthing ward. And at that moment he felt the fool, for Debby Dabby had apparently been writhing in pain for some time. He had heard her shrieks from outside.

Moments later he was in a smock by her side.

He had been at the bedside of his beautiful dear for no more than a moment or two, it seemed, when a scream and a crash was heard from far away beyond the window. Dorma's mind shot to the sight of the great bough tumbling and crashing through the Tanglewall on Race Day. Hadn't that been fixed? He hadn't been back that way since his school days. A sick, black, feeling began in his stomach and he left his wife, to her dismay, to peek out the window. The nurses took her paw as she continued to scream.

Far above them all, the wail of the town's emergency bells began to sound.

Ding Ding! Ding Ding!

"Everybody get to cover! Everybody hide!" someone shouted as the crashing below the window of the hospital became more distinct.

Chaos inside, chaos outside. Dorma looked back and forth, and in a flash he saw what was the matter. Far, far down, there was a dark spot where forest should be, and when it moved, he saw. The tree grumbled and shuddered under the uncommon weight of something far heavier than anything in Hesperia. The black flash darted again, boards flew, and someone screamed.

It was a cat.

No. It was *the* cat.

"It's not possible. It's not possible, not today," he thought over and over, his heart striking about in his chest.

Another crash. That one was closer.

He shouted to the nurses, "Cat!" and they looked incredulous. "I tell you, it's a CAT!" he screamed at the top of his lungs.

"Oh no!" Debby cried, her strength sapped from her body and sweat running down all over. The nurses assured him it was just birth pangs and to try to remain calm. "Nothing to worry about, sir, just please wait outside and you can watch through the glass."

"Apparently, they're used to these kinds of noises," Dorma thought. "What, no, you think I'm crazy! I tell you it's a cat! Look for yourself! The *town is in danger*," he pleaded.

"Sir, please calm down, it's going to be a squirrel, I assure you, now please wait outside." He was rushed out and the door locked behind him. "Is something wrong with my wife? What's going on!" He pounded on the glass, but to no avail.

Just then, a small cry was heard, and everything, inside and out, stopped. It was the faint cry of a squirrel pup.

Then there was a rushing thump. Then another, and another. It was getting closer. The thumping grew louder and louder, and more strained became the creaks and moans of the boards and walls of the birthing ward. It briefly stopped, and everyone stood deadly silent and looked back and forth at one another. Dorma looked at his helpless and confused wife, and she could only stare at the window, perplexed.

Then the window burst into a cloud of splinters and shards as the great black cat, Morgart Wingless, drilled into the room. Dorma watched in horror, trying desperately to somehow open the latch and get the baby and his wife out of there. "Oh no, oh no, please," he screamed and pounded the glass. One nurse threw herself on top of Debby, and Morgart swatted her away with those paws, bigger than anything. Another nurse tried to grab the cat's paw, but the cat threw her, with one flick, into the wall, and she slumped and did not move again. A defensive battle ensued between the doctors and nurses that remained and the bristling black monster that took up nearly the whole room. Her every step shook and cracked the floor, flinging up nails and boards. Dorma's screams could not be heard over the cat's piercing howl.

Then, as Dorma tried still pointlessly to open the viewing room latch, the cat stopped, suddenly turned and, with no one left to oppose her, slowly surveyed Debby, who had rolled from the chair and lay face down on the ground. Dorma frantically pounded and screamed, trying to distract the cat for only a moment longer, but his manic cries were unanswered.

It happened so quickly, and yet so slowly at the same time. Morgart did nothing more than playfully lift her paw and bring it down on Debby's back as if she were a piece of yarn. Dorma had heard the scream and was now wailing and throwing himself at the wall. He could almost feel the claws sinking into his heart, burning and bleeding despair and rage.

Then, all of a sudden, the cat reeled as if she had suddenly taken violently ill, and Dorma realized something had struck her from behind.

Tufts of black hair began flying, and out of the blur he could just make out that odd character Bolly, the only one who could have stood a chance at beating him at the races. But what was he doing here now?

The cat yelped and whirled about with her left back claw all twisted. He held it tightly in a lock hold, threatening to break it off. The cat pounded the walls madly but did nothing to Bolly, and then Bolly did the unthinkable and let go. He held his paws in the air, almost as if to say, "I don't want any trouble." Dorma couldn't believe his eyes for it seemed, for a moment, like the two mortal enemies, squirrel and cat, were having a *conversation!* But it was too muffled from outside to tell what was being said, and anyhow his wife was bleeding on the floor.

Dorma tried the door handle again and found it had been jarred open in the fray.

The scene was even more horrific on the inside. He tried to be silent, but whatever needed saying between Bolly and the cat was over, and they were simply glaring at one another.

Dorma stepped on a piece of glass, and the swallow he made as he gulped a yelp of pain was still enough to alert Morgart to his presence. Bolly, however, had seen him and took the split second Morgart was distracted to grab a bedpost and deal a hard, stiff blow as she returned her attention to him. Bolly saw the paw coming but had no room to dodge. Still he caught the pinky and twisted the claw until she rang in protest, and made a point of digging into the cat's sensitive paw pad. Wherever he turned, she went.

Dorma took the chance to leap on his wife to protect her from whatever happened. He picked up her head and looked into her glazing eyes. He made her face wet as the years leapt, and he kissed her.

The smashing and roaring and meowing continued, but Dorma didn't look. Bolly got one final slug, she got him by the neck, and they both toppled out of the cat-sized opening in the wall. And, moments later, a cheer rose from the town. Dorma looked at his bride and said nothing for a moment.

Finally, she raised her head and looked at him. Debby groaned, letting out the last of her strength to roll over to allow the baby to cry. The baby's already massive wings had to be unfolded to see his face. Amidst all the wreckage the first of the whispers was heard, and at once Dorma hated all of them, but he ignored them, turning to his wife.

"Debby, dearest."

"Dorma."

"You're hurt."

"I can never be hurt, my love."

"You're going to be okay."

"Shhh. I am okay. I'm more than okay. I -g- I have you, and I have my baby."

"Yes...sweetheart. I love you."

"Do you remember what we wanted to name him?"

"Yes."

"What was it again?"

"Mabby. After your mother, Marly."

"Oh, I love it. I remember."

"And after you."

"Our baby. Can I... hold him?" she asked. As a nurse, weeping and trembling, swaddled little Mabby and laid him in his mother's arms, Dorma felt Debby's body begin to ease. "My little baby. I love you so much. Now you promise me one thing, young one, that when you find what it is you want in this life, you remember me, and you remember I told you, you have to do it. Hear -g- me? You -g- you *have* to do it. Have to..." She raised her paw to Dorma's face and caressed his cheek, for he knew it would be the last time. "Take care of him. For me."

He smiled.

"I love our little life."

"Our life..." (Dorma sobbed.)

"Take care of him."

"I will."

"I love you."

“I love you.”
“Always...”
“Always.”

.

Then Dorma’s only forever love drifted from his arms. She flew high above the world, where she could not be touched, and out into the breaking night.

PART 2: The Winglier's Way

Brow to bit and frame to fall, mind will get the best of all.

Feeling, fire, nub to nib, sham and shame, to Rammerie's glib

For what is it thine heart to guard, and yet to follow, speaking hard,

Fill with peace the well repast, taste thy crux on wind at last!

Chapter 7: Don't Cheat, Use your Feet.

The days went by slowly at first; there was more silence in the house than Dorma was used to. He never looked for answers. He just wasn't that type. He just *missed* her.

He had a few more gray hairs, anyway, and there wasn't time anymore for the wistfulness of youth. He had responsibilities: a fledgling business and a son.

He had done the smart thing for once: hired help and moved into a bigger shop. His time was taken up, more and more, by one of the small, shiny-object-seeking projectiles some referred to as a child. It wasn't easy raising him without a mother, but he managed.

Most nights he read or told a story to Mabby before tucking him into bed. And afterward, when he finally had a moment to himself, he would go to his side of the house and take out a box.

In it was all that he had of her: locks of hair, sketches he had made, wedding photos, her diary, and a few knickknacks. Sometimes he remissively picked up the newspaper clipping of the day Bolly Beeley had been made a hero and given an award for saving a hospital. Where in the blue Heaven did he learn to fight like that? Dorma would look at the picture and, after a moment, forget why he had had picked it up. Oh, why don't I just throw it away? I don't know, he would think, and then he would get distracted by her old hairpin or a patch of the dress he had fixed for her, after it had been torn on that first day they met.

He only cried a little anymore, those kinds of nights. Instead, Mabby had him busy answering all his questions.

Daddy, can I have this? Can I eat that? Can I stick my finger in there? Mabby wasn't like the other kids, though.

One day they went out. "I want you to make some friends," Dorma told him as they walked to the park on Lankey, off the Great Commons Hollow, where the biggest play area in town was. They had begun to go so Dorma could catch some sun and Mabby could play with others, or try.

"I don't need more friends, Daddy, I have you. You're my friend." Dorma half smiled, half winced, knowing the little guy wouldn't feel that way forever.

"I know, son, but don't you want to make some new friends your age? I mean, you know, I'm an old guy."

"I don't *want* to go to the park, Daddy, I don't wanna go to the park," Mabby said.

Dorma had learned early on that no logical response was going to work. Rather than making a scene, he would just go silent until something caught Mabby's eye and he was off in some other direction. But today Mabby persisted. "Daddy, I don't *want to go to the park.*"

"Come on, buddy, you've got to try."

He didn't used to be that way. Dorma used to take Mabby to the park, and little Mabby would be so eager it was all Dorma could do to keep him reined in, till off he went screaming like a billybub. There, Dorma would think, this little guy's going to be a hit. No problems making friends at all, not like me.

Nowadays, Mabby walked begrudgingly alongside his father. The other kids didn't like him. He wasn't to be liked, and he had accepted that. Why rattle the bush? "Can we please not go to the park?"

"It'll be fine, buddy, you'll see," Daddy replied. It was *never fine*. "Ah, isn't this just your favorite time of year? It sure is mine." Sometimes Daddy asked questions and then got quiet, like he was asking someone that wasn't there.

They arrived just as the afternoon began to wane, when the evening billybubs and speeder-bugs started to have their fun and the heat this time of year became bearable.

Mabby stood at the edge of the playground, eyeing the swings, platforms, and jackybin courts. His favorite game. He remembered scoring his first goal, the sound of the jackyball going *swoosh, crack,* and all the kids on his team cheering. Just then Dorma knelt down at his side.

"Do you not think anyone will want to play with you?"

"They won't. They all hate me."

Dorma looked down for a moment, trying to figure out what to say. "I know you best, buddy. And I don't hate you, do I? Come on. I want to play jackybin. Would you like to play with me?"

"Really?!" exclaimed Mabby.

"Go easy on me though, I'm not as agile as I—Oof!" Mabby punched Dorma in the stomach, stole the ball, and threw it toward the goal. A jacknut is an incredibly terrible nut to eat, but when one wraps it in Larkspur's yarn and a little leather, till it's nice and tight and round, it becomes fairly bouncy. Mabby was a good shot. "Great," Dorma thought, "my kid can beat me up now."

"Son, I don't think that's how you play," he wheezed.

Mabby was having a ball, or something like that.

As they played one on one, they began to attract some attention from the other pups, what with this little bean beating a grown up. But when they realized who it was, the kid with the *baggy-bag wings,* well, they began to talk. And as we all know, baggy-bags are bags we put our harvest bags in so they don't drag all over the ground before we can fill them up with nuts during the harvest. And we don't want that. So one can only imagine what wings like baggy-bags must look like. And we don't want that either. So when Mabby heard someone whisper, "Baggy," or something like it, he knew what was the matter, even at his age. Swoosh. Another point for Mabby. Back to center and check.

"Syriss."

They both stopped playing, to Dorma's elation, and turned to see to whom the arbitrarily spoken name was attached. To Mabby this was clearly a tactic to distract him from the game. It was unwelcome and whoever had thought of it was clearly deficient somehow.

"Beethorn."

"What?" Dorma and Mabby said together.

"Syriss Beethorn." He paused. "That's my name."

"Oh…" They took this in.

"Anyhow, you clearly are in need of another player." Dorma and Mabby looked at one another, lost again. "Look, my name's extremely important, and you'll do well to remember it. And if I may direct your attention to the opposite side of the court, you'll find there are a few of us awaiting a go. Now not to be rude but, the way I see it, you can either join us or get on. All right? And you, the little one, with your playing you might make the team."

"You, however. Adult or not, we're going to have to take you down a notch." Syriss promptly slugged Dorma in the gut and took the ball. "You can play now," he said to Mabby. Dorma sank off to the side and cradled his diaphragm.

"Life's all about those exceptions, you know," Syriss said.

"You see, Mr., um, Beeth… Syriss, sir, that's exactly how I feel about it with adults and all," Mabby said. Mabby was obviously extremely taken with the young pup's brashness. "But tell me, how do you feel about this?" And with that he stole the ball back, and he had gone around and shot a bin before any of them could turn around to stop him.

The others inserted themselves into the court. One was a tabby (a tabby squirrel! And she was beautiful!), and the other was a pup of rather ferocious enormity. He bashed the ball with his big toe, and it sailed directly into Cyrus's waiting paws. "I'm not getting hit by *that,"* Dorma thought.

"I'm the leader of this band," Syriss said. He bounced the jackyball to Mabby like a pro. "Check. Bo-bo Neebles. Tufa Tankery. These here are my friends, and anyone got a problem with one a' them's got a problem with me, all right?" They were all Mabby's age. They began to play.

Dorma relieved himself of his duties on the court and looked about for the parents of the misfit group of kids that had befriended Mabby with a game of jackybin. Then he understood. They were looking for friends for their kids too. But Syriss, oddly, didn't seem to have anyone there to watch him. He was just...there.

Mabby had friends. "Mission accomplished," Dorma thought and went over to the squirrels of his age and stamina level to introduce himself.

Mabby was on fire with enthusiasm on the way home that evening, giving Dorma a play-by-play of the game which Dorma had already witnessed.

"...and then I got the ball from Tufa and went straight through, charged the basket, and swoosh, in it went again! Oh, Daddy, I had so much fun, did we have to leave so early? Can we go again soon? I just think about how good I can be at whatever I put my mind to, and I feel sometimes like I can do anything! I can't wait to start *school*!" Mabby looked at his father. "Can't you just see me now? Soaring…through… the air? Um, Dad?" Dorma wasn't listening.

The worst part about it all was Mabby just didn't *understand* that he wasn't like the other kids. In fact, it was more like he didn't even understand the word "different." "To a child, and sometimes to adults," he thought, "there are only varying degrees of sameness."

As they walked back to the modest section in Tadwick where they had resided since the "accident," they heard a commotion. Dorma had forgotten that his son was saying something and stopped walking. His ears perked. "Hear that? What do you suppose it is?"

"Let's go see, Daddy!" Mabby said, giving up on the subject of dreams and all that unimportant stuff.

"I think it's coming from the grandstands." The sound was traveling a long way. They traveled cumbersomely, seeing as Mabby was not old enough to fly or, as Dorma often silently reminded himself, not old enough to know he could not.

By the time they reached the grandstand, the commotion was enormous. Someone would yell something they couldn't make out into the speaker for a few seconds, and the whole structure would jump up and down, erupting into a bowel-smashing thunder. They came out from under the bleachers and looked from the east transept. Dorma and Mabby were speechless at what they saw.

Hal, who was nowadays called by his full name, Hallo, was making an absolute scene, yelling into the speaking cone, spit flying everywhere, and pounding the makeshift lectern, and the crown was eating up every word.

"Ah would like to introduce to you the squirrel that saved mah life." The crowd went silent. "Ah'd be cat litter if it wuzn't for him. Y'all would too. He saved us all. Let's hear it for our new mayor, I mean our new potential, um, candidate, mayoral, type...of thing...Bolly Beeley!" He yelled the name into the amplifying cone, flinging his arms, and almost knocking it over. He caught it and looked about the audience, attempting to smile it off, as Bolly Beeley's languid form emerged from the side of the stage. They looked at one another and, after a moment, Hal slinked off sharply. Bolly wore his best jacket, at which Dorma still winced for it engulfed him and was torn at the sleeve and other places. It was also atrociously soiled. These kinds of things a tailor notices.

"What's up with all this?" Dorma thought, "and why? The shy one. Mayor. He listened.

"Well, that was awkward," someone said.

"Shh," replied four others.

Mabby seemed to be having a good time. "That's odd," Dorma thought. Don't tell me *my boy* actually *likes* that bumblehead.

"Hey! Why should we elect a know-nothing farmer boy to be our mayor?" someone shouted from the grandstand audience.

Beeley heard it and attempted to maintain his jovial bearing. He started slowly. "Burying nuts all day and harvesting them is the joyful and natural activity which is, of course, shunned as a task for the low and humble." He started to speed up. "So as they say, education and capitalism go paw in paw, and the farmer and the pauper share a table with the fool. Farmers, for the most part, are perfectly happy with this arrangement, seeing as fools are the entertainers of angels, you see, and often aren't too critical of the paw that feeds, because that's them."

The crowd was completely silent, although neither Mabby nor Dorma was sure if it was from amazement or lack of comprehension.

"Talk squirrel-ese bud! Weh cain't under*staind* yew!"

Bolly smirked. "Progress, my friend." After that he paid no more mind to the heckler. "I'd like to thank you all for coming here today. I know that I am *different.* I have certain features of my character which make it difficult to relate to the working squirrel. I know. I grew up a laborer, I know nothing of politics, rubbing elbows and all that. I can only offer to you one single possibility for why I should, in my own humble opinion, run for the office of mayor of this fine town.

"It's true. I saved the town from a dangerous creature many seasons ago. It's true, for I bear…" and at this he began to unclasp his sides. "I bear…the scars."

The crowd went totally silent. Someone fainted. For Bolly Beeley had lifted the sides of his shirt to reveal not wings but a mangled stripe of scar tissue, bare as day, where wings had once been.

"I know lowliness all too well. I know what it's like to feel like one can never...rise..." He paused for dramatic effect. "...above one's circumstances." His voice cracked. A pup in the audience started to cry. "I don't know what persuaded me, that day, to take on something so...*much* bigger than I." He gulped. "But I remember the many times my life flashed before my eyes…That all I could think about was my fellow squirrels.

"As I said, we are here today to talk about progress. I knew that, even with such a threat gone, nothing would ever be the same. This great realm was no longer going to be our little secret. Nor was this fine town going to know quite the same ease…that it once knew. *Nor did we.* We are humbled. We are known. We are...exposed. I'm sure the question, since the great tragedy of that day, is how do we move forward? How shall we...progress? From this...

"Now, in our society we are faced with a new question: as the world around us becomes more and more aware of our presence, how shall we live? Shall we bury our nuts in the dirt?"

At that, half the audience shouted a "nay," and the other half shouted a "here, here," while Dorma simply said, "That is a bloody terrible analogy."

"Eh...No, I say!" Bolly continued.

"Oh, okay," Dorma thought, "good to know where that was supposed to go."

"Shall we attempt, in folly, to remain forever aloof from the suffering of the outside? *Or* shall we make the choice to firmly ground ourselves, to take up the burden of our fellow forest mates? The groundhogs, the rats...For too long we have thought ourselves better than all others because we have this feature, which is clearly unnatural if you think about it."

"What're yew ramblin' about? Are yew sayin we cain't fly no more?"

"I'm not saying we can't. I'm saying we can no longer expect to survive by living as if this strange *difference* makes us better. It does not. In fact, rodents living aloft...why...it has made us weak."

The crowd gasped. "Where did he learn to talk like that?!" Someone nearby whispered loudly. Then someone replied even less quietly, "He's a farmer, so probably from talking to his nuts." The nearby crowd struggled to maintain bearings.

Bolly, however, held the rest of the crowd like butter in his paws. "That cat took my wings!" he wailed. "But it was not until my wings were gone that I realized I could stand... and *fight!* These *vestigial* occurrences we call wings, they are leftovers of what we were, creatures of weakness, frailty, softness, fear. This new coming world demands more of the squirrel. It demands we learn to take up the weight of progress on our backs.

"It demands strength. It demands the full expression of freedom." And with that statement, he raised his arms above his head, something a flying squirrel cannot do without sitting down. "We have believed for centuries that we are meant to grasp new heights. Well, in my loss, in my struggle, I realized how to do it. When that cat took my wings, he gave me the ability to beat her! Don't you see? A squirrel has wings to fly away from trouble, but the reason he cannot simply overcome is because he is slowed down by these very instruments...of *fear! What dependency! I live because I lost my sense of privilege. I fought back, and from now on I am proud to say, in life, I don't cheat. I use...my feet!"*

The crowd went wild. The heckler said no more. Bolly walked off the stage, waving proudly, as the crowd chanted, "Don't cheat, use your feet. Don't cheat, use your feet." Dorma looked down at Mabby, unsure. They left to the thunder of the chanting audience and remarks like "He's a hero." The newspaper editor proposed a new front-page headline as he spread his paws out wide. "Hero Beeley for Mayor, I'll Save Hesperia Again!'"

Mabby thought it strange that his father was entirely silent the whole way home. The hero that had saved both of their lives was getting all the bad guys. What was bad about that?

They ate dinner in relative silence as well. Mushroom jerky, Mabby's favorite.

"Ready for bed, son?" Dorma said.

"I guess." He looked down at the table.

"Why, what's the matter? You must be exhausted from all that jackybin. I know I am."

"Well, I mean..." Mabby paused.

"Yes?"

"Isn't there any, um, dessert?" Mabby asked.

"Oh my goodness, how could I forget." He leapt up and went over to the cooler. "Dear me, I am such a bumblehead. Don't worry I've got..."

He paused as he looked in the cooler and saw the numpet cake he had bought that morning and had decorated with the words "Happy Birthday, Ace!" and a drawing of a squirrel in the clouds with a "#1" to celebrate the prospect of Mabby's upcoming start in Rammerie's. Since he had bought it, he had begun to have second thoughts. Mabby had talked about it for so long now, and it was beyond Dorma to discourage him. He secretly hoped the phase would pass, however, for he could not see how Mabby could ever pass, not with wings ever so much more massive than Debby's. After all, it had been almost impossible for her.

"Dad?" Mabby said.

"Uh, I mean, I... forgot...what was that dessert you liked again?" he asked Mabby as he rubbed out the words.

Mabby stifled a gasp. "Numpet cakes?"

"Yes, yes, that's right, with um, what was it?"

"Almond frosting?" Mabby panted.

"Ah, almond frosting, your favorite."

"Yeah!"

"Your *very* favorite?"

"Yeah!"

"In the very... *complete, world*, yes? Isn't it?" Dorma stalled as he hurriedly massaged the lumpy blob of frosting into something that looked like it made sense.

"Dad?"

Now or never. He whirled around with the numpet cake. "Ta-da!"

"Aah!" Mabby yelped at what appeared to be a failed version of a sloppy, mentally impaired, furry blue lizard thing with a squirrel tail and one arm falling off.

"Voila! Your favorite." Dorma brought it closer, and Mabby moved back until he realized it was dessert.

"Did you...make that all by yourself?" Mabby asked.

"Well, absolutely, can't you um, tell what it is?"

"Yeah!" No.

"It's a, it's, it's, ah, it's, it's, it is...um. It's... you," Dorma said. The precarious blue arm fell off and plopped on the floor.

"Me?"

"Yes!" Think fast. "It's you!"

"Why am I blue?"

"It's your, um, costume!" Dorma said, to Mabby's shock.

"Well, it's a little rough you know." It was offensive. "Just look at it!" Dorma set it on the table and cut it in half for them to share. "Imagine! Mabby the Hero! Eh, Super Mabbs! Yeah? I wanted to tell you today, son, I saw you out there and I just thought, 'my boy can do anything he puts his mind to!'" He held his arms out and looked at the ceiling. "Right, I said, He's gonna be great.'' He looked down and noticed Mabby had already consumed the entire numpet cake, and the remains of the frosting, blue lizard hero and all, was a murder scene around his mouth. Mabby swallowed and stared at Dorma, who was about to make his next point about how incredible he was going to be someday.

"I… wow, that was, that *was a lot* of cake, son, but never mind. As I was saying, you can do anything you want with your life."

"Anything?"

"Anything. Anything at all, son, and you'll be great, but just promise one thing for your dear old dad, that you'll be sure and use it to help others—" He was cut off by Mabby jumping up in the air.

"Yeah, yeah! That's right! I can do anything. Be a hero!"

"Yes."

"Be a…great fighter!" Mabby flexed and boxed the air.

"Yes! That's the spirit!"

"Just like…"

"R-rrright!" Dorma made a premature fist pump.

"Bolly Beeley!" Mabby exclaimed.

Dorma's face melted. "You mean you don't…want to be… like…" he stuttered.

"Bolly Beeley, Hero of Hesperia, with his trusty sidekick, SuperMabbs! He'll beat up the bad kitties and I'll fly around, and, and, and uh, throw stuff at them. Oh! Father, I do want to fly! I could be a flying ace, the best that ever was, I know it. And…Oh." He dropped his arms and stared at the ground.

Dorma was shaken by the revelation that his son admired someone else, that the time he had been the great alpha in his son's eyes was over so soon, and so unfairly, ended by the words of someone who didn't deserve it at all. Not him. Not Mabby. Is that really it for me then? "What's the matter?"

"You said I could do anything... But Bolly said I can't fly. Flying's bad."

"Come here," Dorma said. Mabby came and sat down. "And wipe your face." Dorma chuckled, wiping his son's chin. "Look, son..." Mabby looked at him. "I have to tell you something."

"Yeah, Dad?"

"You can have anything you want. You can live any kind of life you please, just like I said. I know this is going to be hard. But you c-c—." Dorma got a tickle in his throat. He coughed. "Achem. You ca—." He started again. "Caa..."

"What?"

"I mean, you're very special, is what I'm trying to say. I've waited for you to understand this on your own, so it would be easier for you, but I need to tell you, you're different."

"Different? Dad?"

"You're not like the other pups. You can—nnn—" He struggled to get it out. "You C-C-Ca-han-nnn... Nn—." This was too hard. "You... Can... NnnNnn... t-hhh." Mabby hung on to him, and looking him in the eye made the feat of breaking every rule every father had for being a respectable and decent squirrel toward his boy just too hard. The memories of that horrible old rat that had shut his beautiful Debby up for years—she would have been confined her whole life if she hadn't been the stubborn girl she was—flooded his mind. The years of watching her struggle and the hours and months of sticking that needle into her flesh so she could struggle miserably in so much pain just to do that simple thing, flying, it made him nearly mad. It doesn't have to be this way. Save the boy, he told himself. I can't. I can't be that miserable, weak old simpleton's excuse for a squirrel. That old dog, that Quarles.

"What do you mean, Dad?"

"You…You can't…" No. "T-t-hoo. You can…too! You can too do it!" Ugh.

"Oh, Dorma, you really asked for it now," he thought. His eyes glazed over, for inside he was weeping *and* leaping.

"You mean I can fly?"

"I mean that squirrel on that stage today was wrong, Mabby, he was dead wrong, and you can fly. If that's what you want to do, you can." Mabby hugged him. "And I'll be right there with you, and we'll find a way. Come on. Let's go to bed." They went to tuck Mabby in.

"Yay! Super Mabbs!" Mabby said. Dorma laughed.

"Dad?"

"Yes?"

"Can you tell me one of those stories you said you used to hear as a pup?"

"You mean about the Knights of Elorus?"

"Yeah." Mabby's eyes were lit in a way Dorma had not seen in a long time.

"Sure, why not." Dorma began to regale young Mabby with tales of the great Ekkhorn, Guardian of The Realm, and how he led an army of super squirrel warriors against all kinds of threats against the realm, big and small. And Dorma went to sleep that night long after Mabby, in the chair by his bed, cursing himself.

Chapter 8: The Longest Tail

Out on the court, Mabby held tightly to the jackyball and wiped a line of sweat with his forearm. Jackybin with the gang was becoming a regular thing. He realized that his father was gone from his side, off at home, leaving him and his friends with the day. He could not decide, at that moment, whether he had truly enjoyed jackybin so much or if he had enjoyed jackybin with his dad. He felt the musty late summer breeze, filled with the heaviness of the coming rain and of salted apples. Feeling the tingle of the moist air was a rush, and it brought memories of childish joys, going out to the boughs behind his house, exploring when he was free and season was crisp and exciting as a child's itinerary.

Paing!

His head throbbed. It appeared someone had thrown a jackyball at it. He rubbed his temple and looked to see who had done it, amidst the arising laughter. Tufa stifled a cackle and Bo watched the ball bounce away, in amazement, while Syriss simply stood with an odd look on his face.

"Are you going to do something?" A challenge.

"Oww. What?" Mabby said, still confused.

"Make a play, yeah?" he said. "Or are we here to enjoy pretty sunshine? Hello?"

He had not realized Syriss had gone so far as to take the ball out of his paws, while he had been reflecting, and had gone off into the clouds mid-game. Had he been just standing there that long? Looking silly in front of Tufa was worse than the pain of Syriss's words.

"Give," he said angrily after a few moments of standing there with his head down listening to everyone laugh. Perhaps it was funny. Perhaps.

He got the ball and instantly threw it up in the air, and it sailed and swished in the bin high above their heads. Satisfied with himself, and still angry, he started to leave.

"Oh, yeah?" Syriss said.

Mabby said nothing, only started to leave, not liking where the day was going.

"Throw another. Betcha can't."

"Betcha can." Mabby snatched the ball and threw it with a little hop. It easily sank into the bin.

"Another."

"Fine," Mabby said. Swish, crack.

"Another," Syriss said. Mabby stared at him. "Boys, this better be going somewhere good."

"It's goin' somewhere all right," Syriss said as Mabby took the ball back to the three-point line. "Speakin' of, I bet you, Mabby, that you can't shoot the ball and score from right here." He brought his foot out and pointed his toe at the ground, halfway to the goal. "Just right there. I just betcha."

Tufa looked at Bo then back at Mabby, who took the shot. Swish.

"Right. Got that, everyone?"

"DARD. BEEB," Bo said.

Tufa replied, "Syriss..."

"Just a minute, love. Now we've got that covered, Mr. Mabby Sir, I bet you..." Syriss strolled to the one-point line. "That you can't shoot that ball and score, at *all. From here."* He nodded to the one-point line.

"Syriss," Tufa interjected.

"Just a minute."

Mabby knew Syriss had to be getting to something like a point somehow in the conversation, but couldn't figure out, for his life, what that could be. Perhaps he just really enjoyed looking foolish.

"Step right up, Mister Mabbity Dabbity," Syriss said. Mabby hated his nicknames. Syriss could be a real friend, and a realer enemy.

"You're mister big shot, aren't you? Come on," Syriss taunted.

Mabby stepped forward, almost right under the bin and, without saying anything, held up the ball and took aim.

"Syriss, stop it," Tufa objected.

"Okay, just what are you getting at? What is this?" Mabby was going figs-'n-berries trying to figure out Syriss's game.

"Nothing," He let out his trademark smirk and bowed low. "Just…please. Go."

Mabby shook his head and shot. He barely even had to look, and the other two drew a breath, struck dumb. The ball went in with barely a sound.

"There," Mabby said, but his satisfied grin disappeared as he caught the quiet looks of his friends.

"Now, tell me, mister big...shot. Is *that* why you don't like playing skins?"

Mabby checked his shirt. Buttons all there. He was utterly lost. "Whatever do you mean?"

"*Don't play fool! Mista beeg shot, don't gotta lissen, do gotta show everyone how big he is,*" he barked.

"What are you talking about?" Mabby shouted.

"Wait, you don't know, do you? You don't know?"

Mabby stared at Syriss, who picked up the ball and lobbed it to Bo and said, "Bo, come here, show him. Come, shoot the ball. Just shoot it into the bin." Bo lumbered over while Syriss explained. "I wondered if you were just ashamed of taking off your shirt, at first. Then I noticed you could shoot. Then I noticed you were able to run around like anyone else, and you were better even. So you're not hiding being flabby, Mabby." He chuckled.

Tufa rolled her eyes.

"You have something else. Then it hit me, you could shoot from anywhere, and that…" Bo lifted the ball to his shoulder and, having exhausted the give in his wings, could only desperately flick the ball upward with his wrists. It plopped tiredly on the gravel. "Having great membranes holding our arms and legs together and all, that is something a squirrel shouldn't be able to do."

Mabby shrugged. "So?"

"So, you dolt," Syriss went on, "you don't have any trouble with this game like everyone else because your wings aren't right, are they?"

Mabby stood still.

"You're an infirm, aren't you?" Syriss pressed him.

"Syriss, don't say that." Said Tufa.

"Admit it."

Mabby felt naked.

"*Admit it!*" Syriss raised his voice. Mabby began to shake.

"Syriss, stop it. Stop it right now. That's enough." said Tufa.

Mabby tore away from the crowd that had begun to gather as Syriss taunted him. He couldn't figure out why Syriss would suddenly become so mean and turn on him like that. He had heard that name before, and he didn't like it. He knew kids weren't supposed to use it. He knew it meant something was wrong. With him.

"Mabby, it's all right, stop!" Tufa yelled as Mabby tore off and ran and ran. Tears streamed down his face.

"No, let 'im!" Syriss shouted. Mabby let out a whimper. "He can only play because he's a cheat! That's fine, though, you can cheat but you'll never fly! I'm the leader of this group, all right? ME! Arrogant little…"

"You mean no one gets to be as arrogant as you? Big chief arrogant kid. You're the one that can't take someone being better than you, it seems to me," Tufa said over her shoulder as she went after Mabby. "Mabby? Mabby, stop! Where are you? Ugh! Why are pups always measuring their tails?"

Mabby heard someone calling his name a ways back, but it only made him want to run harder. He grew short of breath and cursed his feet, wishing he could fly. Then he stopped. The sound of Tufa's maddeningly kind voice had faded entirely; instead there was the soft call of the wind through the boughs, resonating against the breathing of the leaves' chorus, audible only to the quiet soul and only in the solitude of the end of town.

"There you go! Run 'cause you sure can't *fly away!"* Syriss yelled after him.

Mabby felt close to the noises of the forest. He had spent many evenings imagining himself going out to explore the rustles beyond the Tanglewall. In the dark, the forest spoke in whispers. It seemed to him those voices called, their words flowing through his wings like the comforting graces of someone who should have wanted to be there. It was as if the wind was that friend in the dusk-time that he had been meant to know. The wind seemed to be calling him to let it take him away and up into its rest. He looked back for a moment, but he heard for certain only breath.

Mabby tried several times to get off the bough and into the air, only to be disappointed by a blow to the sternum. He realized he was going to need more air to prove the little sop wrong.

The compulsion to sail on the promises of his old friend reminded him of his father, who had begged him never to try to jump off of one of those great boughs they traveled on. He looked at the Tanglewall, up at the sky, and then far, far, below, at what he could see in the world, which existed to him only in patches and spots of life under the trees. A scornful gust nearly toppled him, and he grabbed the ledge. "If I need to, I can catch the wall as I go." he thought.

A little more, a little more now. He inched outward, and the Tanglewall below began to look as if it were moving on its own, spiraling closer. An exceptional sickness overtook him, and his fingers shook and his arms buckled. The earth heaved below him, and a strong paw caught the scruff of his neck just as he was about to pass the point of no return. He felt himself instantly back on the ledge and safely balanced.

"What were you thinking? Why did you run like that?" Tufa said. Mabby was surprised she was so strong and remembered someone had once told him that kits his age tended to be tough.

"Hello? Again, really?" she said as Mabby finally broke his trance.

"Um. I..." He had absolutely no idea what to say.

"Well?" she prodded him. "Are you trying to get yourself killed? You've got to pay attention, Mabby." She was clearly frustrated with him, but it eluded Mabby as to why. Couldn't she tell he was obviously very hurt? "And don't you get, by now, that acting weak is just going to encourage Syriss?" She dusted him off. "You've got to stand up to him. He's just going to keep pushing your buttons."

"So you're on his side now?" Mabby said, sniffling.

She sighed. "No, Mabby. He's not a very nice squirrel sometimes."

That must have hurt. Mabby couldn't decide whether to feel bad for not thinking or to feel even more angry that, clearly, no one understood that he was the victim, that he should be defended, not Syriss.

"Look, Syriss can be, no, *is,* very mean. But just because someone has some bad traits doesn't mean you know everything about him. He's mean because he cares so much about every little thing. He's like you, Mabby."

"Thanks?"

"It's true." She laughed. "Syriss is the kind of pup that, if he didn't care, he wouldn't say anything, or *have* anything to do with you."

"Then why are you friends with him? Why do you like him so much?" Mabby asked.

"Look." She stood in front of him and looked all around to see if anyone was watching. "All clear. I'm going to show you something. But you have to promise me you will never tell anyone. Understood?"

"Right."

"Okay." She took a deep breath. Then she unbuttoned the clasps on the side of her shirt that held her left wing. Female shirts, Mabby had learned from his father, took an exceptional kind of skill to work with, as extra measures were needed to make sure they were safely decent while flying. She tightened the extra under-corsets and hook-eyes before she showed her left side to Mabby, who was exceptionally curious, but mostly his head felt just an itty bit tippy.

Her left wing bore a scar near the bottom. It wasn't enough to be visible beneath her fur unless it was pointed out, but there was clearly flesh missing. "I am only a little older than you, Mabby. I am old enough to remember the day Morgart came. And so is Bo."

"But not Syriss?"

"Not by a few weeks. You've seen Bo's limp. Bo and I will never fly. Syriss saw that, and chose to be our friend."

"Really?"

"Yeah, when no one else would. And I bet that was the same reason he chose to be friends with you. He saw something. That's who Syriss really is."

"Well, so, why is he so gruff then?" Mabby asked.

"I guess he tries to lead by example."

"He's a *bad example,*" Mabby said.

Tufa laughed. "Come on, we've got a game to finish," she said as she tucked her wing back in. Mabby's dizziness subsided.

They traveled back quietly and enjoyed the morning air, something Mabby hadn't thought other squirrels did. He smiled at her, and she smiled back. "She is an infirm too," he thought, "I'll have to figure out how to use these wings. Mabby's tabby Dabby. All right, that's enough of that." But he thought it anyway, all the way back to the court.

"So how did you get the scar, if you don't mind my asking?"

"Bo was meant for me," she began. As they walked, she told him the story of how her parents had arranged for Bo and Tufa to be betrothed to one another. Tufa's parents were well-to-do and Bo was an exceptionally bright child, and his physical enormity virtually guaranteed his spot on the professional jackybin team, even as a baby. His father was already in talks to reserve his spot as Professor of Preternatural Rudiments at Rammerie's (His father, Mr. Neebles Sr., was a rather *...nutty professor.*) Their parents put them in a sandbox at the park together as little babies. Tufa was purportedly building a fairy castle while Bo was re-creating, by memory the famous sculpture "*Pieta le Eceurille Fourreure,*" after a recent family visit to the museum. As their parents were off discussing plans for the wedding, they quickly became best baby-buddies. Things were promising.

Then, high above, the sirens went off and the town started crashing down around them. It was all over before anyone could figure out what was going on or what to do. Before Tufa's and Bo's parents could retrieve them and get to shelter, a wall from a nearby peddler's shop had come down on the sandbox. It seemed to all that the two precious babies had been flattened. Then, amazingly, Bo lifted the wreckage from underneath and threw it aside like a kerchief. He had sheltered Tufa from the debris with his body. However, as a consequence, he had taken a nasty blow to the head, and he had from that day forth uttered only unintelligible single syllables. Everyone was heartbroken and grateful, including Tufa, and they were still inseparable as friends.

"Boo!" Bo cried, as they drew nearer. A smile shot across Syriss's face. He had waited for them.

"*Marb-b!*" Bo cried out again.

"Yes, that's right, Bo," Syriss said as they approached.

Mabby stepped back onto the court.

"Come back to get what for again, eh?" Syriss said.

Mabby slammed the jackyball onto the paint so hard it bounced over Syriss's head and went into the overhead bin behind him with a perfunctory rattle. "I came to beat the pants off of you."

"Oh do try, do try that, Mabbs. *Do* try." Syriss was back to his usual sardonic self.

"I propose teams," Tufa said. "And an apology. From you, Syriss. Syriss. Now. Apologize."

"I'm sorry, mate." Syriss bowed his head. "I was just—"

"Right, but that doesn't mean you have to make the world know." Tufa was right. Everyone in the park had seen the incident, and they seemed to be talking among themselves avidly and quietly. She composed herself.

"How about shirts and skins. Tufa…hm." He, to the amazement of all, thought hard about it, when to tell the truth he was actually considering how best to handle Mabby. Tufa shot him a wide-eyed glare. "Oh yeah, um, heh, sorry. You'll be shirts."

"*Well, obviously!*" she screamed.

"My bad. I was thinking about something else," Syriss copped.

"Yeah, right."

"So, Mabby, check. It'll be me against you." With a squinty eye and a nosy grin, he flicked the ball back to Mabby.

Mabby was not about to show weakness again. "Fine." It might be rather nice, for a change, to play against Tufa and maybe actually win a game or two. He took off his shirt. His wings shadowed the ground like drapes. Everyone tried not to look. "Go ahead. Get your eyeful. This is me," Mabby said. "Anybody done yet? Bo, you're on my team." At that Bo snorted and grabbed his shirt and flung it off without unbuttoning it and buttons flew. Someone walking on the park trail got hit, and a faint "*Muthah!*" was heard.

"Now don't you let no one tell you you got to hide or how to be, awright mate?" Syriss clapped his paws to start the game. "Don't worry, Mabbs. I think you're going to be famous too, what with those things." Syriss chuckled as he stole the ball and dribbled down the court, and Bo commenced his hold-arms-out-and-move-at-snail's-pace-laughing defense.

"Famous? Too?" Mabby said.

"Yeah, famous. You know, just like your dad." Syriss attempted to shoot, but Mabby blocked him, so he went in for a layup and passed at the last moment. Tufa jogged amiably away from Bo and shot for two with time to spare.

"Marr-b?!" Bo said.

"My dad is famous?" Mabby said at the same time as Tufa said, "Mabby's dad is famous?"

"Uh. Yeah," Syriss said with his paws upturned in a "how do you guys not get this?" kind of gesture. "His father. Mabby's name is Dabby, ergo Dorma Dabby is Mabby Dabby's father. I didn't know it at first, but I put it together later. Yes, is it all there now?" Syriss went on as Tufa's and Bo's minds absolutely blew bananas. Tufa clapped her paw to her forehead.

"Honestly, guys, how am I the only one that makes these connections?"

"My dad is … *famous!* How?" Mabby said.

"You mean he never told you?" Syriss asked.

"No, I mean my dad...doesn't fly, really." Mabby realized out loud.

"Honestly, I don't know for my life how you got all this time with no one talking to you about this, and your own dad never telling you. Your dad, Dorma Dabby, is the greatest flying ace in all the history of Hesperia! He has the record for fastest time ever at Rammerie's Race Day. He holds *all* the records!" The other two nodded. "*And* he never touched an obstacle doin' it. He's been argued to be even better than my dad, says I! And when a pup says your dad could maybe, prob'ly, almost beat my dad, you better believe it!"

Mabby arrived home several seconds later. The door swung open with a bang against the wall, and Mabby was on his dad with "Dad, Dad, Dad, you absolutely, positively have to teach me how to fly, please, you're the greatest, everybody says so, you're the best, and all I want is to fly, so can you teach me please, please, can we go right now *please*?"

"Get a hold of yourself, now!" Dorma said, laughing, while Mabby still chattered.

"Daddy, I want to learn how to fly. You've got to teach me! Please!" Mabby exclaimed.

"Whatever do you mean, my boy?"

"You're the best ever! Everyone says so."

"Well, who's everyone?"

"I…I don't know, Syriss and like, my friends."

"Well, I don't know how they know that. I myself have never raced against but a few others, and none of the greatest. Who can say they are better than they are?"

"But…"

"Now, I couldn't teach you how to fly."

"But you've got to, you're my dad. Everyone else's dad is teaching them!"

"I can't, son. I'm sorry. But hey, why don't we go to the park and get some pistachio butter ice cream?"

"But…Okay, I guess." Mabby shuffled and dragged his feet.

Dorma hoped Mabby would forget all about it by nightfall. Distraction and delay tactics worked most of the time. But when they got home from their incredibly long walk, at the close of dusk, and the last story and distraction he could possibly squeeze from his brain eaked out and dripped, in tired words, on the floor, Mabby pressed him even still.

"Mabby, I can't teach you."

"Perhaps," Dorma thought, "I had better consider finding him different friends."

"Dad, please! It's two weeks before school, and if I don't learn how to fly…I…I mean, I've just got to," Mabby begged.

Dorma gave a forced laugh. "Don't worry about it. You'll do fine. I'm the best, right? Trust me, you don't need me. Now go ahead and go on to bed." Dorma was beginning to suspect this fad would not pass without a fight. When the pup was younger he had wanted to be a thimble collector, then an architect, without even knowing what an architect was, and then a businessman, then an artist, and he had nearly driven himself mad obsessively squandering each and every newfound passion into dismissive boredom at the faintest difficulty. This flying thing, probably wanting to be an ace or something, was just not possible. That youngrel could entertain every bent and gravitation but this one. It was too dangerous. A raindrop can't break brimstone; no skylark can dine with the peregrine. And no squirrel can fly with broken wings. That settled it.

Mabby went up to his room, defeated on all sides. Syriss thought Mabby wanted to be accepted for who he was but, to Syriss, who he was was an infirm. Mabby wanted to be someone who could fly. "I'll fill my father's shoes. I'll go on and beat him," he swore, as thoughts of Tufa, laughing happily and shaking her tabby tail and her wild locks, a red one here and a white one there, filled his mind.

Chapter 9: On the Importance of Taking Bops on the Head Under Consideration.

Mabby took in a breath of pre-dawn air, smelling of oats and Ballo roastery, with its curious blend of persimmon, rosemary, smoke of heather-spice, which everyone talked about and, somehow, the forest and the air of somewhere close to the top of the world. The view from the back of the house always made him want to fly, pulling him to thoughts of high above. His underarms itched, and his legs felt taut as the fleeting birds spoke to him of a finality of purpose.

There were posters all about town and posted on every tree about Bolly Beeley, "The Savior of Our Town." He was getting an aggressive headstart on his campaign for mayor, although no one seemed to be sure who his competition was, from what Mabby could tell. Still the posters watched him. They watched everyone.

If I am all alone, then that is how it will be done, he resolved, and he bent down, cocked his arms up, and leapt into the dark. As his legs powered him upward, his heart blew open with joy. All the words spoken against this moment became the wind at his back, and he imagined all the againsters staring from below. They were ugly dogs who could not fathom that they should accept him, not as someone too far below or high above, but as someone who was really here and really in love. This image drove his spirits ever upward. Suddenly the world felt alive, and he closed his eyes and felt it all.

Then, since he had obviously not been watching, he felt the special kind of pain that results from unpreparedness as the bough rose up and smacked him in the jowlies.

Dorma's dreams came for him in the night repeating, over and over, the scene from the night before, his life with Debby, and that old cat upon her back. He winced with his eyes tightly shut as he dreamed of a great disembodied black claw carrying Mabby away as he shouted, "I want to fly Dad, I want to fly!" Dorma watched some strange, dark version of himself. He was looking at a wall and would not turn around, and he gave his doltish scolding over and over. "I won't have it, and you can learn to fly in school. There's no need for putting oneself in danger, and there's no need for going outside the Tanglewall when everything is within reach here. Go to bed right now." Everything, that is, but what he needed most. While gaunt onlookers taunted and teased, he got angrier and angrier, but he could only say those words over and over while his little son's voice faded and the piercing laughter of the mockers grew until his ears felt they would bleed.

Then his dream transported him to Debby's funeral. The dream he'd dreamed ten million times. It always played out the same way, with him sitting alone and townsfolk padding silently by. For he knew how it would end, with the strangest squirrel of all to be in his thoughts. It was always Ms. Padduck who came by last, and she was always muttering to herself and sobbing, just as it had really happened. Then she would suddenly fall on him, weeping, and shout, "I'm so sorry! I'm so sorry! I didn't know. It's not supposed to work this way. Please forgive me." She would be whisked away by some figure he had never met who, in his dream, was always cloaked with leaves and branches. Then, alone, he would get up and go slowly to the casket and look on the face of his bride. Then, at last, he would wake in his mask of tears and be on.

Only this time it was not the usual dream. Something changed and Ms. Padduck, instead of falling on her knees in some awful unsolicited repentance, only walked by him and eyed him with eyes like hot glowing metal. He became distraught and rushed to the casket, only to find it was no longer the face of his beautiful, sweet Debby, but his own face, and Mabby was next to him. And then he was in the casket, without a breath's notice, and he looked at his son next to him. Then Debby stood over him, and he wanted to grab her, but he couldn't move, and she just looked at him. Only it was not love in her eyes, but anger, and she said only one thing, "You promised..."

Dorma started up with a jerk, to the realization that he had provided Mabby with the perfect opportunity to escape. He burst through the door to Mabby's room and, just as he had suspected, Mabby was not there. Out the front door he ran, reckless, forgetting entirely about his dream, calling Mabby's name.

He had made considerable progress—progress, that is, in terms of a new record of wounds and bruises to his dignity—as he braved to go higher and higher, and further and further, from the safety of the area behind the house.

He found himself somewhere he did not recognize. Worry started to set in, but he had to figure out how to fly before school so he could be someone great. With only days before school began, there was no time to waste. He rubbed out the pain and pressed on.

After a few more tries the bruises became unbearable, yet his anger grew and he gritted his teeth and jumped wildly into the air. He entered that state of rage in which emotion takes over the body as well as the mind and one abandons all concern for safety. And he became so enraged that, with a desperate primal grunt, he threw his body into the air on the off chance that something would catch. "I shall catch this time or I shall break," he said to himself, holding his arms out and saving nothing for the fall. Then as he was just about to crash face first into the ground, and surely tumble into an ugly unconsciousness, a breath of air moved under his wings and slammed them open. The membranes stretched so that he worried they might break off, and he sailed just above the bough, straining and catching all kinds of branches and knots along the way. He caught most of them in the face, until he skidded and rolled to an excruciating stop.

Flying! It was much more painful than the alternative; that was lesson one.

Where was he?

"Mabby?" someone said, as Mabby snorted and fished leaves and twigs from his cranium.

At the sound of Tufa's voice, Mabby suddenly became very aware of himself. He shook the leaves from his shirt and tried to sound like he could breathe. There was another figure beside hers, much taller than either of them, still behind the shadows. Eyes could be made out, but nothing else.

"Where did you come from, Mabby?" she said. "And what are you doing? You're not supposed to be out here!"

"Neither are you," Mabby said. He had crashed very hard and could no longer hold up the shaking joints that he had wrecked against the wood, and he buckled to the ground.

The figure said nothing. It reached out and gently laid a paw on Tufa's shoulder, and she said, "Don't worry. He's a friend," to him without looking back.

"I'm sorry but I need to go. We can finish some other time," the strange figure whispered to Tufa.

"No, wait." She turned to stop him but he was gone already. "I wanted to introduce you."

"Who was that?"

She looked around for a moment. "Never mind. What do you want?"

"Watch this!"

Mabby crouched and sprang, stretching his wings just as before. "Syriss was wrong, I can fl-" Bap, was the sound his head made as it connected with the bough boards. It's worth noting that one never becomes acclimated to boards to the face. Mabby felt for his nose, as he could not tell if it was in too much pain or gone entirely. He turned away from Tufa, fearing he might cry.

"It's all right, Mabby, I believe you," she said, "That's why I'm out here too. My friend Cal was helping me." Mabby felt a rush of relief. Suspicious pups with names like that obviously couldn't make respectable boyfriends, only nerdy tutors. He held up a paw for her to help him up. She was already off walking again. "I thought I should try and study ahead since I'm going to flight school, after all."

Mabby helped himself up and walked up behind her. "That's great!" He tried to slip his paw into hers.

"Yeah," she said, and ran up ahead to show him. "It looks like it will take me some extra (whoa) some extra work, but…" Her arms flailed wildly but she managed to accomplish a short levitation. "I think if I can do it, you can too."

"Thanks!" Mabby leaned in for a hug, but when he opened his eyes she was already walking off again.

"But just that first little bit was so hard…I can't imagine how difficult it must be to balance myself in the air for so long, like a ballerina."

A flash of determination came over Mabby. "She'll just have to witness my greatness firstpaw," he thought, and he repeatedly jumped up and down behind her, nearly crashing but silently catching himself. She turned around and he stood up nonchalantly.

"You look pretty tired. Are you okay? You took a lot of rolls in that...thing back there. I read somewhere that repeated blows to the head are definitely bad."

"M-hm." He was too busy thinking of how to impress her to hear anything she was saying. "Oh, no I'm *fine.*" No he wasn't.

"Maybe you should get that looked at, and anyway maybe you could work your way up to it. Bit by bit, you know? Less painful."

"Work my way up," Mabby thought. Get higher! That was it! "That is a *great idea!"* he said.

“I know; I scare myself sometimes.” She laughed. She turned around and he was gone. Then she saw him climbing a tree! Oh my goodness, he’s going to kill himself. What have I done? “No, no, no, Mabby, Mabby, I didn’t mean it like that. I’m sorry. Please come down.”

“No, it’s great, it’s gonna be great, just watch.”

“Mabby, I’m scared, please come down! Whatever I said, I didn’t mean it!” Her voice shook.

Does she think I’m trying to kill myself or something? He shook the confusion out of his head and, with a “one, two, three,” he leapt and Tufa gasped, covering her eyes.

He stretched like he had never stretched, and soon he felt the sensation he had before.

“Look, Tufa!” But she wouldn’t. “Look at meeeee! Eeeeeeaaaah!” His wings slammed open, and he had to pull up hard to narrowly avoid careening into her. That sent him into a tailspin, and then…Bop!

Everything went black.

Chapter 10: Inimical Umbra

He awoke slowly.

Where am I? How far did I go? he wondered. The sound of crickets greeted him at an unusual volume. Something was wrong. "What is this soft padding that smells so dirty? Hm. It's dirt! What a dusty tree," he thought. "It must be very far from home. Are there no street sweepers in this part of town? And the moss!" He hadn't seen anything quite so advanced in any of the parts of town he knew. Indeed. As his eyes adjusted, it occurred to him that he was aboard the largest bough he had ever seen! There wasn't a trunk in sight. Then he began to make them out. Trunks were everywhere, but they were much larger and much farther away than he had ever known trunks to be. He stood up dizzily, and it slowly came to him that he was on the forest floor, in that scary place that squirrels in stories didn't come back from, that place every youngrel was made to promise they would never, ever, ever, ever go.

"So this is what the ground feels like," he thought, trying to distract himself from the growing lump of fear in his throat. The scrapes and sores began to make themselves known all over his body. The air was not as cheerful down here. As a matter of fact, he felt as if he were being weighed down by a great blanket of silence. "But it can't be all bad," he thought, and just then he stepped on a thistle.

"Ow!" he yelped, and at the sound of his cries of pain, it seemed as if the forest began to slowly wake. The echoes racketed around and fell dead after many moments.

Mabby looked around nervously. The ladder to the Great Commons Gate to the treetops, the only way into town, was nowhere to be seen. It was an ancient tree as old as the city, and it was as big as twenty redwoods. This must be far beyond the borders of town!

"Dad?" he shouted. No answer. Of course, he scolded himself. Of course, when I don't listen! Now I will never get home and everyone will laugh at what an idiot I am, Mabby the Falling Squirrel. For sham and for shame.

A *woosh* went overhead in the sky somewhere.

But wait, how did I get out all this way?

"Hello? Dad?" he called, and listened to the forest's veils.

But all he heard was its tepid hale, till something out of the venal bode ran behind and around and darted back. A rustle, a snapping twig, a crick, and a crack. Then there was another woosh, and all fell silent as a dead mouse at your door.

Then the breathing started, or what seemed like breathing, but could not have belonged to anything so small as he had ever known. He thought he must have had another knock for there were no footsteps, yet the air was knavish and warm at his feet.

He gave a hard listen. He heard naught of his father's voice, but made out, or perhaps, he could not tell, made up, a tuft of whisper stirring against his brain from somewhere out in the wash of black beyond and it called in a low hum. It moaned in a breath as low as a heartbeat, "In... firm." He listened again. "...Innnnnnnnn.... firrrrrmmmmm."

And it grew closer and louder, though he could not make out what direction it came from. The friend in the forest beyond the Tanglewall did not seem so chummy.

The black knot on his head swelled and pulsed. The hair on his neck prickled, and he started to run, not knowing where he was going. "Infirm...Infirm," the whispering in the wind rustled and droned, and he moved his legs faster. His breath quickened, but the pattering of his feet and chattering of his teeth could not drown out the crescendo of rustling leaves and whispers. He stumbled on a black knot and, as he scrambled, gasps for breath turned to pathetic screams, looking about for some clue as to where to go.

Then, without warning, he was snatched up.

He flailed his arms in a hopeless effort to escape the iron grip of his captor. "Dad! Dad, help me! Help me please! Where are you?!"

Then a familiar voice spoke to him through his rapid-fire screams. "It's me. It's me, Mabby, calm down," he said, wrestling for control as they careened through the air. Dorma managed to swerve back to the Great Tree, already having cleared two or three klicks to the south. "How did you get out here? Stop it! Listen, it's me!"

Mabby began to recognize his father's voice, and he immediately broke into tears.

Dorma said nothing more and took Mabby up to the Great Gate, panting and looking behind him.

"What are you doing!" Dorma started in. "How did you get out here? Where have you been?! I've been looking everywhere for you."

"Dad?" Mabby said.

"What the bloody bing-boggles are you doing? Are you suicidal?"

"I—"

"I don't want to hear it. What is the matter with you?" Dorma shook Mabby by the shoulders.

"I—"

"I don't want to hear it! Do you know what could be out here? Not another word, youngrel, we're going home. What could possibly interest you out here, eh?"

"It's just…"

"That is E-nough! We're going home. We're going home and, we're, uh...we're going home. And you're grounded."

"It's just I wanted—"

"Wanted *what?"* Dorma demanded. "To be grounded?"

That one hurt. Mabby started to cry again. "It's just…I wanted to fly, and you can fly, and I just wanted you to teach me but you *wouldn't—"*

"I've had enough. That's enough, and we're going home. So you thought you could learn to fly by teaching yourself? Didn't you hear me when I said there was plenty of time for that?"

"Dad, listen! I just—"

"No."

"Please! Everyone said you were the best, and I asked you to teach me, and I *know* I'm behind and I can't do it and I want to learn so bad, (sob) and Syriss said you're the best ever, but you *wouldn't (sob) you wouldn't...*"

The storm in Dorma's eyes broke. "I don't care what Syriss said! (sigh) Syriss isn't here pulling you out of danger! I can't..." He let Mabby go and turned away. "I can't...do it. Not again." His shoulders slumped. "You don't understand, Mabby, and neither does Syriss, what it did to me."

"What...*what* did to you?" Mabby asked.

"Being the best, and still not...Not being able to help." His father's voice cracked. "Syriss was right. I was top class and, all the way up, I only ever thought of myself and, in the end, the only person I could help was me. Being better than everybody didn't do anything, I *still* was a failure. (sniff) A lowlife."

"Not able to help who?" Mabby asked.

"Your mother." Dorma fought to choke down the sobs that nearly erupted as he clapped his paws to his face and doubled over. "She...(gulp). She had wings like yours, Mabby. Big, beautiful wings, but she couldn't fly so I tried to help her. But now I understand I wasn't helping her. What I did-I was helping everyone else deal with her. I was helping myself. And I don't *know* how to help. I don't know, but I know I can't do that to you." He stopped and shook between whimpers, saying no more for a long time, till he was almost completely silent and still. "You know they say the Great Nut helps those who help themselves. Well, I say the Great Nut can go to his very own hell, because it wasn't paying attention when your mother was helpless and it wouldn't let me help her. It was like it WANTED this to happen. I should have helped myself, right? Bollocks! I was there, right there watching when you were born... (pant, sob) *and when she died...*

(pant, pant), I died. I died, Mabby, and you're all I've got left. I can't lose you too. I can't…I can't..."

"You won't lose me, Dad. Ever, and that's all there is to it." Mabby, in a most grown-up moment, said nothing more. He put his arms around his father's neck and tried his best to take that burden of pain upon himself. He also felt the weight of Mother's absence. If he dared think her name, the strange electricity of grief rendered him immobile as well, and they leaned on each other. "It's okay, Dad."

Eventually, they silently got up and Dorma took Mabby's paw to lead him home.

Bells rang at daybreak. When the light came, they had only progressed to about back where Mabby had fallen. Shouts clambered in the distance overhead. They were about halfway home when squirrels all over town were taking wing, coming out of their shanties and houses and darting back and forth. Mabby had never seen anything like it. Soon they gathered and began a fast procession, dropping into the lower boughs.

A breathless sentry took notice of Mabby and Dorma. He glided over to them and shouted, "Come on! We're all moving to the gate. Something's been sighted. Hurry!"

Mabby could feel his father's paw clench his. Dorma yelled, "What is it?"

The sentry took a look around and motioned to them. Dorma told Mabby to stay where he was and went over to the guard. They turned their backs, conversing with wild gestures. Dorma looked around frantically, for a moment or two, and barked, "Tufa!"

She was hiding behind a rick of kindlewood.

"Come here. It's all right." Dorma motioned to her. She looked around and realized he thought she was hiding because she was afraid. "Can you do something for me?" Dorma said as she came out from behind the smokestack, straightened her hair, and came over bashfully. Mabby caught her eye—he knew better—and she shot him an "if you tell, I tell" look. Mabby snarkishly complied and innocently looked at the scenery.

"Tufa, I need you to take Mabby home. Can you do that for me? And then I want you to go right home yourself, understand? No doubt your parents are waiting for you, in all this commotion, and are very anxious indeed. I know you are a responsible young kit and can handle this, right? Yes. Then off you go. Get on home, you two. Everyone will be back soon." Dorma gave the two of them a last doubtful look and jumped off the bough, in hot pursuit of whatever it was the town had gone to see.

Tufa and Mabby looked at one another and bounded after him, working their way down branch by branch. "This is better," thought Mabby, "more like it should be."

They were almost down to where everyone was meeting when a figure dashed out of the dark and snatched them into a corner.

"Shh," Syriss said. "Where's Bo?"

"Are you kidding? Nothing could wake Bo at this hour. He sleeps like a stone. At the bottom of a lake," Tufa said. "Inside of a cavern. Under a mountain. On...the moon—"

"Okay, shh."

"Syriss, what are you doing here?" she said.

"Didn't I just say shush?" In an exaggerated gesture, Syriss put his finger to his mouth. "I am everywhere."

"Huh?" Mabby looked at him blankly.

"Don't shush me and then ask me stuff," Tufa said under her breath, but not quietly enough.

"Never mind it's, never mind." Syriss gave up. "My dad said something was wrong, so I went outside before he sent for the bellringer, and I overheard them say someone's been killed."

"What?!"

"Yeah. Isn't my dad terrible at keeping secrets?"

"Who's your dad?" Tufa and Mabby said together.

"I'm not as bad as he is. Duh. I'm not supposed to tell." So Mabby supposed that there must be an ugly reason no one knew this extraordinary person, who was privy to massacres and could possibly be better at flying than his dad.

"Come see," Syriss said, and they followed him out of the knockhole.

Then suddenly, the very moment they were all in the light, they were all snatched up by massive paws and slung over a set of shoulders as big as a police officers'. They all had flashes in their minds about getting a stern talking from whatever adult had found them. "Booboo! Booboo!" a voice called out.

"Bo?! No way," Tufa said, and Syriss laughed. "Under a mountain on the moon, eh?" he said.

"Where's he taking us?" she asked.

Bo carried them down to the tanglefloor, and they got down on all fours, so they would not fall through, and pawed aside the leaves so they could get a clear view of whatever was going on at the forest floor.

"What's going on down there?" asked Syriss as if anyone would know.

They watched as the adults down on the ground, far below the Tanglewall, gathered in a sorrowful crowd. Many of them seemed to be straining to keep it together. One person broke out wailing and had to be carried off, and others shushed and comforted one another and shook their heads. The squirrels in the middle of the commotion held out their arms to keep everyone away from what was going on. Then one of the squirrels in the middle stood up and bowed his head. He must have said something because that was when everyone really let out the head shaking and crying.

Then Mabby heard that strange *woosh* he had heard when he was down there by himself and wondered if it was a coincidence. If so, it was the oddest timing.

The one in the middle was speaking, and then all of a sudden an arm came up and those in between the arm and the middle parted ways, til the outsider was inside. It was Bolly Beeley. What was he doing there? He threw his arms out dramatically toward the still body of the reclusive but kind Hallo Ballo and shouted, "My...*Brother*!" Then Bolly bent over and seemed to be mourning, but from Mabby's hiding place in a hole in the Tanglewall, the body was unrecognizable.

Bolly jumped up and put his fists in the air, and his shouts could be made out with some difficulty. He was vowing revenge. The three of them exchanged glances.

Then it got interesting, for none other than Mabby's dad suddenly grabbed Bolly by the shoulder, put a finger in his chest, and seemed to be giving the old dog quite a talking to. He backed him into the wall of adults, and someone jumped in and took Dorma by the arms. Then Dorma did something Mabby never would have expected. Dorma spit, and it hit Bolly squarely between the eyes. He was then restrained by a few more.

"Heh, my dad's really giving him what for," Mabby said.

"Yeah, but *what for?*" Syriss quipped.

Then something happened which proved the most curious of all things that day. A strange robed figure, whose face could not be made out by anyone, stepped forward silently. Everyone hushed; indeed, it seemed the whole forest, and even the wind, ceased to breathe. There was occasional gasping, so the three intrepid pups above it all could only presume it was saying something, at which everyone seemed as incredulous as they were at its very presence.

Syriss was undisturbed, oddly enough. "Hm," thought Mabby.

The figure slowly lifted its finger, pointing at the deceased squirrel on the ground, and Dorma shouted, for—from the second the figure had appeared—he had seemed to be seconds from a heart attack. Mabby took to hyperventilating, and took not his eyes from the hood on the figure's robe. Others were occasionally whispering to one another and pointing at the design on the hood.

The figure turned its head toward Dorma, who all but fainted, and it said something. Oddly, this prompted Dorma to calm himself. When it turned its head again, it was toward Bolly Beeley, who ducked out of the crowd. Everyone who was paying any attention to the exchange suddenly became very confused, for he had done it so well. It was as if he was as skilled at slipping in and out of crowds as the shaded figure was. The figure merely stood, saying nothing, and jerked its head up.

Mabby realized it was looking directly at them, which took a moment since all that showed of the crested shadow was a small slit for seeing under its black mask, how it could possibly have known that they were there or who they were it was baffling to tell,

"Blathering Broomsticks." Syriss ducked with the rest of them. It seemed to be more out of annoyance than fear. "Spotted. Drat. Nuts."

"Syriss!" Tufa smacked the back of his head. "Don't talk like that!"

Syriss remembered himself. "Come on, we've got to follow that rat."

Off they all three bounded, most of them questioning everything and wanting to get back home as quickly as possible.

"Come on!" Syriss urged them on. "Can you still see him?"

"Yes, but he's quick," Mabby said. "What's going on?"

"I think I have an idea, but I can tell you later."

"No, Syriss. Tell us now, or we're stopping and not helping you one inch more," Tufa said. "(Puff, puff.) We got a right to know."

"Fine. You see 'im down there?"

Bolly Beeley darted this way and that, in and out of view, but generally they could keep eyes on him.

"Yeah."

"He's the bad guy," Syriss said.

"The bad guy? He's running for mayor," Tufa said. "Are you sure he's not just trying to go get help or something?"

"No way. (pant) He's on his way to do some evil thing, as a part of a plot." He paused. "Something. We don't know."

"You're darn right we don't know." Tufa stopped, and so did everyone else. "Now unless you can come up with something substantial against the establishment of authority, then I'm not moving another step. This is ridiculous."

She stopped, forcing the rest of them to stop as well.

"Can't you see someone's goin' around killing squirrels?" said Syriss. "And that's the problem with mysteries. You don't know 'til you *find out*, but we gotta find it out. Now come...on." Syriss' voice scattering off the vaults of the forest.

Bolly Beeley stood still before them, apparently as stunned to see them as they were to see him.

Syriss, for once, said nothing. They all stared at one another for a long moment; then Syriss started whistling and looking around. "Nice day isn't it, lovelies? I think Mummy and Daddy are taking me to the park today."

"Oh. *Oh,* um, yes, most exciting," Tufa said. "That sounds terribly splendid, would you care if I were to join you?"

"That would be most excellent," Syriss said.

"Great, excellent," Tufa replied, "and do you suppose I could bring my dolly and teas? Mummy made numpets and I do love numpets, yum!"

Mabby was entirely lost.

"Most excellent. Yes," Syriss said. "Don't you, Mabbs?"

"Yes, perfect!...Would you like to *play along* with us, Mabby?" Tufa asked.

"Um, sure," Mabby said.

"Great!" they both said, and they all looked back at Bolly, whose eyes had grown wide at the sound of Mabby's name. He remembered himself and looked past them, resuming walking wherever he was pretending to go.

"Good morning, chaps and chap-ette. How do you do?" He barely waved his paw. "Bit chippy to be out this time, don't you think?"

"Oh, it's nothing," Mabby said. "I just love nature." He smiled.

Bolly looked at him as if trying to hide his surprise at seeing a ghost. Then he walked off without another word.

"Well, that was awkward," Syriss said.

"*He's* awkward," Tufa said.

Mabby said nothing, but followed him quietly at a distance, and the others followed suit. Bolly turned a corner into a dark alley and disappeared.

"Where do you think he went?" Tufa asked. They could hear him but he was nowhere to be seen.

"Listen…" Mabby said.

When they came close and put their ears up, they heard a muffled kicking and thrashing about and, after a moment or two, he stopped. After several seconds of sheer silence, they heard only the sounds of rising and falling sobs and trembling whimpers, so they left him alone, for evil squirrels are intriguing, but sad ones are just a bore.

On the way home, Syriss picked up the old conversation. "Now do you two believe me? He's up to something, and we need to find out what it is."

"We?" Tufa interjected.

"Yes. We. You're involved, too, Tufa. Everyone is. Didn't you see all of that back there? Mabby's dad? The…the way Bolly acted? And just how in the *blueberry fluffies* did he get around so fast? Right? Put it all together, something very wrong is happening inside the walls of this town. You can almost smell it in the air. *I swear I'm the only one who makes these connections.*" He trailed off again, holding his arms akimbo.

"No, you can't. I saw the pain of a burdened squirrel. I saw accusations without proof. I see paranoia," Tufa said with a wave of her arm.

"We need to protect ourselves when school starts, that's all I'm saying. We need to look out for each other."

"This is stupid."

"It's only stupid if we're safe."

Mabby was silent, looking at the ground, for most of the conversation. "Then it's not stupid. And we're not safe. Not until we find out the truth, no matter what it is."

Tufa was silent.

"So we're like some sort of club then?" Mabby said.

"We're a secret club. Emphasis on the secret."

"What about Bo?"

"Don't involve him," Tufa interjected.

"We won't. Not if he doesn't want to be."

"Right…" Mabby was a little skeptical. It seemed Syriss had contrived this little club. "I'd say that leaves him suspect too," he thought. "So, what is the name of this little club thing?" Better to be in than out.

"I'll think of one. But this sort of reminds me of those old stories about the old Protectors. You think? You know how they went into secrecy? That's kind of what we're doing."

"Right, I don't think it's quite like that. But anyway, I've got to get back. Dad's probably looking for me now." Mabby said.

Syriss blinked away the contrarianism. "Right, so we meet, just like always, at the court, and we'll go from there."

"All this 'we' business. I said I'm not playing," Tufa said.

"Why not?" Mabby asked.

"A secret society for finding out others' secret societies? It's just so hypocritical. I'm not having anything to do with it, unless… Unless you, Syriss..." She poked him in the chest as he stood proud. "Tell us who your father is."

"Why do you want to know." It was more of a statement than a question, as if they were both merely being rhetorical.

"Because, as the resident logical one, I need you to prove to me that you're not just as bad as the forces, or whatever, you're after?"

"Forces?" Mabby asked,

"Well then, just don't!" Syriss said.

"And what if we don't have any new information?" Mabby said.

"Then jackybin, of course!" Syriss smiled.

"How do we know what information is secret between us and what is not? We need, like, a password," Mabby said.

Syriss looked down and paused; then he grinned. The next two words he uttered struck Mabby, for as far as he knew Syriss was not particularly creative, nor possessed the type of vocabulary for proficient wordplay. And it was for this reason that he decided to join, if not for any other reason than finding out what they really meant.

This he thought as the words, “Inimical Umbra” seemed to slide down his back like nails along some old scar long neglected, the way when someone happened to touch the stiff parts just wrong, and wake the phantoms of memory.

Chapter 11: How Not to Avoid Looking Like a Prating Fool on Matriculating Day.

Hal's body was laid to rest in the great cemetery in East Waldell, between patches of bluebell, where the sun broke through. The gray air below always cast shadows unfamiliar to children in the lifted city. He was eulogized by Reverend Ferroule, who described him as many remembered him, one whose wealth was all the world's before his own. There was the matter of a small fortune that would be left to Callo, but he seemed to pay it no mind, for Ballos held their name to be of more worth than pence of any sort. "The Great Nut is good to us all. We are given work to make a difference..." he would always say in his Southern manner. "And then money to be kind."

Many came forward to say a word, and most reflected on something Hal had given them when they were in times of need, never demanding repayment, even though he was but a farmer. He had even become known as a substantial benefactor to the school. Words were said and, at the private gathering, the body was let down with twine ropes to be accepted by the soil. All passed by, one by one, paying their respects and wiping their eyes.

Hal's funeral had been open. It was said that, in his youth, he had quit flying school but, somehow, he had learned anyway, and though he had been confined to a life on the ground as a farmer, he had still earned his way into the townsquirrels' hearts. While everyone cried, Mabby could only think of the sudden disappearance of Tufa's intrepid friend, but he could say nothing. The four friends only looked at one another, and then went home heavy hearted.

In the very early morning, three quiet days later, classes began at Rammerie's. Dorma picked up the paper on the porch and stirred his persimmon tea while noticing a few pennants hanging from his pockets. He set the paper down on the table inside, sat down, and played with the loose strings. He peeped nonchalantly from the paper to Mabby, who was busying himself with scribbling a death battle between a couple of imaginary squirrel heroes, with a bit of chalk and shale, reciting a poem he was making up on the spot.

Coldy and Moldy, heroes of Oldy
Gold shield and armor foiled and foldy
Swing high lol-lop off a kitty cat's paw!
Come to the tree, ye, ooh and aw.
Shout till all great branches fall
And scratch, drum, striddle
Till the Cat goes, RAW!!!

"That's pretty good, there. You should write that down, or something," Dorma said, somewhere between confused and awake. Then Mabby went on.

Coldy and Moldy, got old and rolly
Lazy, adventureless, drooly and droly
Butterscotch plates and numpet cakes!
Come to the tree, till yer belly aches.
Tell a story of the Squirrel King's hall,
And ratch, rum, and fiddle
Till the cat goes, RAW!!!

It was about that time Dorma noticed an article halfway down the front page: "Bolly Beeley Mayor of Hesperia." He promptly spit out some of his tea and spilled the rest all over his slacks. "Ah!" His surprise was countered by Mabby's, who leapt up in the air and forgot all about his paw-me-down things. Mabby tried to calm Dorma down as he was already well on his way to a fit of clammering and yammering.

"Dad! What's the matter?" Mabby said.

"I can't believe it. I can't believe it. I can't *believe* it!" Dorma shouted.

"I'm sorry, Dad, it was a terrible poem. I'll think of a better one. I promise. Please don't be mad."

Dorma shook the paper, reading the article. "Bolly Beeley, in first-ever mayoral election, wins landslide victory by vote of…Forty-five hundred and six to one...What? Well, well that would mean…" He stopped and stared at the wall as if it had said something quite rude indeed, and Mabby continued to tug on Dorma's shirt, unanswered. "Well, I mean, I thought the poll box was a bit deserted, but…"

"Dad, tell me!"

Dorma continued reading. "Oh, something is wrong, something is very wrong. Very, very wrong!"

"*Dad!*" Mabby yelled.

"In other news, rising fashion trend in young squirrels today, patagectomies...sweeping the Brambleries in celebration of Bolly Beeley's win for the mayoral bid, *celebration!* One youngrel says, 'It's in honor of my dad, who would have wanted me to have concern for the poor and disabled. To go without flight is to stand with them'… oh no…hundreds take to the boards of Hesperia's business district chanting, 'Don't Cheat, Use Your Feet'...Beeley questions the legitimacy and destiny of squirrels who live in trees, says in landmark inauguration speech, 'Remember...*the fallen…*' No..." He squinted at the paper in utter disbelief.

Daddy, what's wrong? What's a patty-tummy?" Mabby asked.

"It's nothing. Nothing, son, you hear? When you hear someone talking about patty-tummies, you go the other direction, okay?" Dorma began to scramble, grabbing an odd thing and a shirt and topcoat.

"Okay, Dad." Mabby shrugged.

"Now, I've got to get to work right away, lots of work to do, that's right."

Honestly, Mabby could not figure out what Dorma's problem was. Mabby loved patty-tummies and, as a matter of fact, could have gone for one at that particular moment.

"Good, now let's get you ready for school." Dorma hurried and fustled and drumbled and fussed with his collar, fighting to get his socktie straight, walking briskly this and that way. "Now go to school. Get right there and no straying, do you understand? Don't talk to anyone."

"Okay, Dad." Mabby watched forlornly as Dorma started out the door, looking back to see that the house was still present, or something. He noticed, out of the corner of his eye, that Mabby was near tears as he messed with his shirt in confusion, having expected that Dorma would walk him to school, at the very least on the very first day. He dropped his paws to his sides and stared at the ground.

"Dear me, what a terrible dad I am." Dorma, feeling extremely stressed and conflicted, let go of his briefcase, bobby-bag, and canvas, knelt down by Mabby, and said, "We can't have you going to school on your first day all dressed like that, now can we? You know," he said as he straightened Mabby's gig line, flicking out a ruler to adjust his pants to the right height, just a bit below his belly button. Mabby giggled as Dorma tickled him. "I bet you've heard others ask why I became a tailor. You know why?"

"Why? Hee, hee," Mabby said as Dorma tickled his neck while straightening his collar and tie.

"Well, it's so you wouldn't have to go off and look like the simpering simpleton I looked like on my first day of school." Mabby laughed. "It's not funny. I literally was wearing the fabric off of my mother's couch from back when squirrels smoked and didn't wash their fannies very well."

"Eww!!" Mabby said, laughing out loud.

"It's true. Society's changed so much." He sighed. "Oh, we're all just getting older by the day, now aren't we? Anyway, you're going to have to start dressing yourself like a big boy now. Remember," Dorma told Mabby as he adjusted buttons, measured ends, fluffed shoulders, pointed at him to straighten up, untied and tied his shoelaces, flushing the tips with the loop ends and tucking his shirt, "houndstooth over herringbone, but never vice versa. Blue over black, but never black over blue. Pat your hair with water; hair gel is the greatest of all sins. The tie makes the shirt, but the shoes make the suit. And the suit does not make the squirrel, but points to the squirrel. Bad emphasis is the definition of idolatry, hear? And a tragedy like that is still a tragedy, however finely written. It's not about what's logical, it's about what makes sense. Got it?"

"I think so," Mabby said. He didn't.

"Right." Dorma tousled Mabby's hair, then smoothed it again, and held him by the shoulders. "Are you sure you want to do this?"

"Yes. I'm sure. I want to." Mabby's self-assurance would have convinced anyone, except of course for Dorma.

"Well, we better get you going. Best part of the look is being nice and *early...* " Dorma trailed off and seemed, for a moment, to be staring at something far beyond the sky.

Mabby and his dad held paws as they walked, and they gazed at the warm blue above. Dorma noticed the light turning to gold shafts driving all around the waking realm and the old familiar birds singing their grand good-day chatter just as ever. The walk, for Dorma, was considerably shorter, being merely down the rows from Tadwick Bough. It was not the usual way he took to work, with the business district being in the Midlevels, across town to the south, rather than at Rammerie's spire. The spire, visible from almost all places, shared the upper level with the upper class, which semi-circled the school in a crescent sloping a bit as it ventured from the peak of Nearly Mountain. It was only convenient to get to Rammerie's from the priciest real estate, so the poor kits and pups climbed wearily and unaccompanied to the point Dorma and Mabby had veritably hopped, skipped, and jumped to.

Dorma couldn't help but look as they passed the old, now abandoned house where Debby had first climbed down from her prison window. Some believed the house was haunted. Dorma knew, and hated that he knew, that they had merely withdrawn from society. They were afraid, as squirrels of their class tended to be, that their little girl, exposed as an infirm all those years ago, had brought shame upon their great and glorious name. So rather than sigh and move on with life, despite some finding out they were not completely perfect, they decided the honorable thing to do was to roll over and die. So they succumbed to a life of seclusion and despair. Or so was the story.

That was not the only thing that was different, Dorma began to realize as he surveyed the walkpaths he had not tread since his yorey days. The old familiar spire appeared less bright and cheerful. Its copper glint had turned a runny green and brown. Now there were guardposts and sentries guarding every this and that. No one could even get yanked into a respectable corner. "And I thought the date stick was bad," he chuckled to himself. Dorma and Mabby came upon the place where a great hole had been torn in the Tanglewall and had since grown over. A redwood had gone to the depths, taking many boughs and streets with it, not to mention nearly taking Dorma's and Debby's lives in that race. For a long and frightful time, this had left a gash in the leafwood floor of the city, where intruders great and tall could enter just as that great cat Morgart had once done. It had never occurred to anyone, until much later, shouldn't there have been many more such threats with the broken wall? Some had many theories and Dorma had heard them all. They made his throat tighten and his visage darken until no one dared deliver such speeches to him. For him, all it had taken was one. Then it dawned on Dorma: why he had always taken such pains to avoid this route to work.

"There, there old boy," Dorma thought, allowing himself to be pulled back to the light by Mabby's gentle tugging. Mabby was skipping, never letting go of his paw.

"Hey, Dad!" Mabby piped up.

"What's up?" Dorma was glad for a little conversation.

“Do you think we could close the shop, after I get out of school, and go to the park?”

“I don’t know if that would be wise at the very moment, but we can see,” Dorma said. That was true, but Mabby’s silence telegraphed his thoughts better than words.

“I just need to see something at work, and then I think we could go.” Dorma couldn’t help himself. Mabby skipped again, taking the concession as a definite affirmative, and Dorma felt the old familiar worry bug settle into his brow line. “I hope these days never end,” he thought. Dorma allowed him out of the house, only to accompany him to work and to the park, less and less and less. Mabby’s friends had begun to wonder about him, but they couldn’t suspect Dorma’s worries. That’s why I’m the Dad, he reminded himself.

Soon the door, signed “J. Marix. Rammerie School for Flying Youngrels” would come into view. Mabby felt a punch of anxiety fill his stomach and a shot of electricity in his flanks.

“Oh… Oh… Preh. Press.” Mabby muttered. Dorma couldn’t figure out what Mabby was trying to say. He was trying to read something. “O-press… (Sigh)” Dorma looked about and found, to his horror, that Mabby was quoting what had been maliciously painted across the facade of the schoolhouse in huge, hurried ugly black letters: “Oppression!” Still other words, “down with the system.” It was scrawled across the doors and windows. Like all over the rest of town, there were posters and fliers and amateur portraits painted all over trees. They depicted the face of Bolly Beeley and, more recently, of Hal. Inside, Dorma marveled, for he remembered a time when all of this had been celebrated, and now youngsters rushed to get inside *before* the bell, so as not to be seen.

Dorma drew in his breath, trying not to let Mabby know that his heart had quickened. His paws shook, and his talk was flitting about more than usual. Mabby had noticed that, but said nothing. “All right, son,” Dorma said, trying to distract Mabby enough to get him past the schoolhouse facade. The painters were out early on the emergency job so they wouldn’t have to worry about it later. “Now, when you go out to try yourself at flying, remember this. No matter what happens, the greatest opponent you will ever have is yourself. It's not about beating anyone else. Understand? That's how we Dabbys get to be the best."

"Got it, Dad." Mabby didn't get it at all. Maybe he would soon. Mabby understood perfectly well, however, that Dorma did not like the words painted across the schoolhouse, and he knew he must consult with the others.

"All right." Dorma patted Mabby's shoulder one last time. "I've got to go. I'm proud of you, son, and so is your mom."

"Really?"

"Believe me, I know."

Mabby looked ahead with a sternness uncommon for his age. It always took Dorma by surprise how old the boy could be.

"Go on now, don't want to be late," Dorma said. "And go straight home. I'll be closing early today so we can celebrate, okay? See you."

"Okay, Dad, see you," Mabby said. He walked into the classroom, waving goodbye, and Dorma began to tiptoe shopward. Nothing further, well, that's good, I think. Dorma quickened his pace. Once Mabby had completely gone from sight, he broke into a run, leaving those around wondering what could possibly make someone run like they were battling a conniption. "Don't worry," one of the other parents said to the pups still saying goodbye. "That squirrel has always been that way."

"*Runs* in the family," another said, making walking gestures with his fingers.

"I guess you'd have to go a mile in his shoes to understand."

"Yeah, it's been kind of a *running joke.*"

"He must have a runner's high."

"Look son, it's a psycho-path! Ha!"

"Oh, I got one, what do you call someone who runs like they still have a hanger in their bum? A bloody idiot! Ha ha ha!"

"Well, that was just rude," said another and they all nodded, agreeing that things had gotten badly out of paw, and promptly dispersed.

Then, *ding dong,* rang the tardy bell, and class had begun.

Mabby sat down in the front, not looking at anyone in particular. He was much more worried about the squirrel slouching at the front of the classroom. Everyone knew her name, but still it was printed across the shaleboard. She said nothing to anyone while she wrote, which made them all uncomfortable. She stopped her feverish writing for only a second, when a bumbling, nerdy kit with an absolutely massive bag bumped in, shuffling. She hit the doorjamb and then a chair and nearly dropped everything as she tried to push up her glasses. Then she coughed and tried to look nonchalant as she wiped her nose. To Mabby's horror, she sat in an empty seat next to him, nearly knocking the chair over in the process, and let her bag down with a thud. To all of this Ms. Padduck barely gave a tilt of her head.

"Deela," she said.

Oh, Nuts.

The thing spoke again. "We have the same birthday."

Well that's creepy. Mabby, extremely confused, was about to ask, "And that means a fart in the wind to me why?" when he realized she was holding out her paw for him to shake. He decided to be nice and shook it quickly, hoping no one saw, but the moment their paws touched an "ooo" rose from the rest of the class. It was cut off the moment Ms. Padduck popped round and said in a booming voice, "Hello, class! What a wonderful day to fly, is it not?" This the class found entirely unexpected and completely disconcerting.

The room was utterly silent. Ms. Padduck went on, "Aren't you all just looking so lovely today! Isn't it such a perfect, wonderful, glorious day to learn and, above all, to begin the great journey that is ahead of you all! It could not be a better day! It is fate this day that you should all come here, and I believe that everything happens for a reason. Not just any reason but, for each of you, there is a definite reason, a reason that has to do with destiny. That's why you are here."

Ms. Padduck's shocking pleasantness, coupled with her alarmingly loud voice, was almost too much for the class to handle. Mabby had been expecting a drone. Only moments before, the class had whispered about "The Tower of Terror, the Figure of Fear, the Sculpture of Scary, the Hard Copy of Horror. The Simulacrum of Sunder." At that point Mabby had stopped listening, but he got the point. He recalled his conversation with Dad in which he had asked what Ms. Padduck looked like, and he'd simply replied, "Well, imagine the devil…" A look had come across his face that had said to Mabby, "We should speak no more of this."

That description did not fit the squirrel that was before him. This old kit was at least as tall as others had described, but a great dumpling, really, not threatening at all. And her personality rang with an endearing sweetness. Mabby could simply not imagine the devil herself as this ginger teacher, with her hair in a poof, wearing pearloids around her neck and a dress from a century ago. The only horns were her horn-rimmed glasses. The class could not figure out whether to be nervous for everything that they had expected was wrong except that her loud voice was blaring in their ears. It was definitely her.

"Mizz Padduck, ma'am?" Someone raised his paw.

"Yes, deary?"

"Isn't there going to be a roll call?" The class tensed.

"Oh, deary, it doesn't work like that anymore. I know who you all are Don't be silly." And she began to point them all out by name. "Yes, there's you, Deela, all ready for note taking now, are we?"

Deela smiled big. "Oh, do they not take notes in Brazil?"

All heads swiveled this way and that nervously for, at that instant, some swore the room had suddenly grown darker, as Ms. Padduck sucked in a breath, and surely there had been a change in the pressure in the room, but no one could say for certain.

"Well, I'm not sure. How *is* your father these days?"

"He's great, ma'am! Did you hear his sermon yesterday on the dangers of perspicacious caterwauling?"

"Oh, well, no. How was it?"

"Oh, it was terrible. But he was very good. You should come down and hear him sometime."

"I shall try."

Deela pushed up her glasses and looked up admiringly at Ms. Padduck. "You're alright, Mizz P. I don't care what everybody says about you."

"My *goodness,* dear. I could just *fold* you *up* and *take* you home and put you in a *stew*, and *eat* you up be*cause* you are *so* precious!" Ms.

Padduck patted her on the head and moved on down the row, reciting names. But why, Mabby wondered, hadn't the marm done anything about her tardiness?! What kind of an example would that set? Either way, Deela was never late again.

Mabby got the chance to look around as Ms. P continued naming names. Syriss, Bo, and Tufa were all in class with him, and Syriss was sitting right behind him. As a matter of fact, the moment that Ms. Padduck turned around, Syriss tried to paw Mabby a note and said, "Meet me at the court after school, much to discuss." He remembered to whisper, "Inimical Umbra."

Syriss whispered the dark password so softly but, strangely, it did not escape the ears of Ms. Padduck, for they bent low and trembled at the sound. She stopped, turned and, almost in a whisper, asked, "What was that? What did you say?" She said again, nervously, "Who said that?" And Syriss was sorely afraid that he had been caught passing the note, which Mabby unfolded later to realize it was but a caricature sketch of Ms. Padduck, containing no risky information at all. So she bent over his face, and said, "Did you have something to share with us, Syriss?" He simply sat up, shook his head, and gave her the fattest, cheesiest smile in history. She smiled, but her tail was clearly not amused as it as it was rigid with anxiety.

"Now all right, children. As I said before, today is a wonderful day to fly!" They looked about, wondering what evil plan she had concocted. Surely she was not insinuating they would take a crack at it on the very first day?! "Today we shall begin our first step in the Practicum. There has been a curriculum change, and… that is all I can really say. I know you have all been on pinions and pine needles to learn the sacred history of our fine town. The provost is… experimenting. So! Up!"

The class stood and snapped together in martial fashion. Mrs. Padduck thought that rather nice and said nothing about it. Mabby simply tried to ensure he would not be caught next to Deela. He sidled up to Tufa, who had sidled up to a tall figure at the very front of the line. Behind him would surely be Syriss and the others. He peeked back, feeling their stares on the back of his head. They were probably wondering what he was so interested in. Deela was looking at him, wide-eyed, leaning over into his line of vision and grinning. A little bit of snot started running out of her nose without her noticing. Then Mabby snapped his eyes forward, as they began to walk single file. Ms. P had finished giving instructions, whatever they had been. Mabby tried to rush out the door, but he was stopped by Deela's insistent badgering. She kept asking this and that question about something or other. He tried to whisper to Tufa and ask her if she was going to the park, but she simply flicked her blonde and brown hair and said, "No."

He asked why and she simply walked on.

A tall squirrel stood behind him, and Mabby noticed that he and Tufa were holding paws. Then Mabby noticed that the rat-faced squirrel was watching him. What a putz, so arrogant to think she needed protection from her own friends, and she just went right along with it! I'll show him, that manipulator, that rat-dog.

He got a tap on his shoulder. He looked back, and Deela was shaking her head. "You shouldn't talk like that."

He realized, to his horror, that he had been talking to himself out loud. But how loud?! He looked ahead, and Tufa was whispering excitedly and waving her paws. The squirrel who held her paw was rolling up a sleeve, and she was trying to roll it back down.

She calmed him down. "Thank the Great Nut," he thought.

Callo. Rat-face's name was Callo, Mabby remembered, recognizing his silhouette. As Callo rolled his sleeves down again, and Tufa relaxed, Mabby noticed strange big bruises and sores all over his arms, and that they were considerably filthy. 'I bet they're fighting a lot,' he comforted himself.

But he felt so bad.

"Now, my mighty, flighty little dears!" Ms. Padduck stopped them at a rickety building, about the size of the classroom they had come from, but inside it was utterly empty with the exception of the platform in the center. She began to explain the rules.

Mabby didn't hear anything for he was too busy thinking of how to explain himself. He tapped Tufa, who kept herself between him and

Callo. She simply shook her head. He tapped her again, and she leaned over and whispered, "Don't talk to me ever again."

"Don't ever talk to me again,"

"Not you,"

"Or…"

"Your crazy friends."

"Ever."

"Ever,"

"Ever!"

Chapter 12: On the Virtue of Knowing How to be Annoying

Mabby couldn't decide what to do with his face. It felt like he could swallow, but the muscles didn't seem like they could work right.

His stomach burned with fear and embarrassment, on top of the anticipation of the fear and embarrassment he was surely about to feel. As the line trudged closer to the contraption of doom, it became apparent that this small jump was simply outside of the mechanics of his accomplishing. He had been assuring himself that all he needed was a little more starting space than the others, and he would do fine or better. But this contraption was clearly designed to ensure, from the get go, that anyone needing just such was sure to be failed regardless of their powers. Mabby felt his wings, sensitive to the slightest changes in air pressure and other such things he had learned only he could sense, begin to tell him of their concerns. His tail looked about nervously for a way out, and Mabby's eyes stayed locked on his fate.

Syriss had gone first, and his jump was a phenomenon of regularity. No flair. He had strolled down from the platform, tucking his wings back in and rebuttoning his shirt with a galumphing air, like in the old "Catterwocky" tales they had been told as babies.

Then Bo went, nearly toppling the whole mass as he landed with a giggle and a grin.

Callo went. Nothing special. Hmph.

Then Tufa nervously approached as Mabby and Callo looked on from either side. Not that Mabby wanted her to crash or anything but, if she did, he sure wanted to be the one to catch her! Tufa didn't so much as look at him, though. She made quick work of the buttoning and sailed across unceremoniously, still wobbling badly. Though everyone gasped, she had no reaction. Some of them began to giggle, but Callo simple met them with his gaze, and they hushed. Ms. Padduck's smile dimmed somewhat, and she interjected.

"Let's not be that way. After all, are we not all here to learn? And what would that be without a lesson or two, now. Tufa come." She motioned for Tufa to go back to the starting platform. "Now, you all know there is no homework allowed, especially study groups, but I assure you it is for your own good, for the blind leading the blind is an endangerment to both." Cal got a little shifty at that, but Ms. Padduck appeared not to suspect anything. "You would all probably be telling little Tufa here to buck up and straighten herself out no?" She said this as she moved over to the far wall of the building and produced a long pole that reached nearly from floor to ceiling. "This is a little out of curriculum, but I will share with you now one of the secrets of the great wingliers." She posted the pole directly in the center between the two platforms, and motioned for Tufa to jump. Tufa shook her head in confusion and fear. "It's quite alright miss Tufa. But I want you to tip to the right, and you will be fine." Tufa approached trepidatiously and jumped just as Ms. P had ordered. However when she tipped, the difference of size in her one scarred wing and her other caused her to surge upward in a singing, tornadic, sideways upward spiral.

"Wonderful, miss Tufa, now bring your knees in and out to break!" Tufa did so, and she found herself far above their heads, and was able to float down, somewhat surprised at it all, and put one foot, then the other on the platform just as light and graceful as the sunshine. The other kits and pups stood with their mouths gaping.

"There now, isn't that better?" said Ms. Padduck. Tufa simply got down. "What you have seen is simple principle put into practice: instability equals maneuverability. Just about anything can be used to one's advantage.

Now, mister Dabby, your turn." She removed the pole and the class turned their focus to him.

No pressure. Deela whispered, "Go-go Mabby-Dabby sis boombah!" as he walked up the stair, too stressed to even think to roll his eyes.

Mabby gingerly approached the takeoff line. The landing was so close, there was no room at all for danger, which was good. But that meant he could get no momentum. He was worried he might not catch enough air. It had taken a launching point nearly twice this height for him to get any airtime, but he had felt what it was like to catch it now. He could find it again. It would definitely be a challenge, though, with so little room for error and so little time. But it couldn't be too hard. All he had to do was get from one small landing to another and, on his very first day at school, he would be able to fly for real, and show everyone how great he was going to be.

He looked down at his toes with extreme self-consciousness as all the other kits chuckled, watching as he undid the buckles and belts his father had fashioned inside his coat to make him appear a normal pup. "Better this way," he had said. Mabby's flaps fell out of his coat, which he removed gingerly, fearful of the mockery of his classmates. "It will be all right soon," he thought. "Soon they won't have anything to say." They sensed, from his hesitation, he was nervous, but they were wrong. He was not nervous. He wasn't just a little skitty. He was terrified. He felt naked as his grossly disproportioned flaps hung loosely like ugly brown drapes. Most of the kits behind him had probably never seen such a thing.

Ms. Padduck yelled up, "Now, little Mabby dear? Can you hear me?" Of course he could hear her. He could have heard a worm fart in mole-hole under Flatrock at the bottom of the mountain at that moment. But nothing in the wide world could get him out of this.

"What's your favorite thing to do, little Mabby dear?"

"Favorite thing?" he yelled down.

"What would you be doing right now if you had any other choice?" That sounded better, for of course flying was the thing he wanted to do more than anything, at least more than anything except be hurt, bleeding, and embarrassed. Other than flying?

"Being alive." Everyone laughed. Then he heard the enemy whispers: "Infirm, scaredy-cat. Can't. Can't, can't. Can't… fly."

"Think, little one." At least her words gave him something else to concentrate on. "When all of this is over, you will go home and *do what*?" Her words pierced him awfully.

He thought hard. "I… um. I like to, um, write."

"Well, what do you write, my little...um...writer?"

"Um, well, stories. That, um, you know, rhyme… sometimes."

"Oh, POETRY!" she exclaimed, and the class burst in laughter. "Oh my, a poet, and he doesn't even, ha! Well, I won't say it, don't worry. Why don't you recite me a poem?"

"Um, now? Here?" he thought. As if this weren't embarrassing enough.

"Well, have you written anything about flying? Come on. Tell me a poem of yours, maybe one about flying? Yes?" She waited. "NOW!"

He saw a flash of that other, scary, Ms. Padduck that he had heard so much about. He started with no further ado.

"Uh, The b- Uh, The bough...*approaches*."

"So stupid," he thought. The class rolled their eyes.

"Walk, don't run." Some more of them giggled. "Fear and love are often one." They fell silent.

"Wait for goodness, wait for light, see the one within take flight."

He looked about. They all just looked back at him.

"Find the place where Heaven lies; Heaven is your passion's prize.

Top of your head, tip of your toe, around the corner and away... we...go!"

"Now… Go!" Ms. Padduck shouted in such a jarring voice that Mabby could not help but jump. But his mind teetered, and he stumbled in hesitation. Trying to push every thought out of his mind, his thoughts fell to his mother and her voice. The poem didn't work, but his mother did. He envisioned her standing next to Ms. Padduck, smiling up at him, telling him to give it his very best. He realized if he were home, he would be writing poetry all right, *about her.* Mom. His heart leapt in his throat, and he realized everyone was watching him standing on the ledge, eyes tightly shut. He thought of the top of his head and the tip of his toe and, with a rather embarrassed last wish, he jumped from the landing with all of his might, throwing his arms high.

The takeoff felt beautiful. It felt exactly the way Ms. Padduck had said it should feel. He mentally checked his form, and it was perfect. He imagined his mother and all the kits *ooohing* and gasping, Tufa and Callo watching him in amazement, and Dad hearing the news. Over the treetops he flew. Maybe he could become someone, and it all started here. Wait till they get a load of me! There was no reason why he should not float right into the landing. "This is great," he thought. "It works this way. I've got to trust it." He concentrated on making his flight smooth and pointed his snout straight to the target with everything he had, straining his neck. The other kits drew a breath as he made his progress from the platform. They watched as he extended his arms straight out to his sides, locked them in, and paused mid-glide, waiting for the air to fill them, for the magical moment when he would start to move forward. As he arched his back, he tried so hard to make sure his flaps had every opportunity to receive the extra lift needed to get such a short distance. But his wings, which had provided him with an extended leap due to their almost slingshot-like momentum, now fell out of form and sagged beneath his arms like wet burlap. It sounded a lot more like gasps now. The vision of his mother, with all her glorious encouragement, faded. When she disappeared from his sight, he ceased moving forward and began to descend in an awkward, horrifying drop. He slammed flat onto the floor. The tears of failure began to flow, and he lurched on the floor in pain, hiding his face.

All the school-pups laughed, delighted by Mabby's fall. He had landed with a pitiful thud, and he lay there for a moment, trying to catch his breath. He had taken harder falls before, but this one seemed to hurt more than any other.

Deela's jump was not even noticed.

Ms. Padduck looked most concerned. "All right, children, that's fine for today. We'll pick up where we left off tomorrow. Mabby, take your time. See you tomorrow." Mabby wasn't listening. Ms. Padduck left quietly. She had taken it rather hard that he did not answer.

Syriss and Deela helped Mabby, who was still trembling, to his feet. Mabby looked up at Tufa, and their eyes met. The worst moment of his short, squirrelly life was suddenly made the best. Forgetting the two at his side, he saw only Tufa in front of him. She, of all kits, had come to see if he was all right. "I would fall a hundred times if you would be there," he thought, unsuccessfully trying to hide his increasing bashfulness. His heart and his stomach were playing merry-go-round.

The other students left, jeering. Disgusted by the crowd ridiculing their friend, Callo and Deela broke away from Mabby. As they all left, Mabby slowly followed Tufa. Lovely Tufa. Beautiful, caring, compassionate, understanding, kind Tufa.

"Tufa?" He looked up at her. Her eyes were so beautiful.

"Yes?" She looked at him half-knowingly. It seemed like she wanted to hear it.

"Will you be my girlfriend?" After having said it, he suddenly became aware of his busted lip, disheveled hair, and torn, dirtied clothes and tried to straighten himself up to no avail. He also noticed another squirrel coming down. It was Callo. Tufa's silence was telling. The wait was like the ache after a hammer blow. He waited for the shock to fade, the shattering pain to set in, and everything to fall apart.

"I'm sorry, what did you say?" she lied. "I was just making sure you were okay. I meant what I said."

Callo approached, somewhat regretfully, and gently took Tufa by the arm. She didn't look back. She really had just wanted to make sure he was okay. "Nothing personal," Callo said, looking intently at Mabby. Strangely, he seemed kind of sad when he said it. How profoundly confusing.

All of the kits had gone, and Callo and Tufa quietly made their departure as well, and Mabby was left alone. "Is class over for the day?" he thought. I guess so. Maybe I just missed it when she said it. I was obviously thinking about flying. I wish I could have just stretched a little farther, then

I would have had it. His thoughts began to berate him, and he began to cry. Maybe they're right, I just didn't try, I wonder if Dad had it so hard, or Mama. I wish she were here. It's my fault I'm here. Mabby's thoughts berated him as his tears broke upon the floor. He listened to the air in the room, as he beat his breath against the wall.

Deela was still there, and he noticed her just as he was about to get up again. "Hey. Pretty poem," she said.

"What are you doing here?"

"Well, I was just wondering if you were walking home alone."

"I can walk by myself. I'm not a girl."

"Well, I'm a girl." She giggled. "And I'm alone. Would you like to walk me?" She looked at him through her thick, bent, googly glasses.

"Why? You're normal. I think..."

"What do you mean? You mean…You think I'm...*normal*?!" She batted her eyes and smiled a wide, open-mouthed smile. She closed her eyes and leaned in for a hug, but fell on the floor when Mabby turned away, totally oblivious.

"I mean you don't want to be seen with me. I'm an infirm. That's it. So just leave me alone."

"I don't think you're an infirm." She picked herself back up. He didn't look back at her.

"Well, I am. Facts' facts."

"I'm sorry you didn't make it," she said.

"Yeah, well, me too, but I don't need your pity, and you couldn't understand, so would you just leave me alone? What do you want with me anyway?"

"I-I, nothing. I just..." She put her paw gently on his arm. "I think I could understand. I can try."

"Well you can't. So leave. Me…*Alone.*"

She straightened her glasses and her hair. Then she left him alone.

Mabby sat for a great long while, only thinking. If any, or whatever, look Deela had given Mabby, he missed it. Suddenly his stomach wasn't along for the ride any more. The stress of the day had finally caught up to him, and he threw up. Then he quietly got up to leave, wiping his face. Everyone had advanced to the next course of difficulty, for he was the only one who had failed.

Mabby heard someone speaking as he left the shelter of shame and embarrassment. It sounded distant, but still directed toward him. He looked about and could not make out the speaker.

"If yuh play by everyone else's rules, my boah, you'll never win..." the voice said.

"Who goes out into town and talks like that?" Mabby wasn't sure he had heard it right. He paused, waiting for the voice to come back. "Hello?" He waited. Nothing. Then he heard a sudden rush of air come from somewhere below.

Mabby was frozen with rage. Nothing was going to stop him, and he was going to go home, drop off his books, and climb to the top of the highest tree. He was about to jump when...

"Hold on there, boah," someone said in the stupidest Georgia-peach accent he'd ever heard in his life. "You've got heart, kid. I'll give yuh that." Mabby recognized it as the voice that had spoken to him from the trees. What did he know? Having a heart means feeling, like no one ever feels, so no one cares, not like Mabby did.

"What are you gittin' ready to go do?" He said, a little suspicious. Mabby stopped, annoyed. Obviously, like too many, Mabby thought he was some kind of crazy person.

"Do you know what it's like?" He turned to face his ignorant new foe. "Huh? Do you know what it's like being…" He paused. It doesn't matter, he said to himself. I don't even know this guy. Why do I pay attention to idiots? "Just…" Mabby looked down, never actually having laid eyes on the old dog that was coming up behind him being so bothersome. Out of his peripheral vision, the squirrel looked haggard. He felt embarrassed, like he was not supposed to continue acting the way he wanted to. Resentment, his lifelong companion, tapped him on the shoulder and he turned away. He tried not to get too angry and embarrassed at letting anyone in his head after just one stupid question.

Mabby was about to leave, still wiping the tears from his eyes and catching his breath. "Hold on, boah. Where you in such a hurry to?" The old squirrel reached out and took Mabby by the arms and spun him around. He caught him by both shoulders, standing face to face, and they silently greeted one another, although Mabby's new elder acquaintance was decidedly more gratuitous.

Mabby simply looked at him with such a mix of emotions that he looked angry but, at this point, it was more an unbridled breed of fear and creepiness. It didn't help that the squirrel was badly cross-eyed. The old squirrel brushed off Mabby's disturbance flippantly. "Don't worry, son. I'm not go'na drag yuh off or somethin' like you're thinkin'." The old dog was looking him over with some kind of decision in mind. "Mh. Uhuh. Yuh." He didn't seem to be in any hurry to introduce himself.

"Uh." Mabby's frustration was growing, as usual, at both the situation and at his sudden inability to verbalize the degree of it. "Excuse me. What's going on? Who are you—"

"Well, that'll be fine…" The old squirrel disregarded his questions, turning him this way and that, walking around him, grabbing his arms and prodding his chest. "I can work with that. No that's no good. Okay, now… okay. Yes. Yuh...Okay..." Mabby felt his unruly flaps being handled from behind and felt seriously offended. His tail was really starting to twitch.

"Ow, hey!"

The old squirrel stopped for a second and looked down at him like a scientist caught off guard by some unexpected variable. "Hm." He continued with his examination.

"Hey! Stop, okay, look, what are you doing and—" he was cut off again by the nameless old squirrel's apparent total disregard.

"All right, I think this can be done. Follow me, my boah." He turned toward the trunk of the tree, as if this meeting were nothing unusual at all.

"No! I'm telling the school on you, and I'm going home to get my dad to come back here and beat you up!"

The old squirrel turned around in a cool, round stride. "Calm down, young'un. I was *sent* by the school." His eyes were a'glim.

Mabby was surprised and a little taken aback, wondering if anyone about town had been talking about how badly he was doing. How else could this random squirrel have known? "Don't be silly, Mabby," he thought, "of course they're talking. You're terrible."

"Well..." Mabby said, striddling up to the old squirrel. As he stopped for a breath, it seemed like he was about to climb.

"Well, what if I don't want to? Besides, how can I believe you? You still won't tell me your name!" Mabby was unintentionally being a little loud. He was angry, but his curiosity was piqued.

"There are little ones who don't do so well in our early courses. It's okay. When there's a student that can't learn, they call me."

"You?" Mabby looked doubtful. This squirrel looked as if he would topple over of a heart attack if he jumped two feet. "I can *learn.* You couldn't—"

The enigmatic squirrel before him had been tested in his patience for these kinds of students one too many times. He looked back sharply at Mabby, who stopped short of what he was about to say. Perhaps he had gone too far. "Do you want to fly?" the old squirrel said. "Why are you here, doing this to yourself? What do you want to do?" he snapped.

Mabby was deeply affected. He wanted to fly more than anything. The old dog could never understand how badly. "I…"

The nameless squirrel waited, still looking directly at him. "Say it," he demanded.

"I…" Mabby could not get the words out so easily as that. He looked down in dejection. Then all the frustration of his life rose out of his heart, swelled in his eyes, shook his fists, and forced themselves out in the surest formation of words he had ever spoken.

"I want to fly." Mabby nearly choked on the words. He looked up, unashamed of the tears that rested on his cheeks, as all the passion in his body prompted him to show himself, in his true depth, to someone who was probably the most genuine squirrel he had ever laid eyes on. No one had ever demanded such candidness from him, *all at once.* And he gave it, gratefully, and for once in his life he felt free in front of someone. He straightened up his shoulders and turned to the old dog. "I. Want. To fly. I don't know you but, if you must know, I want to fly more than anything. Anything." He wiped off a tear in anger, so hard that hairs came with it.

"Then. Come with me." The stranger took Mabby by the arm, guided him over to the tree, and motioned for them to ascend. The old squirrel held no quarter for ceremony. He jumped up the tree. Mabby followed hesitantly. "Besides, where would the fun be in all that telling stuff, anyway? Where would it get you? I…" He paused, looking back at Mabby for effect. "Am y-oh private tut-ah."

They leapt up Rammerie Trunk in tandem.

"Don't compare yourself to the other squirrels. Never compare yourself. Just don't. Because you'll get lost in the fact that they are actually right," he said as Mabby trailed behind him, up, up, up, and up, till they stopped at a branch so high that Mabby shook in his boots and could see all the world, and all the world could see them. "At least partly, that is. You are different. Really, they will always think less of you because you can't do what they can do as easily. But what really makes them not like you is the fact that what you CAN do most naturally, they can't do at all. Most will work their whole lives at it and nevah get to where you have to start." Mabby looked at him in sheer confusion.

"They can run and jump and glide away at will, it's easy for them. Look at them. Don't it make you so angry how easy it is for them? See how they give it a little hop-hop and off they go? They don't have to move their arms, they just ...*look* at where they want to go and, if it's lower than where they started from, they just ...end up there...no work, no sweat. But look, they are designed to be on the ground and sometimes in the air. But you are designed to fly high, not float, and *sometimes* come down." The old man drew a breath, having reached the top of the tree, and Mabby came up shortly thereafter, panting only slightly. "Ah, look at that. I never get over that sight." They both looked out over the horizon. Mabby took it in. He had never imagined he would ever get to be up here with permission. He stared out over everything, watching the shadows of a flock of geese pass over the Acheron, as its waters wound their way out to the end of the forest's infinitude.

"It's so beautiful," Mabby reflected.

The old squirrel spoke. "Doing what you do takes being different. The force you need, with which to soar above the others, just takes an extra...PUSH! To get yuh started!"

That was the last thing Mabby heard as he tumbled into the air, high above even the boughs the young kits were not allowed to climb, tumbling through heights that were only unrestricted because no young kit would dare climb so high. The old dog had brought him entirely too far up, and no one had offered the courtesy of telling him there was a different means of going down. Mabby screamed and screamed until he ran out of breath, and the hopefulness of his life fell from his heart, into his mouth. He tumbled over and over, and in each pass over the ground he saw a scene of from his unkempt life. He was as angry as he was surprised and terrified. He felt the hairs on his body tighten, and the air rushed by until he could almost press his paws against the force of the fall. He instinctively reached up and out in attempt to stop his death. Then, out of nowhere, his wings caught the full force of his velocity and slammed open. "Omygosh I'm gonna live," he thought.

He soon realized that he had not ceased to travel at a rather dangerous velocity, but only changed direction. The trees ceased to shoot up around him and began to whiz by, and he still felt his cheeks peeling back from the wind resistance. He wasn't sure how to stop. His screams of brief elation returned to screams of terror as he blazed by trunk after trunk, each one coming closer and closer as he attempted to steer. He barely evaded one, and the next grazed his wing, setting him off in a tailspin. He whirled in a frantic sinusoid, reaching out for anything he might be able to grab to help stop the momentum. Twigs snapped, limbs slipped out of his grip, and his paws slapped uselessly in the scream of flight. He heard faint words swirl into his head. "Try to flap. Look upwards! Just a little farther now! Almost there!" How could that old rat be following him at such speeds?!

Mabby passed through a wall of leaves that seemed to have been configured, by paw, to form an artificial barrier, and between midair tumbles, he saw what the squirrel was talking about. It was a giant platform with what, in the brief glimpses he got, looked like lines going to and fro, with numbers here and there and various types of strange gear. It was some kind of hidden training ground. "Aim for the middle, boah!"

He slammed into the deck of the platform, barely missing the edge, and tumbled over once, then twice. He was unable to gain control before he blundered into a conveniently placed pile of leaves just before he would surely have been stopped by the wall of a very solid-looking tower in the center of the platform. Mabby remained motionless, lying precisely as he had landed, in a petrified mix of mortification and adrenaline overload. The world settled around him. The only thing that further disturbed the bubble of existence that was this strange, empty enclosure was the chirping of birds who didn't agree with Mabby's offensive and inferior flying shenanigans.

"Flying. Flying," thought Mabby.

"Perfect*ish!*" The old squirrel hollered. At least someone was happy. The old squirrel landed with quite a bit less ruffle and flourish than he had and began walking toward him. The old fart wasn't even panting. Mabby attempted to gauge his descent, unsure of how he could possibly be alive, much less have been followed with ease by any squirrel. The trees, at one point, had been going so fast he had only seen a blur. He remembered the moment his flaps had opened and his stomach had turned into a lump of dough.

The old squirrel burrowed through the pile of leaves to get to him. As he struck body parts, he wiped them away fervently. He blew the last of the leaves off of Mabby's face, which still held the same expression as it had in flight. It resembled the physical incarnation of every emotion he had ever felt. This was the lingering effect of all those moments that had flashed before him. It caused the old squirrel to instinctively dodge then become highly curious and lean in closer. This expression resembled a walnut and rhubarb pie he had once bought and then immediately dropped.

Then, caught by surprise, the old squirrel reeled back as Mabby suddenly came back to life, yelping expressions of both elation and fury. "I'll kill you! Why did you push me like that? Why I oughta…But I flew! Oh, thank you! Thank you! Why did you do that to me? Next time I'm gonna push you and see how you like it! I thought I was gonna die but I flew, I flew, I flew, I flew, I flew, omygosh, omygosh, omygosh! I'll kill you if you ever push me again! I CAN FLY." The two of them tumbled and rolled over and over, and Mabby soon had the old dog pinned to the ground by his shoulders.

"Get off, before you get the horn." They shared a dislike of bodily contact, and Mabby had forgotten himself. Old Dog elbowed him off and got up one knee at a time. Mabby's emotions came to a consensus on pissed off. "Why didn't you tell me you were gonna try to kill me?!" Mabby exclaimed.

The old squirrel didn't answer.

"Hey. Fart-head." The stranger was on him in a heartbeat. Mabby hadn't expected that. He kept underestimating him. Now Mabby was the one pinned against the wall of the central tower, not sure how he got there. "YOU! Are in my verbal touch bubble." He scowled down at Mabby over the top of his engorged, very angry nose. "Don't call me that." Simple. Effective.

Mabby remembered all of the parts of his body that happened to be screaming at him. "Okay, that's gonna work," Mabby said. The stranger let him down, and Mabby slumped in the realization of physical pain, from tumbling and tumbling, and the exhaustion of flying at supersonic speed, the exhilaration, the fear, the fall, the crash—it had all been so, well, perfect. There had never been anything else like it.

"When can I go again?"

"Are you serious?" Normally squirrels like Mabby wanted to die, or kill someone, after experiencing the real power of their abilities. But this one wasn't anything like those others, who were angry or just quitters. A twinkle of hope lit inside him. "Are you...okay?" He suppressed his hope in case Mabby was crazy.

"What do you mean am I okay? Well, I suppose yes, I'm, yes and no. Since you tried to kill me, I am badly in need of medical attention. But since I flew, I think it cancels that out. Unless you were just, you know…"

"I know?" He found that even he struggled to follow Mabby. Wow.

"I mean, you, whoever you are, do you know what you've done?"

Mabby tried to explain. “To me? Do you know what this means to my life? Or were you just improvising?”

“I suppose I do,” the stranger said.

“Perhaps...” Mabby said, letting go of the conversation and looking around. “What is this place?”

“This place is a special training ground, built for squirrels like you, with your abilities, to help you learn the way you need to learn. You struggle because you are not the same, not because everyone else is better.” He led Mabby to the edge of the platform, a landing strip that must have exceeded a hundred yards. There he gestured toward the forest floor, and Mabby noticed a huge net around the sides. “We must teach normal squirrels to fly as well, but here you can learn as easily as them. This is a place to help you do what you can do, rather than trying to get you to work like everyone else. Being different, quite simply, means learning different. See the height of that center platform all the way up there? It’s very simple. Most young squirrels need lots of little hops lined up for them to get through large courses. You, in fact, need all those little things taken away, and to be given the space to guide yourself.”

“But that’s risky, isn’t it?”

“Life is risky.”

Mabby was nearly in tears all over again.

He led Mabby back to the center of the platform and, after a few moments, he said, “If you’ll notice, there is nothing to do here but fly, nothing to look at, nothing to think about. And not hop, skip, and jump.”

“Sounds boring,” Mabby said.

“Exactly. Boredom is the product of an impoverished mind, not surroundings. Patience is the resource of the skilled winglier. Ever so much more than air gives one lift; it is truly patience that elevates you to fly. And not glide, like what they really mean when they say flying, but real flying. The other school was built so they can do what they are built for, so we let you do what you were built for, then we fill in the rest later. Most of them back there, they are obliged to do small things that lead toward their destiny. Their learning unlocks their passion.” He motioned for Mabby to follow him up the tower ladder, and up they climbed, higher and higher, till

Mabby felt nauseous. "You, however, your passion unlocks your learning. Some say you need to learn to hop before you can fly, but what about those who can fly better than they can hop?"

"Everything is going to be different now…"

"No it won't," the stranger said.

"What do you mean?"

"It's not going to get better. Or different or whatever. It might get worse. Don't get yourself confused." Now Mabby didn't follow.

"No, everything! My life, my father, my friends..." Mabby trailed off.

"You have friends?"

"Well, no."

"Look. I am not here to fix you. If that were the case, there would be a nice soft landing pad, pads everywhere, and cuddly things for everyone and chocolate and candy and a therapy session after every time you escape the ground." The stranger's head went from nodding to shaking. "I am not here to fix you. You are here to fix you, and you've been given a process to do it. I'm here to show you what you should have always known if our world were different, and it understood its..." He couldn't believe he had almost said it. He sighed. "Never mind." Mabby was confused now. "Just understand this for now. That flight here was the only thing you're going to get for free from me. Your job here now, our job, is not to fix you and all your feelings. It's to get you to fly through the small obstacles to be successful, and for that you have to work just as hard as others have to work to get through the big ones. It's not easier, it's just different. If you want to be the best, you still must work harder than anyone else."

Mabby groaned but did not answer, and the tutor motioned for Mabby to follow him up to the top of the central tower.

Once at the takeoff point, he started again. "This will be your first lesson." He took Mabby's arms and held them up in the standard flight position over his head. "Not here, not for you." He lowered Mabby's arms to straight out to the sides. "Here, lower slightly for acceleration, pull your wings tighter to slow down. The biggest problem is the easiest to fix."

Mabby gave a few wiggles. It sure felt more natural.

"Don't reach for air. Flap, like a bird."

Mabby looked back. "That's what's going on? It's really that different? Wow." He tried the mechanics out for a few moments.

"And don't point your nose or straighten your tail. *Your tail* is a rudder at high speeds, not your nose. You see? It all changes. And if you move your head the way you need to turn, you will instinctively do likewise with your tail. That's how it works. You don't harness the wind, boah. Yuh beat the crap out of it, heaw?" He pointed outwards. "Now, jump."

"What, from all the way up here? I'll die!"

"You'll only *die* if you do what you've been doing. Do what I told you instead. Besides, you'll just hit the leaves below. So if you fail you'll really only be critically injured. That's all."

Mabby positioned himself. "All right. Fine."

"And if all else fails, reach backwards as far as you can and clap your paws hard."

Mabby stood for a moment longer. "Clap mah paws," he joked.

"Dagnabbit boah jump or I'll jump yuh!"

Mabby sighed. "Why does he have to say it like that? Fine...Nub to nib, top of your head, tip of your toe, and...go. Ahh! I'm gonna die!" As he was, perhaps, just about to jump, the tutor yawned and kicked him. Screaming like a lark, he forced himself to refrain from stretching his flaps to their utter capacity, and he pointed his tail straight up like a rod. Then, in near panic, he reared back and clapped his paws as hard as he could, but his wings slammed open so hard it hurt, and he went for a loop.

"Woo!" The old squirrel heard a yelp and looked down to see where the splatter was. He was nearly knocked over by Mabby, who came whistling in a tight spiral around the tower. He rocketed up in the air so high he nearly touched the clouds. He really is going to be the greatest. The others weren't kidding. We're back. The tutor tried not to get emotional as he took off to meet Mabby on the ground. The youngrel happily circled down like a poised hawk. 'I can't believe it,' thought the old squirrel. 'But don't get too far ahead of yourself, old boah.' There were still too many opportunities to fail ahead for him to imagine such fantasies.

Mabby was breathless when the old squirrel met him again. "I never imagined that it could be so different. I would never have guessed that the way they were teaching me was actually teaching me to hold myself back."

"Well, squirrels like you, but yes. Some don't consider the old texts very useful. They don't know what the books really mean. They were written by great fliers, the true wingliers, the legends. Those legends were like you, not like them. Why else do you think they could achieve sustained flight? But don't let anyone know that. It would expose the truth, and we would be found out here. You can tell no one, ever, what you are doing here. No one can know."

'Mabby, you have no idea how special you are,' thought the old squirrel.

"You mean there used to be more squirrels like me?"

"Perhaps, but at least certainly the ones that overcame; they were always the ones who wrote the books. Most of us only want the simplest explanation, not to be given all the facts," he continued, "but given only the facts we want. But you will begin to learn what is real now, here. But it will be more difficult than how you have learned all this time. It's difficult to learn something most squirrels don't know. It will separate you, not join you. It will hurt you as much as fix you. It will cost you everything, before you ever get to…Before you get to fly." He didn't say what he had wanted to say. He couldn't believe he was already believing in this kid.

"Why do you keep skipping things?" Mabby was getting frustrated. "That wasn't what you were going to say. Before I ever get to what? Its what gets to what? I'm going to bother you until you tell me, so tell me. You know I know how to be annoying."

"Fine. Before you ever get to be a hero. That's what you're going to be if you can stick it out. Heroes get to change the world." He took the risk of giving Mabby a little hope to chew on. "Go bury that in the dirt, boah."

"Heroes? I get to be a… hero. From someone with no name," Mabby thought out loud.

"You don't get it. You'll learn my name when you've earned it. You don't GET...ANYTHING. You'll learn what you'll need to know to get through school here, and if you do better, maybe you'll learn more. But only if I say you've got what it takes to go that far first. Understand?"

Mabby was a little surprised at this sudden very official-sounding type of authority. This was real. He could really do what he said he can do.

"Uh, yeah." The old squirrel's eye crooked back at him. "D- Uh, *yes.*" More eye crooking. "Uh, yes, *sir.*" Mabby suddenly felt the compulsion to salute.

The old squirrel sighed. "You're a smart-mouth. It makes all your other words less valuable. Don't worry, son, I'll flush that out of you, too." He turned back around and held out his arm, pointing straight down at the deck immediately before him. "Front and center." Mabby got there.

"For now, all you need to know is your next lesson, for which you will report forthwith, tomorrow, following your last hour of class, and you will travel the fastest, most direct route, or you will not receive authorization to enter these premises, thereby receiving a demerit for every day tardy, punishable at my discretion. Do. You. COPY?"

"Uh, uh...Roger. Aye-aye. Ten four!" Mabby stammered. The old squirrel eyed him again.

"Just say 'copy.'" He said in his stupid Georgia-peach accent.

"Copy."

"Yeah. Whatever. Now, get out of here."

"They're always like this," he thought. "Just keep reminding yourself. Maybe you've been doing this too long. Maybe you're not up to snuff for this anymore, but it must be done."

Just before Mabby left, he looked back. "So, what do I call you, anyway?"

"My call sign is Bumbleroot. But you can call me Mister Bumbleroot, or sir. Hesperia is that way." Bumbleroot pointed. With that, Mabby left.

Mister Bumbleroot put on his black robe, decorated with leaves, for the journey home, where heroes hide to put on the tea and prepare for a long night of thinking.

Chapter 13: On Down the Boughway

The very next morning Mabby woke up sore but elated. "Bumbleroot. Huh. What a weird name. Sounds strangely familiar," he thought.

He got dressed, stumbling over himself, grabbed an oat cake for breakfast, and ran out the door before Dorma could stop him to say "goodbye and good luck at school."

Mabby burst through the doorway, bubbling He took off and, after a moment, spread his wings, caught the air, and was soon whistling down the alleyway. Unfortunately, he crash landed, rolling to a painful stop. A minor frustration. At that point he was happy simply to have flown. Not wanting to have to nurse too many bruises, he got on his feet and ran the rest of the way to school.

"Hello, Mabbs," Syriss said with his usual bright sarcasm as Mabby walked in. But his old friends were all surprised to see that he greeted them, not with a shrug and a suspicious side-glance, but with a "Hello!" and a "How do you do?" He even managed to continue smiling when Deela pushed up her glasses and attempted to high-five him, noticing his superior mood as he sat down to lecture time. He pretended not to see her paw, and a chuckle rippled through the class, but she only said to herself, in a whisper no one could hear, "He smiled at me."

He buttered through lecture time, so excited at the prospect of passing praxis marks that he could not stifle a grin. He actually wrote some things, although he would later look at those notes and realize he should have looked at what he was doing and tried to actually write real words. No matter. He would quickly blaze ahead of all others as the master of all things flightful when they saw his newfound skills.

Then it was over, and Mabby went this way and they went that. He watched them depart, all hopping up in the air and gliding, all wobbly like for a few feet, all the way to the secondary course. Then he ran to the platform and jumped. And jumped, and jumped, and jumped.

And jumped.

And with each successive failure his frustration grew as his pain tolerance shrank.

Mabby left, disappointed, after an entire day of failure.

As the sun began to wane over the western wall, the intrepid tutor padded about on the floor of the secluded training ground about the time Mabby crash landed onto the deck as usual. This time he took it rolling and jumped back up to his feet. He started running around, looking for the old squirrel that had led him into believing in some kind of trickery. "Where are you? Come out! We need to talk, you and me."

The old tutor came out from behind the shadow of the central control tower, but said nothing as Mabby grabbed him by the shirt and yelled, "What did you do to me yesterday?"

"What do you mean?" the old one replied.

"I mean you did something to me that made me think that I could fly. Maybe you put some kind of potion or spell on me or something, but you lied, and I don't know what your game is but I'm onto you!" Mabby said.

Mabby's tutor laughed. "You didn't pay attention, did you?"

Mabby only looked at him blankly.

"I told you that it was not going to get easier. As a matter of fact, the truth is it might not ever get easier. This is not for everyone and there are some who have been given the gift that you have that did not deserve it and there are some that could not handle it."

"Then why did the Great Nut give me this gift in the first place? How is it a gift if all that it ever does is make my life harder? It makes me to where I can't be with my friends, to where I can't be understood."

"You're right," the tutor said. "It's not fun. This life you've been given...it probably never will be. You will probably always wonder where your friends are, what it would be like to have a life and be able to live just like them. I can only tell you this: not all gifts are for the one that receives them. Sometimes we get hurt and the injury makes us stronger. Mah boah, what you did last night, it was real. And if you succeed here, others will look on in envy, but it will never change the fact that you will always be somewhat alone."

So after this hard lesson Mabby, dejected and defeated, went home.

When he arrived at the house, he noticed a note from his father on the kitchen table.

"Mabby, help yourself to the cupboard. Had to stay late and try to find some customers. Hang in there. You're doing great! Your Dad."

"He has no idea," Mabby thought.

The days wore on into weeks and, though his training progressed and he soon leapt to new heights with the strange dark one showing him the way, Mabby's frustration only grew and grew.

As for Dorma, he had arrived at the business square, panting, just a few moments after delivering Mabby to school. At first it all seemed fine, and he breathed a sigh of relief that he might not have had anything to worry about after all.

But then the parade came, if a parade was what to call it. A drowning, cantankerous noise, cheering and clapping and yelling and singing and kazoos and trumpets and rattlers and streamers and screamers and the rattle of shakers and the flag bearers whistling along the boardwalk, bearing down on the business parts. Fearing the worst, Dorma closed the door of his shop, shut the windows, and stuck his head outside to see what was causing the commotion. And there was Bolly Beeley, mob in tow, marching right up the street.

The papers had told Dorma the story of Bolly Beeley. He had soon become the richest squirrel to have ever lived, purportedly, within the walls of the realm, and perhaps even among all the creatures of the ancient wood and all the surrounding land of Nearly Mountain. From the rock-river to the Acheron, his had fame spread, but how he had become so wealthy so suddenly none could explain.

But Bolly's success had not been shared, for it seemed there was no money left in all of town for anyone else. Especially those who had not come over the line Bolly had drawn at the rally on the day of his election. Dorma had known there would be trouble, but he'd had no clue that rally would turn into a riot, and he had not had a chance to talk to Mabby about not coming to the shop anymore. Mabby would object, but he must not know about the destruction that had ensued. Beeley had given a speech at the square in which he'd said that anyone who was not for "The Lowest" was not for him and named the shops that "aided in the business of flying" as part of the sinister and elitist establishment. But all Dorma could think of was how badly Mabby wanted to fly. That meant Dorma must do what he was best at to keep him in school, whatever the cost. Nearly all of the businesses had crossed over and given up their signs to be repainted with his name on them, which Bolly had burned. Dorma, however, had stood in front of the shop, giving the mob nothing.

So they had taken it. They had thrown him out of the way, ripped the sign down, smashed it before they burned it, and trashed the store, taking everything. Dorma had only just managed to rescue his bobby-bag before they pulled him out of the store and all but tore it down. They destroyed his expensive sewing machines, his presses, and his mannequins, all irreplaceable in this economy. Now all that was left was the walls, and the floor was covered with indiscriminate garbage and dangerously rife with stray needles.

Dorma was glad Mabby had school now, for he could not see how hard things were becoming all of a sudden. Dorma's shop sat lonely, and customers continued to dwindle, but he did what he could. He was a wreck because he had not had a chance to talk to Mabby in so long. It would not be long, if things kept going this way, before he would have to close up shop and walk about town for work as he had, so long ago, when he was trying to get started. Oh, the ruin that had brought to his feet, the strain it had brought to his wings, and the worry it had brought to Debby and the unborn baby. Oh, the many nights they did not have much more than a crumb cake between them, and Dorma went hungry so little Mabby would not starve inside Debby's belly. He thought, "Perhaps it is best that I haven't told him."

He did his best to keep things clean. Mabby would come in and Dorma see the bruises, but wasn't sure if he should say anything. "Let the boy try to handle it first, maybe." He knew what Mabby was going through, what Debby would have gone through, if he had not been able to be there, and he admired Mabby for his bravery. But Dorma could not be certain that he could ever bring himself to try such a thing, if he were in Mabby's place.

These days Dorma welcomed struggle and heartache and hard times. He had found that life always worked out better for those that played the long game, since one's first plan for success was so quickly snuffed.

It wasn't long until Dorma found himself joining the lengthening line at the teller window at the bank at the center of the business district dug into Melliverin trunk. Each time he struggled more and more to convince the teller, who saw from his own window the daily operations of his shop, to let him barter a ring for a coat and a bag of pine nuts. That very penny merchant used to pay Dorma for his services at patching up the poor beast's only trousers. Quite a job that had been, for little pay. Dorma scuffed the floor, so dejected at having to stoop so low to procure a nice meal for his home that he barely looked up from the ground most of the time.

But on this day in particular, Dorma and Bolly could not help but notice one another. As it happened, a certain cantankerous squirrel was making such a fuss at the teller window, with half the district in earshot, that to pretend not to notice him seemed even more ridiculous than the situation at paw. The two tried not to look at one another.

Now this squirrel was aged. And it seemed he had a bit of a chewing problem, for his squeaky eye and his jaw moved incessantly. And the more the banker insisted that there were no funds to be had, and that the times were lean, the squeakier the squirrel's eye got, the more fervently he shook his jaw, and the louder he got, until the conversation happened as follows.

"Very sorry, sir."

"Now how can you tell me that after all the years that I've been a patron and a patriarch of this fine furry town? How can you tell me that, after all mah years of doing business with you, now my word t'aint no good?"

"I'm very sorry, sir, but we are under new management, and new policy states that all members must show valid identification and must have standard collateral before funds can be accepted or distributed. There are no more barters or fraternal benefits. I'm very sorry, sir, but there's nothing I can do." The teller simply looked down at his receipts.

"Well, that sounds like a whole lotta fancy talk in place of yew just telling me yew ain't gonna allow me to improve my financial situation until I improve my financial situation. Is that about how that oughta be summed up? Is that what yer tellin' me?" The teller stammered and stuttered. "I can, um, if you like, put you down for one of our fine credit lines, starting at a paucit...um, 5 percent interest...?"

"Per whut?"

"Just a d-d-d, um. (Gulp) Day. Per day, sir."

"And if I taint got no money how's I s'posed to git more money? Youse wants to charge me to pay off the money I don't got? Huh, y'idyit?" And at the silence of the teller, the old squirrel banged his fist on that counter and coins when a'flying, and he said very loudly, "You know for a banker yew ain't too good at fig'rin!" and he whirled around and stormed out, hopefully never to be seen in those parts again. Everyone breathed a sigh of relief, happy to return to their own worries.

Now, since such scenes had become so commonplace in that office at Melliverin Bank and Trust, Dorma had made it a special point to be as gentle a squirrel as a gentlesquirrel could be. However, that day, the teller became distraught halfway through Dorma quietly and gently asking for but a few pence to buy the smallest loaves, just to hold his son over until business picked up again. But the teller shuddered, shook his head, and snapped his window shut right in Dorma's face, and he would answer no more pleas for help.

Not a sound was made beyond the glass partition after the "Line Closed" sign flipped up and everyone dispersed. Then Dorma could see why, for it seemed everyone in that building, including the tellers, was ragged, patched, tired, sunken, and clearly lacking the means to keep themselves up good and proper. They all left slowly, dejected. What was happening?

Dorma was thinking that maybe he could venture beyond the Tanglewall to the edges of town where Ballo's farm was. Perhaps there was still some spirit of generosity left over in that place, and he could procure some nuts from the edges of the orchards there. Then he saw Bolly Beeley still standing in the other disappearing line to Dorma's left. His stomach growled. He was handing in a note through the teller window, in another line, smiling as wide as he could and stuffing a bright, shiny quill deep into his pocket. The teller's eyes flitted across to Dorma, and then he disappeared to retrieve a bag. Bolly very cordially thanked the teller and tapped his nails patiently, leaning on the glass. He looked over, and his eyes met Dorma's. Bolly smiled his mayor smile. And as Dorma turned to leave, saying nothing, he heard Beeley say to his back, "You know, Mr. Dabby, it's all about attitude."

He heard the murmurs, and no doubt there were nods of approval, from the crowd. "Richest squirrel in town, he's got to know what he's talking about," a little bit of, "successful business-y" type talk, and a plenty of "So and so helps those who help themselves," which only made him angrier.

Dorma turned around, strode up to Bolly Beeley, and looked him square in the eye. Then he adjusted Bolly's tie proper and motioned to his buttons, which were askew. "Mr. Beeley, sir, you could come by later if you wish to have that polka dot patch replaced with something respectable and decent for a fine mayor such as yourself, and I would be happy to sew up the seam of that pocket that held your fine watch for free." Dorma wished him a good day. This time Bolly said nothing and Dorma turned off and left. For a moment, however angry he was, Bolly actually looked sort of regal for a moment. But he shook it off, and his hair stood on end and his tail twitched with a rumbling fury.

As soon as Dorma walked out the entryway of Melliverin B. and T., the roastery air and the sickeningly freeing feeling of fresh poverty hit him. Somehow it occurred to him very strongly that he hadn't flown in so long. It was very arresting having a non-flying companion and a flightless bumpkin to haul around to boot. And here was everyone he knew these days thinking it was out of honor. He chuckled to himself, thought, "Hey, what the heck," and placed his bobby-bag down. No doubt Bolly was still watching him. Some passerby stopped and asked Dorma what was the matter as Dorma performed some side-stretches. He reached back to un-fix his sideclasps, the cumbersome little attachments that made flying possible while still being decent. "Oh, nothing, nothing at all. Good to see you. I'm just out getting a little *air*." A few squirrels pretended not to notice him. Still others pointed discreetly, and he noticed some heads popping out over the banks of the boughs above.

Whispers traveled to his ears saying that he was preparing to defy Beeley's mayoral decree that any public flying would be fined and repeated offenses would land one in the gaol with charges of mockery of the peace and shaming the status-disabled. Or whatever.

He turned and stood for a moment, then ambled down the boughbank and stood a moment more with his paws on the rail. Then he heard footsteps behind him, running.

"No time like now. Dear me, what am I even doing?" he thought, sucking in his breath, and he hopped up, put his feet on the rail where his paws had been, and pushed himself off with all his might. A paw barely grazed his pant leg, and Bolly's voice shouted, "No! Stop him! Stop!" but he did not look back. He had never been the type. He dove and spun faster and faster, and the crowd gasped. That ought to get their attention. Oh no, where did that thought come from? Why am I doing this? To hell with it, he chastised himself again, while he plummeted to the floor. Bolly Beeley shouted down something unintelligible and, just before the point of no return, Dorma opened his wings and jerked his neck, sending him into a spiral pattern. The leaves blew about gently at first, but then they began to follow him. He banked hard, then slowed, then moved slowly toward the outside, and repeated the pattern. Very quickly he etched a giant spiral in the tanglefloor. Then he went up, flipped over, and twisted under, again and again, making star patterns, and the wind carved lines in the leaves like a knife. And then he chuckled to himself and went in for one more motif, banking to the outside. He swirled up, and up, and up, spinning for centrifugal momentum and sending it out to get more speed and height. He coursed up, and up, and up, and up, touching and going, and he felt the fresh breeze of the upper boughs and the glow of the sun. Then he stopped.

Everyone in town was watching as he began his last descent, repeating the same feat, only this time he sped faster and harder till his eyes felt they would bleed. And just as he was about to hit the floor, he banked again, but so hard that it hurt, making a splash, and he cut like a saw, so close to the floor that it was all he could do to keep from punching through it. He stayed on course, slicing this way and that through the leaves, sending them up in a flurry as he made his way cursively around the outside of his starry designs.

"How is he doing that?" everyone up above was asking as they watched Dorma perform.

Someone interjected, "If you get angry enough, you can kill a horse with a peanut."

"Almost, almost, and that'll do it," Dorma thought. He used up the last of his momentum to glide to a halt, and then he surveyed his work. He climbed the nearest trunk, panting, and read the words out loud to make sure his spelling was good. "I, heart-sign, flying! B. Beeley. There." He basked in the shade for a moment, wondering what would await him when he ascended. But he did not have to wait long, for the sound of uproarious laughter and lighthearted cheering descended upon him, followed by the outraged shouting of an upset civic leader. Then a bobby-bag and briefcase crashed right through the tanglefloor, probably never to be seen again. Dorma looked up and found the face of Bolly, his hair pulled straight, his coat even more torn, and his eyes burning. Beeley shouted and this time Dorma heard it.

"Take that, and see if you ever work in this town again! You just wait, you liar! Fake! Thief! I'll get you, I'll tell everyone! The truth!" And though Dorma had absolutely no blue bloody clue what Bolly meant by that, it certainly sounded like he meant to do it, and could. But what was this, "truth?" What had he stolen? Needles from the foundry market? Precious moments of time stitching the cuffs of awfully styled topcoats, forever gone? Stolen *the show*, perhaps? That he had done. Dorma laughed out loud, and Bolly saw it. Dorma said nothing more and simply went over to the nearest trunk that pierced the Tanglewall to climb up, electing to rest his tired wings and enjoy the scenic route home out of view of the center of town. He went to the bottom of the world he'd always known. A long walk it would be. He went slowly, taking time to wonder and to chuckle.

But the branch he grasped, on the nearest trunk, broke off in his paw, and he looked at the dead heart of the tree. "Hm... interesting," he thought, not remembering having seen any dead trunks along the boughways, well, except... And then, to his dejection and horror, he realized he held a shard of the remnant of a memory long wearied and mourned in silence in his mind. For it was the trunk that had nearly killed his sweet Debby. He went off, being careful not to fall through the tanglefloor, but he could not tear his mind away from that day. Oh, how he missed her, and she had been taken from him so unfairly.

"It's not…It's not fair at all!" he shouted, throwing the broken husk of death in his paw at the rotten trunk. It hit the crumbling bark with a pathetic pit-pit, and more bark fell away. "A pathetic throw. Like my life," he muttered, but then the bark crumbled some more where he had hit and, behold, a shape had been carved into the musty gray wood. After a moment he traced the pattern and realized he was looking at some kind of secret passage.

He approached fearfully and quietly raised his paw to press on the door, holding his breath.

Then he simply thought better of it and found another way home. "Nope, don't care. Don't want to know. No scary doors for me," he said out loud, dusting his paws. "Those kinds of things are for squirrels who enjoy dying, and that's not something I plan to do with my life. I'm going to *live forever."*

He arrived home very late and found a municipal citation had already been tacked on his door. "For disturbing the peace, general rabblery, and conduct unbecoming a squirrel…" Dorma read on, scoffing to himself, and said aloud, "Nuts to your fines." Then he quickly looked around to be sure no one had heard him talking like that, and he went inside,

Now, if it hadn't been for the incident at the bank and the long time coming home from the tanglefloor, let alone the many pawshakes and even more numerous jeering calls, along the way, from all those who had seen his public display of defiance, he would never have guessed that Mabby had come in only moments before. As a matter of fact, the covers had only just been pulled up over his head, and sleepy noises had just begun to be faked as Dorma opened the door of Mabby's room and pondered bothering him awake to ask how his day had been. Then he thought better of it and closed the door. He whispered from the other side, so as not to wake the sleeping pup, "I'm proud of you, son, and your mother is too."

"He has no idea," Dorma thought.

Dorma spent a little while in the living room, icing his ankles and looking longingly at the old box. "Oh, sweet wife. I miss you so very much. I think you'd be proud of me and what Mabby has done. I think you would." He wiped a tear, and his gaze drifted down till something caught his eye. Something was wrong with the picture. Dorma couldn't place his mind on it, but somehow he knew something was wrong and he began to feel very angry. The same feeling he had always felt when he looked at the picture of Beeley and his award, the key to the city, for his bravery in rescuing the town by battling that great cat. Oh, that was it. Hate.

It wasn't long before he drifted off to sleep.

Chapter 14: The Ding.

Bo Neebles was a remarkably happy being.

Very few in the realm of Hesperia demonstrated the concern for the ill-fortuned to take notice that Bo had a unique communication system worked out for himself.

For example, "Boo Boo," meant somewhere in the range of, "I'm hurt," to just a deep insecurity about a particular situation.

"Murf." That was anything related to food, from "Does anyone wish for a bite" to the most imperative sense meaning, "Give me something to eat before I devour the nearest furniture." Determining the meaning of this complex and nuanced expression was the result of time spent immersed in Bo's presence and a great deal of interpretive capacity, the latter of which was why only Syriss understood him completely.

"Ding," though. There are words and then there are words. When some say "ding," they mean "perhaps that one is correct, or even incorrect," or, "someone is late," or just "ding," imitating an arbitrary bell-like noise. When Bo said "ding," he meant "The Ding."

The first time Bo had ever heard "ding," at first it had made all the pretty colors come on, and beneath the pile of rubble that he had suddenly found himself under, on that strange day, the ding had kept going. It was the first thing to welcome him to the bright and cheery world, full of candy-colored clouds and walls that smiled and laughed at all his jokes, in which he had lived ever since. But Bo could not be completely happy in this world. The ding that made him such a happy boy made everyone else very sad. And the ding had almost made Tufa go away. It would have made her go away if he hadn't been there. In fact, every time the ding happened, it made someone he loved, which was anyone out of the pool of *everyone,* go away. All in all, it was a reminder that life could otherwise be beautiful, but instead someone was being boobooed. So he kept an ear out and, even in his sleep, the only thing in the very complete world that could possibly wake him was the ding.

It was on the very night after young Mabby's own father, who had bravely defied the nefarious Bolly Beeley and the whole of the new Hesperian social order, went to sleep still holding a box of worthless keepsakes. Being so tired after such a long day, Dorma was not in a position to be alerted to faraway bells. On that night, if he or Mabby had not been so completely exhausted, they might have heard a dark whisper and seen a black flash passing by the window. They might have heard the muffledest of muffles on the wall beyond the pantry and a scratch, a flick, and a light glassy tink-tink, and a not so hushed "hush," hushing something or someone that no one even heard at all. And they might have noticed a gloomy sliver of silvery smoke crawling silently over the bare, hash-marked, dry-as-a-bone wood floor. Then they could possibly have heard that breathy, happy sort of rumble that lights up the colder nights when the old squirrels sing their kits and pups to sleep and tell stories of thinner years such as these.

They might have heard the distant sound of a bell.

But all was not lost, for on ding one, Bo's eyes were wide. On ding two, Bo's bedroom door was gone. And on ding three, he was out of the house and far away shouting, "Ding! Dingding! BooBooBooBooDing!" And Bo's father, the experienced handy-squirrel, was shouting, "Ah, rats! Not again. I just fixed that!"

Bo did not move well; this was no secret. He could fly just like any normal squirrel, despite his size, but he had never been seen doing it. Bo's secret, though not for lack of trying to tell it, was that he was afraid of heights. So he only flew when he absolutely had to. But on this night, there was only one thing to be more afraid of than not getting to whoever was in trouble fast enough. And it was not long before he spotted the flames far away toward the eastern walls and off the long hill, where the squirrels that everyone talked about as if they were giants lived, that led to the school. "Booboo," he said to himself and was off again.

On that night, he flew. Like a lion raging through a lily-heather, he flew, closer and closer to the red, silent dawn that had come before its time.

Mabby was a-dreaming, asleep in his cozy room, when he was awakened by a slight cough. He didn't bother to open his eyes and rolled over. He coughed again and, when he tried to recover his breath, he quickly found himself on the floor, feeling as if there was fire in his lungs and his eyes would explode. Then he looked about in utter confusion, and he saw that his room was a frightening red all around and his window but a scarlet night. Then he heard an awful thud, and his father began to scream from somewhere, but he could not tell where or what he was saying over the growing roar. Mabby tried to get up, but his muscles were paralyzed by desperate hacking as his lungs tried, in vain, to expel the deadly blackness, only to draw in even more. He gasped for oxygen. The room began to swirl. He was too asphyxiated to move, much less scream to save himself, and the blackness began to close in.

Then something did explode.

Debris flew overhead. The next thing Mabby knew he was being draped over the back of some great hulking beast, the likes of which should probably not be allowed to roam around town. As he was being laid gently down, he heard the comforting burble of Bo's deep voice, and he passed out.

He could not tell how long he had been under, but the moment he came to consciousness, he thought first of Dad and he woke screaming. A cheer went up, and everyone that was there started congratulating one another the way adults do when they have had absolutely nothing to do with the situation.

"I'm here, son, I'm here." Dorma put his paw on Mabby's shoulder, and Mabby came around. More folk were running up and, as Mabby started to make out faces, he also began to make out that he, along with everything else, was covered in a soulless white ash. He could still feel the hot breeze of the smoldering fire behind him as the helpers jettisoned the smolders they could not put out with their scrambling and their buckets. Almost none of the house remained.

Dorma helped up his boy, and Mabby noticed, in his father's other arm, a box which he had never seen before. His dad was covered in soot, and some of his sweater had been burned away, and Mabby realized he must have gone back into the flames to get it. But what was so important that he had never seen until now?

"Mabbs?" Syriss's voice poked through. The whole gang was there. Including Deela. "Ugh," Mabby thought.

"Oh, thank the Great Nut you're okay," Tufa and Syriss said.

"Both of you there together, not fighting about something even?" Mabby said, cool as a spring breeze, but then he took to hacking again and was on his knees.

"We were so worried about you. We didn't know if you were going to come out of it," Tufa said.

Syriss nodded, looking down.

"But it was Bo who saved you."

"Yeah, you'd have been toast without him." Syriss pointed over to where the house had stood, and Mabby saw a blur of flying soot darting this way and that, batting out the remaining embers with no concern for stray nails or for himself. Apparently he had already forgotten about the emergency for he was gurgling and laughing happily, squealing at each little glowing remnant of the fire and batting it into a sparkful oblivion.

Dorma watched in horror, as his life's toil was doused and beaten into history, only to be distracted by the sound of childish laughter. Mabby was laughing at Bo with Syriss and his other friends at the scene. "Well, he's found himself a fun game then!" Syriss chuckled. Dorma looked back at the scene and could not help but see the utter hilarity, rather than the loss and escape from death's black gate.

"Marrb!" Bo shouted in mid-swing, evidently happy to see that they enjoyed the game as much as he. He dropped the enormous plank he had used to save his friend's life and came over and patted Mabby on the head, giggling to himself. "Boo!" he said, poking Mabby in the stomach, which had the effect of causing a small puff of smoke to come out of Mabby's mouth. They all laughed and Bo did it again and swished his tail about, at which point Tufa shouted, "Bo, your tail is on fire!" It had actually been on fire the entire time, and all the helpers doused him with water. He said nothing, looking around. Mabby coughed another puff of smoke.

They had all nearly forgotten about the brush with death that the house fire had been only moments before. But amidst the sudden jollity that Bo had managed to make out of it all, Mabby still could not help but hear an old familiar sound: that rush of night air, the kind that was often accompanied by a soothing breeze. But these, Mabby knew, were of a different nature. They did not seem as friendly as they once had. The first rush of air only managed to catch the slightest bit of his attention. The second one was different, stronger. He stopped, realizing that they were going in different directions. So he listened, determined not to miss it if there were any more. Then there it was, going off the same way as the first.

While everyone else laughed and hugged each other, thankful that they were all alive and staying to make sure there were no further threats of respark, as was the town's usual emergency protocol, Mabby slipped away.

The bough was long and open, as the great trees that comprised the higher-class neighborhoods were set in older and higher redwoods on the mountain. Back when the forest had been but a grove, and the squirrels of yore had taken great care to bind their boughs into great long paths and borders that grew high and dense, much more care and time had been taken. Thus it was hard to get around without being seen. The others spotted Mabby and called after him, "Mabby, where are you going?"

He pretended not to hear, and they called louder. The longer he walked, the more quickly they followed him, till he heard his dad shouting. He looked back to see his father running, his tail tucked low. Mabby broke into a run, taking a hard right toward the edge. They were screaming now. He looked back one last time, and his friends were in the lead. "What's wrong, Mabbs?!"

"Where is he going?" They asked one another.

"I don't know, he's… chasing the wind, I guess," Syriss replied, and Tufa gave him a look as if to say, "Really?"

"I'm sorry, but I've got to find the truth," he barked as he took a flying leap and went off the deep end.

"No! We'll rebuild, Mabby! It's okay! Don't, you'll fall—-" But Dorma was too late.

"Eek!" Deela said, and some were a little shocked for she, for some odd reason, sounded excited that Mabby had apparently jumped to his death. Tufa looked at her, quite judgy. Deela only chirped once more, grabbed Tufa's and Syriss's shoulders, pointed, and thumped her feet.

Dorma was startled to see his son, who he thought was committing suicide, and now felt silly for Mabby the infirm had disappeared into the abyss, and Mabby the Flying Squirrel had emerged, soaring to the sky. They stopped and looked on as Mabby banked out of a gloriously executed sextuple upward tailspin and clapped his paws together, sending his wings into full tilt. He all but disappeared, once more, off into the distance. "My son…is flying?!"

"What?!" They all said in unison.

"Well, we've got to follow him! Maybe he knows something," Syriss said to Tufa.

"But, how?...And... How?" They all asked.

"Probably, I don't know, by trying? Yeh?" Syriss could be annoying sometimes, was the collective thought among the rest of them. "So come on!" Syriss started running.

Tufa looked at Deela, whose paws were over her mouth, as she stared starry eyed at the puff of soot that had been shaped like Mabby's midair takeoff pose. Then they both smiled. Tufa motioned for Deela to join them, and she gave a little overjoyed hop and caught up with them quickly.

They followed Mabby before anyone could stop them. The adults pursued them until they ran out of breath, but the gang was long gone. Bo, Tufa, Syriss, and Deela continued down the boughway.

"Oh, goodness me," one of the adults said to the rest after about a minute. They were trying to still their hearts. "If that kit comes back in one piece, she is so dead meat." The others concurred and discussed the most effective methods of punishment according to the latest book, *How to Train Your Hellspawn* by mammal psychologist R. L. Levant, "Oh, it's diamonds luv, just *diamonds!"* they said between laborious gasps.

"I think I'm going to puke," another said. But Dorma could not help noticing that no one had anything to say about Syriss. Where were his parents? Was he a latchkey pup? "Well look, everyone, I'm not one to start a rabble, but we need to come up with a plan. Let's fan out and find out what our kids have run off and gotten themselves into, awright?"

Reverend Wally was there, and Dorma quickly realized he was the one who had been puking. "Well, we're all good squirrels, one as good as another. This is a safe town. These kinds of things, they're accidents, you know? I, (huff) I mean, (puff)..." Dorma took the time to note Wally's dad-bod status was clearly hard won. That Deela must be a hurricane. "Well, w— (Barf!)"

"Oh, aw, ick, disgusting," they all said. "You literally ran for eighteen seconds, old boy."

"I (h-ugh, hunh) I mean, they couldn't be *un*safe, right? They're fine. I mean, everyone in Hesperia is basically good, (huff) and there's no way they could go *outside* the wall. So let's all just go home, and relax, and (hunh)…" But Reverend Wally did not get to finish what he was saying for the moment he said the words, "the wall," the parents became hysterical and came to three conclusions: one, they all very much liked the Reverend safely *behind* the pulpit; two, that red hair must indeed be of some birth deficiency; and three, that the children must be found post haste. Then the good Reverend simply lay down where he was and passed out.

"My goodness, old boy, we didn't even leave the bloody neighborhood!" someone shouted.

"Party up!" shouted another. And they did, concluding that whoever had thought of forming a search party was a jolly fine chap, and Dorma got a few more pawshakes. It was all the same for he was a jolly fine homeless chap.

"Okay, so we'll need parties to look for Mabby, Syriss, Deela, Bo, and Tufa," Dorma said, but then someone interjected with, "Mr. Neebles doesn't worry about his pup. Look, he's not even here. I say Bo can take care of himself."

"Right," they all said in unison. "And Syriss's parents aren't here either. We say if they don't take care of us, we don't take care of them." Then they all got into a squabble.

"All right, stop. Does anyone else not care about their children?" Dorma asked. "Okay, just so we don't lose ourselves, let's make a tally of who's here."

"A roll call!" Mr. Ferroule said.

"Yes, a roll call," Dorma said, rolling his eyes, as everyone immediately snapped together, shortest to tallest, in perfect military fashion. "Right, so there are about twelve of us…"

"Well, would you look at that, Wally's gone!" Dorma looked back to find he had squirreled off and was nowhere to be seen.

"Uh, okay, that makes eleven. We're odd," Dorma said. "If the fire says anything, it's that there may be danger. So would anyone like to stay behind or take a third wheel—"

"Well, I can't go, asthma and all." One of them started to wheeze. "I-I'm afraid I'd just *cough* slow you all down."

"Danger?!" another said. "Well that's...dangerous!"

"And, uh, I've got, um…" said another, "lots of… hungry little kitties at home. Yes, oh my goodness, and a stew on. Oh gracious, they must be starving. Oh I've got to go, so sorry. Bye, knew you'd understand." And that one slinked off.

"Eh! Didn't Bo go with them?"

Another piped up, "I bet they're safer than WE ARE!"

"Here, here, a good wall he makes, that kid," said another, and some began to leave. "Someone ought to give him a medal. Protecting our babies and all that. We really ought not to worry."

"Right-o! He just saved your life, didn't he, Dorma?" And Dorma stood speechless at that one. "And what, have we taught our children nothing? How could they *really* get outside the wall anyway? About impossible it is, if one doesn't know the way. I say old Wally's right, we should just *go home* and wait for their safe return." The remainder of them murmured in agreement that that would be the most conscientious thing to do. "Our lives are more important! We wouldn't want ourselves to get hurt because then what would they do? They need us to make the tough decisions."

"A fine one, that Neebles kid. Born hero." That was followed by many "here, here's.

"All right, I'll say it." Dorma tried to stop them. "I know my own son has gotten out of the wall and has probably done it lots of times, knowing kids."

A few of them muttered something about the "age of exploration."

"Well, how do we know that just ain't your shining parent skills. Can't even teach your boy how to fly. What, are you gonna carry him all his life?" He looked around and then said no more about that. "I mean, after all, you just sit in your shop all day not watching him. That's just terrible, letting a latchkey pup run around all day long doin' whatever, bein' a deviant. It's no wonder he took off without saying anything, and he led our poor children off with him. A fine parent you are, now you got the rest of us sitting at home wondering where our children are all times of the day. I say this is *your* fault!"

None of them knew what being a single dad was like. As offended as he was, Dorma knew he was losing them. He just looked down, walked back to the rubble, and dug out the rags he had tied together as a makeshift bobby-bag. He meant to do a quick check to make sure everything was in it, out of habit, but he immediately realized the journal was gone, the one he had used to write his letters to Debby, after she had died, and simply kept. He quietly gasped, but resolved that he would find it later if it hadn't burned up and, with that pain in his heart, he got up. He placed the box in the bag after making sure it was good and latched and started walking, slinging the sack over his shoulder.

"Where are you going?" said one of the few parents still left.

"I'm going to go find my boy. With or without you all." And as he took off, he shouted back, "And you're all crazy!"

To which the last of them shouted, "Remember, don't cheat. Use your feet!" And they laughed. One could expect children to break the law now and then, but it had been made clear to everyone that any adults caught flying would be made an example of. "His body, his choice," they said. Still Dorma went. A faint whistle went through the woods, but no one heard it for they had cleared off with all their talk about fines and things being in the oven too long.

Through the trees they whizzed and whistled. Mabby was far ahead, though, and none of them could hope to keep up. "How is he doing that? I thought he couldn't fly at all!" Tufa exclaimed.

"Well, he obviously can," Syriss said as they huffed along from tree to tree, trying their best.

"Obviously!" She laughed. "But how?! I mean, hasn't he been sitting in first course? He's not flying with us, but he's way faster than anything I've ever seen."

"I duh—" Syriss was out of breath. "I dunno (pant)," he said, unable to talk and scrambling for dear life at the same time.

Bo sang alongside them, giggling and burbling happily, though he went through more branches than he went over. Nevertheless, keeping up with Mabby was hopeless. He seemed to propel himself through the air under his own power. It was like magic.

They followed desperately for a long while for the sun came up while they chased him. By the end they could no longer even see Mabby, but were following the trail of falling leaves and the rush of his wings. It got harder and harder and they just kept going in the same general direction until they came upon the Tanglewall.

There were two puncture holes. One was about the size of Mabby, and there was another, much larger, hole.

"Oh my goodness, he was following someone," Deela said.

"Or something."

"Well, that is a little cliché, don't you think?" Deela said more than asked.

Tufa chuckled.

"And what is a 'Klee-Shay'?" Syriss asked.

"It's when you wear the same shoes as everyone else, and you think it's quite novel when it's not."

"But I don't…wear shoes. *None* of us are wearing shoes."

"My point is that that hole, while much larger than Mabby's, is not so big that it could not have been created by an adult squirrel, or a bird, which would be cool to imagine Mabby keeping up with, I'll give. However, to say that it couldn't be easily contrived that it was probably just another squirrel is like something out of a scary kid's story, for no other plot purpose than to give us—"

"Goosebumps. Yeah, I agree," Tufa said matter-of-factly with her arms folded.

"I would say pigeon or duck bumps at best, really," Deela said.

"Well, topple my mammy's dear sweet nut bowl, we've got us a voter-ship," Syriss said.

"Much better." Deela smiled.

"Hey. Duck bumps. Can we just focus on the real issue here?" And with that Syriss pointed to the hole Mabby had made, and they all went over and looked at it.

"Murf?" Bo said, looking out into the forest with a worried expression like the rest of them.

"Ugh, we can eat later," Syriss said. "For now, we go find Mabby."

"Um, we didn't vote for that." Tufa raised her paw and put it back down.

"Argh!" Syriss exclaimed, pulling his hair. "Says the one who's only around to be a friend when it suits her!" Tufa looked down. He had a point. "Mabby is our friend, *so* we *go*." And with that, Syriss fearlessly cleared the wall out into the forest.

Deela looked at Tufa for a moment, offering a consoling smile, and then they went together, right behind Syriss. "Ma-r-r-b!" Bo said and jumped through as well, excited as could be.

It was Mabby who was the most amazed on that day, however, for even he, with his great speed, was unable to keep up with the elusive culprit. Or so it seemed for Mabby did not know who he was chasing, but he knew for certain that this creature did not wish to be caught. Its course was astoundingly difficult, winding over, under, around, and around again, in every ridiculous direction, while Mabby struggled to go relatively straight after it. This freak of nature was literally nothing but a blur, and its sheer agility kept Mabby from being able to attain full speed, starting in one direction, then the other. He realized just how far he had to go in his training. He lost track of his direction and was losing sight of the blur he was chasing when, in an instant, the thing just disappeared altogether.

Mabby caught up quickly to the place he had last seen it, but no trace. Not a nockhole to sneak into, nor any odd shadow in the brightly fading morning. Just the branch of a dead tree, still wavering from the suspect's departure. He realized he had been chasing the figure for hours and could very well be irretrievably far from town. Fear caught up to him for he began to hear the sounds of the forest again, through his exasperated breath, as it briefly slowed. But Mabby had to continue on, for the culprit could be impossible to track down if he stopped any longer. He took off again, alone, as fast as he could fly. "You nearly killed my dad! Whoever you are, I'll get you, you hear me?" he shouted into the woods.

"Did you hear that?" shouted Tufa, far out in the lead, and they all listened for a moment. "It sounded like Mabby! It came from over there." She pointed. They took off again in their new direction.

After Mabby was long gone from the dead tree, and the forest had grown silent once more, a section of the tree's bark separated, and a tall, dark figure looked out from inside the secret passage. "I'm sorry, Mabby." Then it silently closed again, and the figure began a slow descent, weary from the chase.

"It's nothing...personal."

Mabby was sitting silently on a branch, sulking, when the others finally found him.

"Oh, thank goodness you're all right!" Tufa and Deela said together.

"You shouldn't have come. I'm fine." At this the girls were extremely offended but said nothing. "Shh. I'm trying to track him."

"He got away? From *you?"* Syriss whispered.

"Be quiet," Mabby said.

"Mabby, that back there..." Tufa said. "That was the most incredible flying anyone's ever seen!" They all nodded, "Everyone in town's going to know that you're the next flying ace of Hesperia. You're going to go down in history!" she exclaimed, forgetting to whisper, and a few curious birds flew out from behind a nearby tree. They all looked about, a little more worried, except Mabby, of course, who simply gave an exasperated huff and got up. "What's the use, he's long gone."

"He?" Syriss said. "Does that mean you got a look?"

"No," Mabby said. "I mean I did, but he was dressed in this crazy black leafy robe, or gown, or whatever. I only guess it was male because he was, you know..."

"Faster than you?" Deela completed Mabby's statement, and Mabby looked apologetically at Tufa.

"Yeah. Sorry, I guess," he said.

Syriss said nothing.

Bo had become slightly agitated and, after a moment or two, he found a bit of bark that was leaking sap, which he licked furiously and then began to gnaw.

"I don't know where I am anymore. I don't know how to get back. That's what I meant when I said you guys shouldn't have followed me here. Because now we're all stuck in this place."

"Nonsense, we'll find our way back to town," Deela said.

"How? And what if we don't?" Mabby countered.

"Well, then we'll not find our way back *together*. And we'll figure out how to help each other make it 'till someone finds us," Deela said. "Right, guys?"

Tufa and Syriss were silent.

"I mean, they're coming to get us, right?" Deela said.

The others were not so sure, and they all looked back to the sound of Bo's chewing. He had begun feasting on the inner wood of the branch he had snapped off.

"Oh no, stop that, Bo. It's all right, stop. We'll find some food, just not that. Can somebody—" Syriss wrested the tree limb out of Bo's mouth. "You know, help...Please?" They got the tree limb away from Bo, much to his dismay, and he began to protest. "Murf! Murrherfff...mmm*murf*," he said, whimpering.

"Oh, boy. We're in trouble," Syriss said.

"Wait!..." Mabby held up a paw to silence them, and silent they were. "I think I hear something."

After a moment of no one even breathing, Syriss whispered, "It just sounds like wind." And Mabby promptly took off once more, careening upwards, nearly leaving everyone in the dust once more.

"Ugh!" Tufa exclaimed, and they all followed, even Bo, who was glad they had found a new game. But not before he snuck a last big bite of that delicious maple.

Then Mabby realized, in midair, that he recognized the area they were in. He stopped, catching hold of a branch and holding on.

The others caught up again after a few moments. "What's the matter, Mabbs?" Syriss asked. "Oh! Is that town? Did we just come in a circle?"

"No, it isn't."

The others just let out a collective, "Whoa."

"Oh. Well, it must be a part of town, or town is nearby, right? That up there was clearly made by squirrels. I say we go in there and give our culprit a stern talking to. You mess with us; you get the horn!" Syriss said as they all looked up at the massive structure, hidden from view, cocooned by a great encasement of tanglewood that they all knew so well. They looked around at the golden day, feeling a little more able to relax with the prospect of familiarity nearby. The forest seemed almost peaceful, not scary at all. They began to admire its startling depth and the sight of the forest floor on all sides, in the middle of a world that seemed to be truly without walls. They began to wonder if they really wanted to go home just yet.

But Mabby was looking straight at it. "He never brought you to work, did he?" he said to Syriss, who looked at him in confusion. He had been considering much and, at that point in time, he decided he felt something that was entirely different than the rest of them.

He said, through clenched teeth, "You guys want to know a secret?"

"Ding ding…?" said Bo.

Part 3: The Battle for Hesperia

Is passion not thine heart-song's reed, and vigor not fury's own seed?

So fear no mind, nor closing door, for channels new from small things pour!

Except that one can learn to fly, how else shall we live to die?

And how else shall we splice the strand, for Heav'n's to be understood...

And understand.

Chapter 15: Beethorn

Just as the rest of them breached the Tanglewall, Mabby rolled and bounded back up again, shouting in anger.

Mabby called out, "I know who you are. All of you. I know everything! Come out!" When that didn't work, he shouted, "Inimical Umbra!"

Syriss put his paws up as they descended behind Mabby. "Mabbs, you can't say that, it's our secret pass...word...uh." He was struck dumb when Bumbleroot emerged from the base of the control tower with a snarl in his weathered lips and his one straight eye on them.

"Dag-nabbit, boah, I told you to be my eyes and ears, not to amass yer own private child militia."

Syriss piped up suddenly in a similar Georgia-peach accent, "Well, maybe you ought to be better at keepin' secrets and I wouldn't have had to. And I'd have a good one by now if *somebody* wasn't always trying to *keep me down*!" Tufa laughed for a moment, thinking Syriss was making fun of the old dog, but Syriss turned and looked at them and said, "What? I told you, he's the one bad at keeping secrets."

"That doesn't help your case with me." Tufa smirked.

"Well, I wasn't trying to!"

"Then what were you trying to do?" Tufa asked. "I think that's something we all want to know. So tell us, why are you so insistent on having this little club of yours going? What has it accomplished?"

Syriss blushed, embarrassed. "I…"

Tufa went on with her momentum. "Because I think you're just out to prove something. You just want everyone to think you're really special."

Not everyone, Mabby began to realize, but someone. Syriss just looked at the deck, disarmed.

"What I want to know is where on earth you're actually from," Mabby said.

Then Syriss burst out, "I can do it! I told you I could do it, and I've been doing it, all right? I can do it."

"That's not the point. You can't because you can't. You weren't born this way. I didn't decide that fact. It's just life. That's all there is," Bumbleroot said, somewhat under his breath.

"Um, excuse me, do what?" Tufa said.

"It doesn't matter, it's between them." Tufa nearly pressed the matter again, but Mabby fixed her with a look.

At that point everyone but Mabby had an extremely confused look upon their faces. Bo was simply wondering, very desperately, why there was no food.

"Is he going to be all right?" asked the tutor, pointing cautiously to the absolutely massive squirrel behind them all, who was not paying the slightest attention.

"Look," said Mabby. "Syriss, this is a training ground where squirrels like me learn to do what I just did all morning, but somehow I think you already know a little about that. Mr. Bumbleroot, these are my friends, who saved my life from the one that led us here, whose identity I intend to expose shortly. And yes, Tufa, Syriss is the son of my tutor here."

"What makes you think that?!" Syriss and Bumbleroot said in unison.

"Well, besides *that…"*

"It don't matter, boy. Just you all get out of here, right now I said, b'fore y'all get the *horn!"*

Mabby looked back at Tufa and Syriss. "Oh," they said.

"And anyway, I know it was you, and whoever is back there that just tried to kill me, and I want to know why!" He raised his voice so whoever had been hiding inside the tower base could hear.

"You don't know anything of the sort!"

"Oh, yeah? Well, how?" Mabby said.

"Because! It's…not true."

"Look, I saw you. You led me straight here. You set my house on fire, and my friends nearly died pulling me out."

"Mabby, that's not possible."

"Just because we don't like or understand the facts doesn't make them impossible. Facts' facts, and you tried to kill me. You dragged me out here, and you've had me here all this time, doing your bidding, just so you could try and kill me? You can't tell me it wasn't you. I saw your robe. Why is everybody always trying to kill the Dabbys?"

"I don't think I can explain everything, but right now we think there is a connection…" Said Bumbleroot.

"Who's 'we'?" Mabby interrupted, running behind the tutor to the control tower. "Tell me everything, now! Inimical Umbra! Inimical Umbraaaa!" Mabby was silenced by the tutor grabbing him from behind and clapping his paw over Mabby's mouth. Mabby struggled, but Bumbleroot was too strong.

Then a voice came out from behind the tower base door as it opened with a creak.

"Yes. Inimical Umbra, the codeword for our operation. You're intelligent, my young one. Surely you know it simply means—"

"Dark and sinister shadows," Mabby said. Bumbleroot released him as soon as he stopped fighting and screaming like a fool, but he wisely kept his paw on Mabby's shoulder.

"Who's that?" the others asked among themselves.

"And those shadows are why you must learn to be discreet," said the voice as its body emerged from the door and into the light. "But continue, please. Tell us all you know…" The others gasped. The figure wore the black robe Mabby had described, embroidered with lifelike designs of red, green, and gold leaves and branches about the shoulders, descending down the mantle, and around the opening of the hood. Mabby caught a glint of metal under the folds of the robe. "I think it could really help us out a lot!" The figure drew his paws from his sleeves and lifted the hood to reveal his face. He smiled.

"Daddy!" Deela exclaimed and ran up to give her father a big hug.

"No, Reverend."

"Are you yankin' my tail?" said Syriss in his native accent.

"It was *YOU?!"* Mabby said.

"Of course not, silly. Ho ho!" Deela and her father, Reverend Wally Ferroule, with his now knightly white hair, laughed together. "I just showed you my face! Now, you say you saw someone with a robe…" He motioned across himself. "Like this one?"

While Mabby considered his reply, Bumbleroot interjected, "Yuh, and that means someone knows! Led him here. Probably knows every*thang*. That means our cover is blown, and we are ruined."

"On the contrary," The Ferroules both said, then stopped, and Deela went on, "I've got this one, Dad." She grinned and turned back to Bumbleroot, pointing her finger in the air. "On the contrary, it is more probable the assailant has known for a long time, since he had the pretense to plan and execute such an elaborate ploy to lay the blame on us and no doubt manipulate Mabby into giving up, and even that was a plan B to getting away with murder, which they apparently might have. It also shows us that this enemy is also reliant on secrecy, both ours and his. By allowing some flexibility to our secrecy, we may actually be giving ourselves the upper paw."

"An upper paw that doesn't matter since we don't know who it is and they clearly know who we are," Bumbleroot said.

"Yes, but no one knows what they don't know." Wally paused, perhaps thinking that was enough to have made his point. It was not. "So, clearly, no one can know what anyone else doesn't know either." He paused again. "*So,* if the obvious is, in fact, the truth, then the assailant will expect Mabby to quit, and obviously he will not, signaling to the perpetrator that his plan has failed because it has, and *that…"* He waited.

"That," Mabby attempted. "That…we know!"

"Exactly! The safest bet will be for them to lay low, giving us the time to find out who it is!"

"Yes. The best course of action is for all of us to give the impression that we know everything."

"So how do we do that?" Syriss asked.

The Reverend held a finger up. "...I have no idea."

Bumbleroot exhaled. "This is useless. We need to act on what we know."

"And that is?" Mabby said.

"No. I mean us, as in the Reverend and I, and the rest of us, not you kids. You all need to go home right now and say nothing more about what you've seen here."

"No, I think perhaps they could be of use."

"No!"

"The enemy has someone working in the city, so maybe we could use a few little information gatherers ourselves."

"This is unacceptable. This little meeting is over. You all young'uns need to go on home. Right now." He took Mabby and Syriss by the shoulders. "Get out of here, and never tell anyone. It'll be your own heads if you do. Go." He shoved Mabby and Syriss to the edge.

"Now, Bumbleroot, sir, you can do more with gentleness than you can with force," the Reverend said, but that did not stop anything.

"Go! Get out of here!" Bumbleroot shouted.

"Just a minute!" a voice shouted from above. Everyone stopped and looked up. In the sky, from the tallest visible tree, something leapt and circled down. "Paws off my son!"

"Dad?" Mabby squinted as the silhouette came closer.

Dorma Dabby landed with a thwack on the platform with his fist on the ground. "Just what are you…hey, oh this place is...whoa, wow, eh! Really big. Didn't see that coming..."

Bumbleroot smacked his own face.

"Whoa," Syriss said. "It's really him."

"What? My dad? Yeah," Mabby said. But Syriss walked over to Dorma and shook his paw. "Great to see you again, sir. I'm actually a big fan. About that time with the jackyball, um, sorry, I didn't know who you were." Dorma just nodded.

"What? More?!" Bumbleroot exclaimed. "Can everyone just leave? You're not supposed to be here! This is…" He gave an exasperated sigh. "This is a secret! There's no use in a secret that everybody knows!"

"It's all right. You can tell them." Two more squirrels of unseemly age hobbled out of the control tower base door. One had a rickety jaw with his twangy tweed jacket that made Dorma wince, and the other wore a soiled duster, holey pants, and nothing else.

"Who is that?" Dorma asked.

"They are like me. They have kept a silent watch over your city for ages. Well, mostly. Their codenames are Masters Bang and Bone. And, in this place, whatever they say goes…My name is Bumbleroot. You, Dorma Dabby, are well known even in this place. It is an honor, sir."

"And what is 'here'?"

Bumbleroot looked back at the one called Master Bang, who nodded. "This is the training ground of the ancient Protectorate. You might know us as the Knights of Elorus, but understand we have many names."

"Is there anyone else?" Dorma said.

"Grandmaster Cloudsparrow is not here."

"And?"

Bumbleroot looked around. "That's it."

"That's it? You mean this is your whole army?'"

"Well, yes," Bone replied. "It's all right, Bumbles. You can tell 'em."

"Well, don't call me that, first of all," Bumbleroot said. "As little as it means, our numbers have dwindled, and there are so few born with Guardian's wings that now, save young Mabby here, we're the only ones left that have not perished in the protection of the city."

Dorma could not reply to this out of sheer speechlessness.

"But nothing really happens?!" Tufa said.

"Yes," Bumbleroot said. "You're welcome."

"Are those your real names?" Tufa asked.

"No," replied the one called Bang.

"But if we told you our names, we'd…we'd all *die*!" Master Bang unexpectedly shouted.

Bang took hold of his collar. "Don't worry about him. It is important that we maintain secrecy as well as we can. So yes, the formality of codenames is necessary. The mere whisperings of our real names in some places could spark a riot, or worse."

"But everybody knows the Reverend," Tufa argued.

"Of course. He's one of our moles."

"A mole!" the gang cried. "But he totally looks like a squirrel."

"No, not an *actual mo—*. Oh, buttsticks."

"Look, we were banished. But not because we are dangerous. Never mind all of that," Bumbleroot interrupted. "Reverend Wally and I have been investigating on different ends. And if we are right, you all knowing what you know now is going to make you a part of it. Something is deeply wrong with Beeley's movement to undermine flighted Squirreldom, not just on a moral level—"

"Now hold on, hold on. Mabby," Dorma said. "What are you doing here? Did you know about this?"

"Yes. I have been in training here."

"What?! For how long? And you never told me?"

"Secrecy, Dad."

"But, but I'm your Dad! This is, this...it's…amazing. Is this where you learned to do what you did back there?"

"Yes, and they've taught me a lot more. I can show you!" Mabby began to get excited.

"You can and you will, okay? Show me first chance we get. I want to see everything."

"Okay." Mabby grinned, and Dorma turned back to Bumbleroot.

"So you taught my son to fly like that back there?"

"Yessuh. Ah dee-id."

Dorma was having a hard time with the accent, but he stuck out his paw, and Bumbleroot shook it. "So what do you plan to make him into? Like, one of you? Is that dangerous?"

"Are you opposed—" Master Bone put his paw on Bumbleroot's shoulder. "I have a better question. Are you...with us?"

"I'm sorry, hum?"

"You now know who we are and why we are here, and we must know now if you are with us or against us."

"Well, I suppose that would depend on what you plan to do."

Bone crossed his paws over his cane. "We are going to destroy Mayor Beeley's hold on the city, by any means necessary, and return our exiled selves to our rightful stations. We are the keepers of the Hollow and the Mountain, and it is our desirous and rightful power. Are you with us or against?" Master Bone struck the deck with his cane.

Dorma was struck by how easily Master Bone's words assumed the mantle of authority. "Any enemy of Bolly Beeley is a friend of mine."

"I've got *three buttons,*" Master Bang said to himself, away from the crowd, who, it should be noted, was entirely in LaLa Land at that moment, which is very far from Hesperia. "FOUR buttons!" He grabbed his coat in abject shock and then promptly resumed staring at the sky.

"Good. And we are not in a position to refuse a willing ally. Now, as we were going to say, there have always been sightings of Morgart out in the deep valley," Bone said. "But we once saw her too close, way too close. Not to worry, this particular instance was long ago. We took the necessary precautions, drove her off with ranged attacks…" At that the one called Bang cackled a little, for he seemed enjoy the way Bone put it. "And we thought nothing more of it. Then it was later that day, afternoon time, the bells began to ring. We rushed to the gates, but somehow the cat was already inside the city. As prisoners of exile, we watched in horror as the cat took Hesperia apart. She had caught us off guard, and we have no idea how she got inside undetected to this day."

"It was the day that Mabby was born. Essentially the day you all got your scars," Bumbleroot said.

Bo clapped his paw to his head. "Bobo Booboo…"

"It was to our amazement that Bolly Beeley was the one who ultimately fought the cat off, all by himself at that! No one could believe, at first, that he was actually so strong a fighter that he could hold off the cat unsupported, but we received clues suggesting he was the one to blame for the infiltration. Someone was meeting with that cat that day, and she was spotted unawares. We found squirrel tracks."

They gasped.

"That led us to the strange nature of the attacks. The cat seemed to have a predetermined course, for it knew where to attack all the houses of the families opposed by the Quarleses. But you, Dorma, you have no relation to them, and you were attacked. Not only that, Bolly showed up at *your* hospital room. Debby was a Quarles girl, we know, but I doubt after keeping her alive but under wraps they would suddenly elect to have her killed. Someone had to inform them, but it had to be someone that knew about Debby when no one else did. Do you understand? Now this may be all coincidence. We are not certain, but we suspect Mayor Beeley to be the one conspiring to destroy the Knights."

"But he's the one who saved the town. Why would he want to turn around and put it at such risk?" Dorma said.

"We know only that it has something to do with Mabby here. He is special. He somehow managed to escape the clutches of Morgart. So we have been watching since his birth and anticipating his entry into the school. There is some connection between all this and Mabby. The fact that no Guardians have been born in a long time, Mabby, you, Dorma, and your late wife, bless her soul, and that dratted Bolly Beeley, and that cat. But we were not completely sure what until Hal was found where he lay. But even with that we don't have any leads to follow to find out what he is up to, just that, after all these years, Bolly Beeley's thirst for vengeance still burns."

"What happened to him?"

Bumbleroot looked down for a moment. "He was incredible. He was the strongest winglier that there had ever been, at least in memory."

"A phenomenon," Wally said. Dorma's mind flashed to the day, at First Practicum, when Bolly Beeley had performed that impossible flying feat. Everyone had been so impressed, and Ms. Padduck had simply insulted him for his eagerness to make sure everyone saw how good he was.

"He was genuinely dedicated, so much so that we took the liberty of awarding him the Armor of Elorus, the seal of initiation to the Protectorship, which we all wear." He showed the metal beneath the robes, which Mabby had seen, and it glimmered a glorious gleam. It was a well-worked single-piece breastplate of silver and gold, which no claw or splint could penetrate, with all manner of forest scenes surrounding a shining sun. "But he was as arrogant as he was talented. The moment we gave him his honorary plates—"

"And robe?" Mabby interjected.

"Yes, we have also had a disguising robe as part of our official uniform ever since our exile. Anyway, he believed himself to be on equal standing with us and no longer needed to finish his learning. He was angry that, as he put it, there was a certain kit who was like us, and needed our help, but...the teacher would have none of it. He claimed the kit was being held back and that Ms. Padduck had it out for her simply because her family hated the Protectorate."

"Debby? Debby knew about you all?" Dorma said in disbelief.

"No, I think if she had known about us, it would have been by mistake. She was a Quarles."

"And?"

"The Quarles family was among a number of families that believed that the strength of a squirrel was in his sameness with others. They believed this because even the advantages of real flight were a disability in some ways, rather than merely a difference, on account of its drawbacks." Dorma could see how they could believe that. He had tended to agree. He nodded, but gave no clue of his position on the matter. "They believed in the natural state of squirrility as being the obvious perfect state, and that the advancement of our kind to the eventual rule of all the Lands of the Acheron, even far beyond Nearly Mountain, beyond Nockshin Wood, was dependent on perfect universal conformity. Beeley believed she was being forcibly disguised as a "normal" by her family, and Dorma—yes, you—were planted by her family to make sure she didn't act up, even that they had arranged for your marriage to her against her will."

"It can't be. Do you think that Bolly Beeley…was in love with my wife?"

"We know he was," Bumbleroot said. "The whole time.

"So he could definitely see that we were in love…And he just didn't want to believe it? But why would her family want to deliberately discredit their own daughter?" Dorma's face fell as he asked this, having realized everything he was hearing was the likely truth, as unbelievable as it was.

Bumbleroot continued. "Bear with me. Long ago, a warrior of the Protectorate, by the name of Ekkhorn, fought against that great cat, Morgart. No one knows why she came other than that she just seems to have an insatiable thirst for squirrels. And though Ekkhorn did his very best, he lost, and the cat was able to punch through our defenses and ravage the town with no one left to stop her. Morgart was the only being that had ever caused the Protectorate to fail in its ongoing mission."

"The day my wife died—" Dorma said.

"No, but I will get to that," Bumbleroot said. "This was Ekkhorn's first battle, so he was inexperienced and, in many ways, as cocky as Beeley is. He didn't listen to his strategic commanders and charged ahead in the fight, and his line broke off from the others. His defeat left the defenses compromised."

"And that one stupid move cost us everything we'd ever worked for!" Bang said. "Like, ever!" And with that Bone knocked Bang on the back of his head and eyed Bumbleroot, indicating that he should go on.

"Well, enough about that. Back then there were many more of us, and our presence was quite public, but it was that loss that caused everyone to doubt us. Panic swept the boughs, businesses barred their doors, and Hesperia recluded itself from all contact, and the townsfolk summarily demanded the Protectorate be dissolved. They believed some narrative that we had let Morgart into the city to prove a point and it had backfired."

"But why would anyone say such a thing?"

"Take a wild guess."

Dorma thought for a moment. “The Quarles family.”

“They led the movement, taking the opportunity of our failure to seize power, and so you, Dorma, and every squirrel since has grown up in a Hesperia that has fostered only the most regular, most common, forms of flying. All else has been named heresy, infirmity, misfittery, etcetera. They monitor hospital beds, making sure to prevent ‘too many infirmities’ from occurring, and encourage the segregation and even deportation of such squirrels. If any made it out of the birthing ward alive, the Quarles family made sure the curriculum was impossible to pass for anyone but the ‘natural, ideal’ squirrel.”

“So when Debby was born…”

“It was only because it was their daughter and not someone else’s that she was allowed to live. Being born into evil and hypocritical power has its privileges. Yes, if Bolly was right, and she was one of us, they saw what they were doing as protection. Bolly came to us shortly before the final day of school and declared himself in a conflict of interest. You see, at first he was on our side, but Ms. Padduck, he told us, was obstinate and continually denied what he felt was completely certain.”

“What was that?” Dorma asked.

“That Debby was Eloran.”

Dorma sighed. “She was. Goodness...”

“We felt, at Ms. Padduck’s behest, that the little one should be made no fuss about. Ms. Padduck also felt that, as long as she was passing, there was no need to start another political battle on her watch. She was really doing what Debby had asked her to do. Protect her and keep her in school for all she wanted was to be normal and live a normal life. The Quarleses, we discovered after some digging, punished her every day she went to class, sometimes physically. Ms. Padduck had seen Debby’s wings herself and certified them as normal, but we guess that Debby must have found some way to disguise them.”

“You mean you kept someone on the inside?” Syriss complained.

“Secrecy, we discovered, has served us as well or better than publicity, for now we can continue our work protecting the city with little interference, with a little bit more effort towards not being seen…”

"No!" Dorma exclaimed unexpectedly.

"We told Bolly to stop his nonsense and leave her alone. He didn't realize what she had truly wanted, for Ms. Padduck had shown us something, a hand-scrawled note, begging for help. Bolly didn't know about this, so he refused to trust us and vowed that day that he would expose the truth or that he would lay down his armor. We took heed to those words, at least, and were all watching outside the city, waiting with three hundred and sixty degrees of surveillance on Rammerie's Race Day, waiting for whatever Bolly would throw at us. We were all too far away to do anything but helplessly watch our beloved city crumble from within. By then there were too few of us, and he knew where we would be, and we were too foolish to see it coming."

Master Bone went inside the control tower and came out with something wrapped in cloth.

"Oh, my love, my sweet Debby, my dear. What have I done?!" Dorma fell on his knees with great heaving sobs. "I can't hear any more! I can't! It was me. I was the one who disguised her wings! I sewed them up so she could fly, so she could pass! I just wanted her to have her dream, to be happy. I didn't know it would lead to all this." He was consoled by Deela, who sat with him. Tufa joined and Bo knelt silently to weep, bowing his head over the group. Mabby had once heard Syriss explain to Bo the difference between when children and adults cry: "When children cry it's because they are hurt, but when grownups cry it's because someone *else* is hurt." Mabby's chin quivered, and he sat down, weak and helpless at witnessing his father's pain. He had been so insensitive, so wrong, more wrong than anyone. Ever.

"Debby Quarles Dabby was quite possibly the bravest of all, having so quietly endured such remarkable pain every day of her life, with the torture of her family punishing her for pursuing a dream and going every single day to that school with her wings clamped shut. Protectors' wings are far more sensitive…their sensitivity gives us an amplified spatial perception, a sixth sense about fighting, but it makes us often unable to stand being touched. Like I said, drawbacks."

"Why are you telling me this?!" Dorma shouted through his tears.

"Because you need to know how much more important being able to live, hell, just being allowed to dream, was to her than you ever could have imagined without knowing the pain she willingly suffered. So what you gave her, which was impossible for us, was more than just a paw up. It was more than having a hero. It was being understood."

Dorma continued to sob, and his tail slowly relaxed until it trembled on the deck as Bumbleroot continued talking.

"We don't know for absolute certain how Bolly could have done it. Or even what he did exactly. We just know that this..." Bumbleroot motioned and Shin threw the cloth wrapping on the deck in the middle of them. "Showed up on the landing, right over there by the straw-keep next to the door, the morning after Morgart attacked your wife, and Bolly was never seen in this place again." Deela bent down and uncovered what was inside, and everyone gasped at the sight, for all who had been to Rammerie's on the first day of school recognized the word "oppression" scrawled bitterly across the sun relief of the charred and mangled Protectorate armor, so badly beaten that it could never be worn again or repaired. It was the same angry writing that had defaced the schoolhouse doors and windows.

"But," Mabby said, "he didn't give back his robe, did he?"

Bumbleroot postured. "Well, no, I don't think he did now that I recall. What is the fixation on the robe?"

"I saw it."

"What?"

"I saw him. Remember? I said the person I chased here was wearing a black robe just like yours."

"So you thought it was me?"

"Yes, wouldn't you?" Mabby asked a little sheepishly.

"Yes, I think I would. It's all right, I understand." He looked at the rest of them. "But it could not have been Beeley."

"Why not?"

"Excuse me, but I have a question." Everyone looked at Syriss. "Why does the armor have nipples?" To which the Reverend leaned his head back a bit and sighed. "Dude…" was all he said, and the matter was dropped.

"Do you remember Beeley's initial campaign speech? Were you there? Then you must remember his revelation that he had no wings for, while he was saving the city, the great cat cut his patagiums off."

"Patty-tummies," thought Mabby, and winced at the ultra-corny level of his stupidity.

"Y'know, come to think of it," Syriss said, "none of this explains how Bolly got around so quick that day—"

Mabby motioned behind his back for Syriss to shut up, and Tufa interrupted him. "Well, I think we've had a long morning. Better rest up for tomorrow. We've got a hard day ahead of us at school, now…"

"No. You'll all three stay right here and tell me what happened."

"Oh, um, heh." Syriss realized his mistake and tried to backpedal, which only made things worse. "Well, we were kind of all really awake on the day of Hallo Ballo's death, with all the bells, you understand. Um. Bless his soul, and all that. And we were um…"

"We were there. We didn't see his death, but we saw everything after. I know, it was wrong, but it wasn't all we saw." said Mabby.

"Ugh!" Tufa said.

"It's all right. Tell us." said the Reverend.

"We followed Bolly after he left the scene of the crime, watching from up above the Tanglewall. I don't think he knew we were following him. But at one point he simply disappeared. Then, seconds later, there he was right in front of us. He has some means of traveling instantaneously." Said Mabby.

"That's it! That's why we couldn't arrest him then and there. He claimed he was at his farm down on the ground, and we couldn't argue that since he was the first on the scene. The bell had been rung immediately after Hal had fallen, and those few who saw Hal pushed could not say for certain in the dark of the morning, but they all said it was Beeley who pushed him. Then they said Beeley simply walked off and disappeared. It couldn't stand up to the fact that everyone saw him there, 'mourning' with the body, when they began to arrive only seconds later, and already claiming he saw the fall from his farm. Somehow he had beaten the witnesses down, and he wasn't even breathing hard." Said the Reverend.

"He traveled faster than flight? Impossible!" said Bumbleroot.

"But he had to have done it, and we don't know how. And we also don't know how it is that Hallo Ballo couldn't have survived. It would have been easy enough for him to just tail about and glide off." Said the Reverend.

"He never passed Rammerie's. He could have just not had the know-how to fend for himself," Tufa said.

"Ah, beg to differ, my dear," Wally said. "He was one of us, or he could have been." And at that the four of them removed their covers and placed their paws over their hearts for a moment.

Dorma kept silent, but he somehow knew that the insignia on the old fallen tree had something to do with all of this.

Wally looked up again and said, "We think Hal was on to something. We think he had learned Beeley's secrets and had gone to confront him, and that's why Bolly killed him."

"Well, that person I was chasing disappeared the same way. I thought he had gotten out of my sight, but there's just no way, now that I think about it. If it wasn't Bolly, and it wasn't any of you, then…" Mabby trailed off.

"Then we need to figure out how this mysterious figure is gettin' round, and then we can figure out who is working for Beeley and the rest we can beat out of 'im," Bumbleroot said.

"I think I can help," Dorma said. "Just give me a couple days to investigate, and I will let you know, back here, if I find anything," Dorma said.

"Someone on the inside might be just what we need after all this time," Wally said.

"Sounds fine." Bumbleroot tried not to sound too grudging.

"And we'll help any way we can, Mister Dabby," Syriss said, and about that everyone in the gang was on board. That is, except for Bumbleroot.

"You aren't going to help with anything. You are going to go to school and make passing marks, and not mess around in adult affairs—"

Master Bone interrupted. "Here is your task, Syriss." Bumbleroot grudgingly took a step back. "You are going to…keep doing what you are doing now for that has been valuable enough to us since we cannot enter the city. It is our one weakness. Watch over our town from the inside—that is invaluable to us—and send your reports back with Mabby. And be Mabby's friends. He will need it."

"So…" Syriss paused. "Mabby's in charge."

"Over your party, essentially, yes."

Syriss paused again, then looked up and grinned his foolish grin. "Got it, sah!" He saluted. "There's no one better."

"Now, once we can figure out who is helping Beeley, then we can know if Beeley's goal is to help the Quarles family destroy the Protectoracy. They can figure out how to stop it. Heaven knows we will need to nip this in the bud if he plans to get that cat involved. We will be helpless with so few," Bumbleroot said.

Tufa said, "I know! I will let Cal know about everything and see if he can help."

"No!" said every single one of them, to Tufa's surprise.

Reverend Wally said, "Sorry, but our operation needs to be secret. We told you all in confidence."

Bumbleroot added, "Trust no one beyond this wall."

Tufa immediately replied, "Except for you? Callo is the best, most honest and capable, he *can* be trusted."

"My little ma'am, those very same words were once spoken about Bolly Beeley."

"Well, how do you know you can trust *us*?" she challenged.

Bumbleroot said, "Because you didn't know. Even when you didn't think you were being watched, and if you didn't know then, it's because Mabby has been doing his job—that is, up until now—but I think we can sort that out."

"Well, I mean, I knew," Deela said, smiling.

"That's because Wally sucks," Bumbleroo said. Wally only smiled and tousled Deela's shiny red bob so that she giggled and had to straighten her glasses.

"Agreed," Wally said. "It was clear no harm was intended by any of you, and you only sought the truth, and you have found it. But to be sure, there is an enemy out there, not only seeking to destroy, but to destroy *us*. Mark my words, if you mention this place to the wrong person…"

Tufa only looked more enraged, but she merely put her head down for a moment. "I am going to try to trust you. You know the trouble with secrecy is that you inevitably end up hurting the ones you love. And if it comes down to it, you won't get me to hurt Cal."

Mabby's heart fluttered a little at that one, but he had always known anyway. Bo, however, slumped to the floor, did not look up, and said nothing.

Tufa let out a short gasp. "I have to go." She ran off without another word.

"Mabby, Syriss, home's to the north. I'll see Tufa home." Dorma left with that.

"S'alright, big guy, she didn't mean it like that." Syriss gave poor Bo a pat on the back. Bo's tail flopped on the deck, and he began to sniffle, the great ridge of his eyebrows furrowed.

"I hope she's right about him," Wally said.

Syriss replied, "Well, I do know that Tufa is the smartest kit I ever knew, and if anyone's going to be right about anything, it will be her. I don't think it can hurt, and he would be good to have on our side."

Reverend Wally motioned for Mabby to come over, and he knelt down. "I had to give it some thought, but I need you to do something for me. When you go to school tomorrow, I need you to act really mean. I mean I need you to give literally everyone the 'I can see your soul' kind of stare, like, you know, like you can…"

"See their souls?"

"Precisely, yes. I mean do it real good, that ought to flush out whoever is working for Beeley in that school."

"Got it." Perhaps. Mabby and Dorma left next, and Syriss and Bo followed.

Master Bone approached Bumbleroot and said, "You, Ekkhorn Beethorn, are the greatest commander in all of memory. You have held us together much longer than we thought possible, and don't listen to anything else."

"On the wisdom of children," Bumbleroot said, "we hang the future." After everyone left, leaving only the Four Knights in the one great hope of Nockshin Forest, he added, "If indeed there is one."

Wally sighed as the others went back in, Bang and Bone shaking their heads at one another in contention. "Yes, well, hasn't it always been so? Perhaps if we truly can no longer protect this place, then something better should rise up," Wally said. He looked as if a ten-pound sack of worry hung from his mind.

"You're not even going to think about the safety of your own daughter?"

"That hurricane is the least of my worries." He laughed.

"Well, we should have stopped the other one, the tabby, or at least told her what we know about the son of the one who would have commanded me, nay, even the grandmaster."

"Yes. The one who could have even stopped Bolly Beeley."

"Exactly!"

"Except Bolly got to him, too. Bolly left him a broken heap, like that piece of armor."

"That was not Bolly's surrender. It was a symbol of what he planned to do to us. These kids don't know; we are not playing some game. We shouldn't involve them. It's not safe, and it's not about them."

"No, it's not. It's about power, and Beeley's got it all. But you know what is more powerful than power itself?"

"What?"

"Truth. When you contend for the truth, you contend for the truly oppressed. And everyone else destroys each other. It's the only hope we have. It's all we've ever had, for the sake of our children. We'd best not be ashamed of it anymore."

"You want the boughways overrun with mobs? You think that's the solution?"

"No. But they will do that anyway. The uncivil are not the fault of the civil. I'm simply saying…" Wally picked up the broken armor before he finished, and they began walking back to the door. "that silence has killed, stifled, and oppressed many more than we have ever been accused of. I'm saying the Elorans first conceived the tree-world. We are the ones who protect it because we alone understand its power, because its truths were our truths, OUR hopes. Our dreams. So in truth, if there is even one of us left, we can only fail if we stop doing that."

"Doing what?"

"Dreaming." Wally walked off, leaving his commander with a long time to think.

Chapter 16: Friends.

Dorma had found a spidery hovel for them to stay in, "Until things blow over and business picks up," he had reassured Mabby.

Mabby got ready for school that morning, the start of the week. Bolly was in the papers again. "Beeley closes MB&T again as shares drop." There were stories of lesser importance such as, "Habitat concerns arise as trees die variously" or "Estate sale tomorrow featuring prized old dirty shovel collection." Dorma sighed, then folded and tucked the newspaper in his arm.

"All set, SuperMabbs?" he said as Mabby put his shirt on, clasping his sides, and moved toward the door. Dorma went to grab the doorknob, but there was not one. Adjusting to the new surroundings was difficult. All the old pictures were gone, and the bright checkered cabinets, yellow walls, and window-filled halls had been replaced by holey boards. There was nothing to speak of in the way of furniture but a dusty gray stool. They had the clothes on their backs, and Dorma had a satchel, which now occasionally carried a loaf of pankeybread. He could touch the front and back of the home, which was little more than a converted hallway in a run-down bungalow. All the other rooms had also been converted into single-room dwellings. He could hear the slumlord owner knocking on doors, making sure no one was marking up his barren floors. Dorma sighed again over the muffled nagging, in the next room, over rent. A dish crashed somewhere. Someone had room for a dish? Sigh.

He pushed the door open to take his son to school. A small pennant emerged from Mabby's sweater as he went out in front, looking down, and Dorma instinctively attempted to snatch it off. His sweater came unraveled, and Dorma let go of the string to let it hang till he could fix it. He walked right behind Mabby, in his unraveling sweater. "A clothier," he thought. "What will they think of this sight?" He sighed again. "Debby wouldn't care. I shouldn't care. But I suppose I do."

"Care about what?" Mabby asked, and Dorma realized that he had been thinking out loud. "Well, I guess, *everything.*"

"Eh, it's fine, I suppose..."

"What, though?" Mabby pressed, but that was the end of their conversation, apparently.

They trod, for what seemed like hours, up the winding boughs from the poorest parts, even poorer than the Brambleries, that they called Promise's End. There was no sign that they were in that area, only signs, if one understands. They had to get past the thieves, hustlers, and panhandlers, all up at dusk to work in a full day of stealing from each other. Mabby looked at one homeless chap covered in soot.

"Are we like them now, Dad?"

"Well, I don't know."

"Don't know what?"

"Well, I don't know that we are *not* like them...and anyway, when you've run out of options, you'd be surprised what you might do to survive, who you'll become, without even realizing it."

"That's terrible."

"Even when it looks like squirrels are all bad, you can't give in. You gotta believe in others, even if only for your own sake."

"You mean like in Bolly Beeley?

"Even Bolly Beeley." Dorma kicked himself for saying that.

"Do you believe in me?"

"Of course. I believe in you more than I believe in anything."

"That I can fly?"

Dorma hesitated, wanting to say yes but, at the same time, not give him false hope. He realized he was a complete and utter hypocrite. He tried to stutter out a quick answer, but Mabby just looked away, having gotten his answer already.

They said nothing more, and Dorma hurt all the way. "Why," he thought, "is it so hard to say for evil squirrels, but not good ones?" Why? Even when I've seen what he can do? What is wrong with me?

"Well good luck in—" he started when they got to school, but Mabby interrupted. "I can do it, Dad. I know I can."

"I know you can too, son." He bent down to meet Mabby's eyes. He's getting so big. If Mabby believes in himself, then it doesn't matter, I will too.

"Bumbleface says I have to trust the process." Mabby started walking again.

"Sorry, what was his name again?"

"Dumpleboot."

Dorma choked on his laughter. "I really recall it was Fumblenuts. Or something."

"Rumblepoop," Mabby said. "I've had a long time to think about this."

And on they went with a Stinklefoot, a Wrinkletoot, and so on the rest of the way, which was still a long way to go. They behaved as if they were very much enjoying their breakfast. Dorma didn't bother to tell Mabby where he had gotten the pankeybread. He also didn't bother to tell Mabby what he planned to do that day. "Plenty for him to worry about," he thought as they laughed.

At school Mabby picked the best time to perform the Stinkeye Experiment several minutes before class.

Ms. P wasn't there yet, but all the students waited patiently and quietly in their seats. "As good a time as any," thought Mabby.

The first victim would be little Riffa Tadwick. She was automatically suspect for never once having said anything in class. No one even knew she was there most of the time. She was a poor being with dreadlocks, not the good kind, and sometimes smelled of an old house that had been rained in and never swept. She always fiddled with a silly bundle of dirty white string. He could tell the moment she felt him looking, and her eyes shifted. A look of incredulity came across her smudgy face, and just as a curious smile appeared, she apparently thought of something very sad and looked straight down again. Mabby found her too pathetic to be harmful, or helpful, to anyone.

But who could do some real damage? He suddenly realized Callo was nowhere to be found. Syriss saw Mabby looking about, motioned to Callo's empty seat, and shrugged.

Bo snuck a log of cheese from his packed lunch and crammed the whole thing in his mouth when he didn't think anyone saw. His eyes closed in a wave of relief.

Ms. Padduck hobbled in, now quite late indeed. "Well that was stupid," Mabby thought.

"What a heavenly morning, my dears!" She set her things hurriedly on the teacher's desk and clasped her paws. "We have a few things to discuss." She was interrupted by Cal, of all beings, who entered without a word and sat down without looking at anyone. He was out of breath and appeared to have been sobbing, his flushed red cheeks and jerking chest giving him away.

Mabby stared at him and, while Ms. Padduck was momentarily silent, he squinted at Cal, who did not look up. Cal never saw him for, as soon as Mabby perked his ominous sneer, he began to feel a funny feeling in his bowels. Mabby realized Tufa, seated directly behind Callo, was eyeing him. Her eyes glowed like oppressive, intestinally upsetting embers.

"Dearies!" Ms. P snapped. The class jumped, but she quickly returned to normal. Bo, unfazed, simply stared ahead with his palms on his desk, which was tiny (for him), and chewed slowly with his mouth covered with yellow stuff. "I want to say, first of all, that you have all done so well! Well, for those of us left, of course, eh, em…" She hadn't meant to say it like that; that much was obvious. "You must know that, due to unforeseen circumstances, there will be no more curriculum. Instead of dealing with all of the complications of making you understand why things have come to be, the higher ups have thought perhaps it would be better to simply not worry your minds with it. Live in the present, and such."

The class looked about as if they had all just been given a bushel of lollies, and could not help but wonder if it was some kind of trick.

"But I assure you there is nothing to be afraid of. Nothing at all that should threaten your very existence. In fact, I can no longer teach you anything ...eh, since you have all al*ready* mastered so much. I cannot tell you why, to *save my life,* as they say. We cannot continue with classes a day further."

The class looked about incredulously.

"So from now on, only recess. All day."

And again.

"Now, let's stand up!" They all shuffled to the door while Ms. P continued. "Yes, in truth, we have all done so well that this is our reward, and I cannot tell you how proud I am. Now, out the door we go. You must play, you must, until the bell rings. Yes, congratulations, you now do not have to listen to a word I say. I will be here, my dearies, if you need anything."

But there they stood looking at her.

"B-well, GO!" She tried to laugh it off. "I can't...I can't..."

The message was loud and clear. The class persisted until she waved her paw. "I'm sorry, but all I can say is that the school has been sold off. The philosophy is different now. Now I cannot tell you whether to go or stay. I cannot tell you anything unless you ask, not even how to *defend yourselves* from...you know, falling to the ground, I suppose, if that is not what you want. So go on, then. Go play. I know I have been hard, so I understand."

"Miss ...Miss P?" It was Riffa. The class was now quietly hysterical. "I... don't know how to play."

"What do you mean, deary?" Ms. Padduck said.

“I want to know, but I can’t. Would you show me?” She tugged ever so gently on Ms. P’s dress.

“Yeah,” Syriss said, “show us please, Ms. P. Show us.”

The class gave a round of “Show us, Miss P. Show us.” Then they all walked out, with Riffa leading her by the paw.

As they trudged, Mabby turned to go his own way, and his thoughts turned to his failed experiment. “My goodness, why didn’t Wally just ask Tufa or Deela to get the truth out of everyone?” he thought. That would have been failproof, just trap everyone in town and give them the look. If she wasn’t so in love with…It hit him just as he arrived at the shed. He turned to run after the others but was met by Deela, Bo, and Syriss, just the ones he needed to see. But no Tufa.

“Let’s go, Mabby!” they cheered as he almost ran into them.

“Whoa, what’s going on? Aren’t you guys supposed to be going out to practice?”

“Nonsense!” Deela and Syriss said together. “We’re here to cheer you on since you’re going to pass First Practicum today.” Deela smiled and shook her fists in the air in premature triumph, with her sweater sleeves flailing.

“I don’t think you guys understand. It’s not going to work like that. But anyway, listen…” He whispered softly, “Wally asked me to do something for him, but I just realized we can help him better than that.” Syriss looked confused, but Bobo was not. “I was told to draw Cal’s attention, make him think I know.”

“Know what and why, Cal? And why not us?” Syriss said.

“Because I don’t think they know whether or not Cal knows about you! They want me to keep an eye on him, probably because Tufa can’t tell him, but you guys are out of danger, and that means they know Cal is really the one helping Bolly.”

“Well, why wouldn’t they just tell us that?”

“I think they want to see something. And if they want to see something, then they want to see what he will do if he thinks we’re on to him, which means I have a better idea. Let’s make friends with Cal.”

“What?” Syriss said, while Deela considered.

"Let's get him in our club!"

"That's..." Syriss paused. "That's, that's a pretty good idea! I think I see what you mean. Yeah, let's do it."

"Then we can get Cal to lead us right to Bolly, and whatever is going on, himself!"

"Great idea! He won't suspect a thing. Now, let's get to jumping."

"I don't think..."

"Come on! We haven't got all day," Syriss said, and Mabby looked at Deela, knowing he wasn't going to win and they would just have to see. He climbed to the top and jumped. He stretched his hardest, but they watched him fall and smack the floor.

"No problem, just a fluke," Syriss said.

"You can do it!" Deela said.

"Yeah, we seen it!"

Their cheers went up once more, and once more he fell. "Mabby, if you can't pass the simplest test, then what is all that work you're doing at the training ground for?" Syriss said. Tufa elbowed him to stop. "No, seriously, how could all that he was good at possibly apply to the real world?" Syriss asked.

Mabby looked at him, his eyes turning red.

"I mean, what are you supposed to do when you think you can do some good, but everything you can do just ain't worth nothin'?"

Mabby yelled at Syriss to stop. "Leave me alone!"

Then Deela held up her finger, but her sweater sleeve was all anyone saw. "What he means..." She yanked her sweater sleeve down, and her glasses fell off. "Ugh, hold on." She picked up her glasses, huffed on them, cleaned them, and put them back on. "What he means is that when the world won't accept you, or doesn't understand you for who you're meant to be..." She helped Mabby up and led him over to the takeoff stand once more. "Then change the world."

"Yeah, sure, you know..." Syriss condescended, more or less angry that his pep talks always get interrupted before the turnaround, making him just look like a sod instead.

"It's easier said than done." He made his way back up one more time.

"You can do it!" they said.

"Let's go, Mab-by, let's go!" Clap clap clap! Syriss led the cheer and Mabby poised, feeling himself grow stronger, feeling everything around him, sensing all, drawing it in.

Another thud rattled the boards. Mabby didn't get up. He just gathered himself up on the floor. His head bowed and he shuddered for a while, and the rain gathered between his feet, and he covered his head with his tail so no one could see his eyes go red. After a few moments they left, Syriss shaking his head as usual, confused that Mabby could not pass the Practicum even though he could fly so well the day before.

Deela waited until they were all gone. "If someone is your friend you don't leave them," she said. And with that she plopped down next to him and waited. "No matter how hard it is to stay..."

After a moment his shoulders eased, and he gathered himself. "I can be okay with that," Mabby reflected out loud. "Friends," he thought. Deela pushed up her glasses and wiped her nose with her sleeve after looking to see if anyone was around. She put her head on his shoulder and her paw on his elbow. "I'll never leave you." Her tail curled as he slowly moved his paw on top of hers.

"Yeah." He said without moving. "Friends forever."

Deela's eyes drifted to the floor, and a look of bittersweetness crossed her face, but Mabby never saw it. He looked up at the open slats in the makeshift pallet-ceiling once his eyes had dried. "I did get the farthest ever that time."

"Will you tell me a poem?" she said and he looked at her, but she did not meet his eyes.

He paused. "Well, there's this one I've been working on but I don't quite know how to fix it."

"How does it go?" she asked as they slowly got up.

"I'm thinking of calling it 'An Honest Squirrel.'"

"Sounds forthcoming."

Mabby snaffed (which is the opposite of having sniffed), but didn't quite get it.

"Yeah...Well, it goes something like ..."

In the minutes that followed Dorma and Mabby's departure, it only took Dorma moments to relocate the old tree. Although many rafters had been grown over and homes had overtaken the old neighborhood, where a single level held the whole neighborship of Glimmer Commons, he needed only to close his eyes, and the fall of the major support tree crashing through the boughs and taking much of the north Tanglewall by the Hundred Trees took over his mind's eye, as always.

The problem with trees is they are always growing or they are wasting away, one or the other. So when a tree dies it is no longer built upon, the properties are sold off of it and, slowly, it is allowed to turn white. Wood that could not be salvaged and traded off is allowed to slowly crumble to the floor. All things can be done, with small actions, over time. So a new tree, well, it was easy to set the course for new paths by simply tying the green ends of a couple of trees together. This bond made both trees stronger, so they would grow together quickly. But when a living tree fell, all of those strong bonds went with it, affecting every other part of the city.

So, naturally, squirrels of the flying variety were highly concerned with the secret lives of the trees, and they paid attention to the rates at which trees died throughout the forest.

Dorma had resolved to investigate the night's events. Nothing had been found in the initial investigation of the fall at Rammerie's, but there might be something now. After some searching, he found the place, on the floor of the Tanglewall, where he had found the crumbled bark, and he brushed more of it aside.

"Stupid squirrel. You're a stupid squirrel. The opposite of smart...yes, that's right, keep being a stupid squirrel." The bark crumbled until it began to avalanche, revealing a completely barren half of the tree with scrawlings all around it. The dead bark had outlived the honey-and-hogtooth adhesive that had, apparently, been used, leaving a dusty yellow stain all around the strange carving of the door on that dead tree. But no way could it actually be a door. It looked like it hadn't been used in some time.

"Well, here goes, um, probably my life."

With a feather of a push, the door gave away easily. He held his breath to run but, out of the darkness, there was only a cool rush of air. The dust cleared and nothing ragefully killed him, so he peeked inside. It looked like someone had made the hole and figured out some crazy way to burrow through a massive amount of solid wood. How is this possible without anyone noticing? Dorma wondered. Are we all just floating around in our lives, just not looking at anything at all? Mabby would not have missed these kinds of details. He missed the things everyone else saw, and saw the things everyone else missed.

The dust was gone, and his eyes adjusted, revealing the contents of an empty shaft. There was nothing in it but a couple of old ropes clinging to something far above.

When he tugged the rope, it shot out of his paw with a yip and moaned as it picked up speed. Whatever was coming down was coming fast. Dorma rolled out of the way before it gave him a skull polishing, and they both landed with a thud. He looked around. The air was as motionless as ever, and a few birds chittered overhead.

Dusting himself off, he found the cause of his near demise was nothing sinister, only a large ball that looked as if it had been honed to weigh a precise amount for some purpose. There was a third rope taut along the wall. A strange device that looked like a pair of kitchen rollers was clamped over the rope and attached to a painter's handle. Then he noticed the weight had rolled on top of a couple of disc-like pieces of metal that were attached to the floor of the hollow. Ropes were tightly wound around the discs. Dorma rolled the weight off the wheel contraption. Two knotted hooks seemed to hold it suspended a certain way. He held it up. "It looks like it was designed to get out of my way if I stand over here," Dorma thought and, voila, he found himself next to the roller handle. He grabbed it and gave it another tug. The rope banged around up above, but nothing. Then it hit him that this contraption was upside down. Yes, this tree had fallen over, and he wondered if he needed to send the weight up. Would something happen? He looked at the weight, which needed reattaching on one side. When he repaired it, he found it went up and down the rope it was suspended from with ease, even though it weighed as much as he. He grabbed the roller stick and gave the weight rope a tug. Up it went and, after a moment or two, he realized something was coming down on the other side of the rope.

It was a platform. Down it came and he backed up so it could come to rest on the floor. It had a hook for the roller thingy and a guard attachment for safety from the weight. "Now that's subtle, old dog," he thought. As soon as he stepped on the platform, it seemed as if the whole thing counterbalanced and it actually got easier, actually effortless, to pull himself up and down, even with the slightest jerk. Genius!

The strange thing, as if it weren't all strange, was that everything was, apparently, rigged to be upside down. However, the platform inside the upside-down tree was upright. Odd indeed.

But ah! He smacked his forehead, for it suddenly occurred to him the only reason for that must be that this lift-hickey thing had been re-engineered after the tree had fallen, which meant it had been built before that, which meant…whoever or whatever waited for him at the top of this shaft was at the bottom of the matter. He now knew the undeniable truth, that someone had gone to extraordinary lengths to ensure Debby's death would look like an accident.

"And I will know it presently," Dorma said aloud and, just then, he noticed something odd.

It was writing, perhaps done in blood, for it had badly faded and dirt clung to it in the dark. He blew.

The writing was upside down, and he had to turn himself into quite an awkward position without letting go, but the dust gave him the words, and the words were hard.

"'I... claim...them all,'" he read, "the savage…"

Hm. Well, that was obscure. "Salvē, brute." He gave the middle rope a hard tug and sent himself zipping up into the blackness.

The counterweight rushed by and he knew he was at the halfway point. A light came into view. He was glad he had kept hold of the roller, realizing it had helped him slow down. He brought the platform to a stop just where the sunlight came in.

It had only been a few seconds but, when he stepped out onto the bough, he was amazed to find he had traveled upward hundreds of meters. He was still outside the Tanglewall but, judging from his bearings and the age of the trees, he was under the old neighborhood, near the entrance to the Hundred Trees. A flash of memory of his first encounter with Debby went through his mind. The old Quarles house, his own burned life, and then there was a flash of anger. "This was why I wanted to tangle with the well-to-dos, right?" he thought. All because he had looked at this dead reminder of the damage wrought by hate against his own: the white boughs upon which he stood. Now he knew it. All because of foolish dreaming, he mocked himself.

"And I just bet…" He did a little calculating and quickly found the tree most likely to lead to the empty place that he just bet wasn't as abandoned as everyone thought.

Sure enough, after a moment he found the lines carved into the bark that, upon close inspection, revealed the door. Like the other door, it was covered by glued-on bark, but it was much better attended to.

This time, without a moment's thought or hesitation, he flung the makeshift door open wide and jumped.

When he stepped out again, it was not so light. For the "abandoned" Quarles residence stood around him, just as he had theorized. It was terribly unkempt and smelly and full of scrawled letters, all over the floor, and holes in the wall from mice and anger.

There began to be a terrible taste in his mouth as he stepped off the platform. He had never been in the home of his late wife's parents. That didn't bother him too much. It was the different-yet-sameness of it all. The yellow walls and white window sills, the whole idea of being in the house of someone he despised, having to note the similarities between his enemy's life and his. Imagining the tink-tink of one's keys upon a drawer stand, embracing the lady after a hard day's work, and being a totalitarian bigot all at the same time makes the whole story so much more difficult, does it not?

"Yet here we are," he thought, "in the examination of a life well ruined." Pages and torn scribblings littered the floor of the whole filthy, cracked house. He picked one up. It was unreadable.

He found the main foyer, apparently the most lived in, judging from the savagery of the filthy floor and unwashed, overworn clothes.

"Okay, anything strange, anything at all…" He reminded himself of his directive, as if there were not a full panoply of strangeness before him. Most of the notes looked useless, and he couldn't read the writing. He noticed that they tended to propagate from a door in the foyer, probably to the smoking room. The door seemed to bear the marks of heavy use, and it had been recently used, judging from the brass handle, which was quite shiny and starting to come loose. He thought perhaps he should give a listen, and behind the door there was only silence. So he turned the knob.

The room was dark all over around the bare floor and back baseboard illuminated by the light behind. The moldy smell was nearly unbearable. There were deep scratches on the finished floorboards, from the kind of squirrel that occupies a house in Hundred Trees and doesn't wear houseslippers. He felt about what seemed to be shelves, making sure not to bump anything, until he found what felt like candlestick holders, and the matches were nearby. "Well, I had the presence of mind for that," Dorma thought, and he lit one of the candles, and then another, and the room got lighter. He could see the desk, with stencilboards and loose shelving packed all around. There was a notebook on the desk. It seemed to contain patched-together scrawlings, and pages and packets were falling out. And those were packed with tackings upon tackings, notes upon notes, lines going here and there, and familiar names and places with deranged circlings and scrawlings. It was full of craziness, and he put it down. He traced the lines, and they tended to lead to a particular point, close to the wall before him. There were several journals, one of which looked familiar but, at the moment, he couldn't place it, so he passed it over for one that looked exceedingly curious indeed.

There was what appeared to be another, large diary, well worn, lying open on the desk in the only place there was really room to put anything. Many pages had been torn out, and many more had fallen out onto the tabletop. It contained many torn bits of paper with handwriting and old signatures, with the documents long destroyed. He found the first page that was still bound.

It read:

"Long after those days I sought out the great cat where she lived.

"I saw her... I met Morg...she showed me...the shadow of the forest far enough away. She came to hear my proposal, and she liked it very much, she did. I went with her, to understand, for she said she came from a world unlike the one the fools know. I should record everything I can to preserve it, for I at first only wanted the damned fool Dabby to meet a just end, but (scratched out) she showed me what the next world looked like. ...

"Then, I am not sure who saw us, but they attacked, ambushed us. We shall meet again, but for now I know that Dorma shall surely die, that waste of life, he took her. He TOOK HERRR—"

It became illegible, so he flipped a few pages.

"...So you see, my friend, my crimes are not crimes, for one cannot commit crime if one is above the law, and in order to be above the law, one must simply place himself above the law, and to do that is only to believe in something better, it's truly better, so much...for what is law but a thing that prevents the necessary changes from happening to us when they should. What are those things others would call crimes then but the price of progress?"

He flipped back a few pages toward the middle of the book.

"...For, you see, I believe we are at an apex, but an apex is also a precipice, and the risk of our future stands on how well we are able to shed this unnecessary weight, so that from this final platform in the advancement of our kind we can be ready to fly from our raised prison, unabated by cheatery and these...Abominations! Which are an affront to our unity!...But each of us can excel just as well as the least, with work, work, work! Blast the Protectoracy!

"There was a time...Morgart the cat. She said, 'You asked to meet?' I said, 'I believe those I represent have asked me to meet with you is more accurate.' (A fool was I to be so patronizing, a fool!) But I was indeed there on an errand for my patrons, for the cat's services had been messy but effective in overthrowing the Protectorate. She is from a place where everything is cold, she explained to me. Where there is order and anyone who does not serve the Toolegs or, as they call themselves, the Peepulls, is relegated to a life of starvation and suffering. While those lucky enough to be chosen never want for anything, yet they are completely subdued, and are imprisoned as toys for the pleasure of the Peepulls for all their lives. Anyone who challenges the power structure gets sterilized, made an example of, or thrown out to make room for those who will submit. This is for the reason that Toolegs believe that those beneath them exist for their pleasure, therefore, they are the ones that determine population and food, they control everything, down to the possession of happiness itself. The system was perfect, and of the nature of absolute lack of disruption or disorder, and no one lacked a thing, and no one had a thing to hold above any other.

Everything was a realized and perfect sameness, and thus realized and perfect order.

"I, however, did not feel quite the same way as my patrons, for they lacked vision. They saw only to the point of overthrow, like all would-be revolutionaries. These endeavors have failed in the past because they replaced it with nothing. Order cannot be replaced with chaos, only order, or they will only return to their old and obsolete way. As I pondered my next inquiry, this truth entered the front of my mind, and I say it was destiny that this was so, for the full revelation (of revolution! Viva Risorgimento!) to be revealed to me in our proceeding concourse.

"It was at this point a strange thing occurred to me, to ask why Morgart was speaking so favorably of this system, if she herself had abandoned it, by evidence of her being before me, and of course I spoke most respectfully. She told me that she realized it was her destiny to rule, since so many of her counterparts saw nothing beyond this system, but were totally and ineffectually absorbed in it. Only one who is truly capable of such is graced with the temperance to see all things and still embrace the truth, that there must be someone with such a superior mind to rule and all others are meant to be tamed. So she began to look for her window of destiny.

"Upon this chance, one day, she came to a book, as she had in many of the places she had lived in. It told her of a faraway land where squirrels were living in the disgusting filth of wishy- washy ideologies and contending with one another all the time for trifles. She realized this must be her destiny, to rule as the Peepulls rule, over the squirrels, and perhaps eat a few, but that's just business, for why else should this glorious thing be shown to her? Why, pray tell?

"Seeing as she could develop no other answer, she waited patiently and watched for her escape, whereupon to keep her Peepull from the futility of attempting to retrieve her, she ended the poor

simpering's life instead. Better that way, for she should never return, and the Peepull would surely be rendered to a life of despair and lostness. It was a mercy killing indeed, I most agreed.

"While she spoke I became arrested with astonishment and joy, for at every turn her elegant story rang through my person with the whole analogy of my life, and I too realized that not only was she meant to rule, but I was like her. I shared her mind as well. This was indeed not a meeting of dueling tribes, but one of the fates. I, most honored reader, have realized that I was chosen by the Great Nut to beautify and resolve the whole history of the place of my birth, for as the great cat herself possessed such tools, I must have them all, I must see it, this perfect civilization. I must do it, for it shall end the hurt of my kind forever!

'"Why," Morgart asked, "do you want to see?" She smiled as my eyes grow wider at this and I simply said, "Show me the future..."

"...When I returned, I shared my ideas, but they were not receptive, and they tried to stop our future. At that point there was nothing else to do! It was fight or flight! I could not understand their change of heart, but it was the greatest tragedy I have ever known. Before my eyes I saw them change and I knew then and there that I, and I alone, must carry out this task. (Traitors, for they abandoned me and sided with him. Him!) For no one would, or could, understand, for squirrels are entirely lacking imagination, and that is all simplistic squirrels' most tragic, and unfortunate..."

"...Demise." Dorma looked up. "The old dog is insane." Smart but, as they say, all that headroom is also room for a bigger mess.

“So Bolly sought out the cat, and that’s part of how he became so powerful so quickly,” Dorma thought. It also occurred to him that he was not reading Bolly Beeley’s diary, but his manifesto. He had made a deal with a cat.

He might have gone on to discover much more, but his reading was interrupted by the dripping candle wax, which spilled rudely on his toes as he leaned over. In the heat of the moment the sting gave him a fright, and he jumped and lost his balance. The candlestick fell and went out. He tried to prevent his fall, but only brought the table and shelves, brimming with dusty books and scraps and nails and boards, down upon himself, for it had been dreadfully unsecure.

The conflagration eventually settled, and he poked his head above the jagged pile he was buried under. He finally got a paw on the floor and pushed up to sit. He was dazed, and it took a moment to ascertain that the dusty innards of the wall had come down with the stuff. There was another room behind it about the size of a shoe closet. And that was the moment he received the great fright of his life for, as his eyes adjusted, plainly before him were the white bones of Mr. and Mrs. Quarles, no doubt in the very clothes they had died in. Aye, in the very position they died in, it appeared. He had just killed them and left them there.

“They came around after all,” Dorma thought. They hadn’t left town out of embarrassment. They were murdered. And the book, he realized, was his confession! This proved everything. He saw that he had flung it out of the way in the commotion, and he snatched it up.

“I’ve got to get out of here.”

He tried to climb over the fresh rubble, but it gave out beneath him several times, and he fell forward. Fortunately, he rolled out of the room and tumbled across the hall, where the back of his head nearly cracked against a statue.

Huff “I’m too old for this.” He sighed and let his head rest against the foot of the statue, and his tail went limp.

Then the statue moved, shifted, and rattled a bit. And then it rocked over to the side and, to his bafflement, completely disappeared into the floor! Then, with a rattle and a crack, the floor shook, then gave way.

All of the loose papers and filth began to shake and fall away. The center of the floor opened and let the morning in, and Dorma had to jump to a ledge. "Oh my!" he exclaimed. For the room had transformed into a sort of hangar bay with a ramp extending down. He followed it with his eyes. It led down into a large bough that had been drilled out, just like the dead trees he had seen, but this one had been built upon and had an archway and ceiling of boards. It had probably been made to look like a walkway above, but it seemed to have been meant to accommodate something very large passing through and up into the house. At the end of the tunnel, as he leaned in, he could just barely make out, in the distance, the windblown grasses of Nearly Mountain's western slope. A tunnel to the outside! Or...a tunnel to the inside.

Then he was startled by a head poking in and looking right up at him from the other side.

With his good squirrel eyes he made out that it was Cal Ballo! That son of his most honorable friend.

"Cal! Hey down there!" he yelled. "Shouldn't you be in school, m'boy?"

But Cal's once friendly face lowered and his eyes narrowed. Then, without a word, the pup sprinted up the path straight to Dorma. As he emerged, Dorma was shocked to realize that the young pup was wearing a faded indigo robe, embroidered with once bright gold leaves about the shoulders. "The reasons for that," he thought, "are possibly many, yet doubtless one." And with that he shoved the book in his trousers and bounded out of the house by the back way with Callo on his heels. However, as soon as Dorma entered into the bright view of the public, Cal coursed off. And that was all the proof Dorma needed. It was still early morning, but Dorma didn't go to this shop at all that day.

Instead, he lingered about the top of the mountain a ways from the entrance to the school. Cal soon appeared, huffing, and went inside, probably pretending to be late. Dorma kept an eye on everyone from overhead for the rest of the day to make sure Cal didn't try anything, and no one noticed him.

At the end of the day, Mabby and Deela emerged from the First Practicum building, smiling, at the end of that day, which warmed Dorma's heart beyond all belief but, frankly, it was not time for such things. They stopped when they saw the look on his face.

"Hello, Deela. Mabby, we need to go," Dorma said.

"Can I come?" Deela asked.

"I suppose, but what I have to tell you must be behind closed doors." He took Mabby's arm.

"Am I in trouble?" Mabby asked.

"Why, have you done something? What did you do?"

"Nothing!" Mabby exclaimed.

"Oh." Dorma paused and shook it off. "Well, then of course you're not in trouble. I just need to talk to you, yes, maybe you both."

"How did you know I was here?" Mabby asked, feeling rather ashamed.

He went silent for a moment and leaned down, as they walked, and whispered into Mabby's ear. "Don't react. Don't say anything. I was attacked. By someone you know. Let's go."

But it was just about that moment their journey was interrupted. Dorma had been leading them upward, and Mabby had accurately guessed he planned to make their way to the Training Grounds. However, as they passed the school, standing in their path were Mabby and Deela's friends, and Cal Ballo as well.

They looked at him oddly, and Dorma spoke first. "What's the meaning of this?" They remained silent.

Syriss spoke. "We want you to say hello to our new friend, Mabby." Cal stepped forward and eyed the two of them. "He's been through a lot, and he wants to help us take down Bolly Beeley."

"You can't be serious! This youngster is *helping Beeley!*"

"No, Mister Dabby, sir. You've got it all wrong," Tufa said. "Cal is in trouble. He came in crying today because Bolly just bought up Cal's inheritance, Ballo's whole estate. And Beeley has been forcing Cal to do his will or—"

"Nonsense! Rubbish! Cal just took it upon himself this morning to…look, just come with us, Syriss, and I'll tell you everything. Let's go."

"Well, can Cal come?"

"No. I'm sorry, but I cannot allow that, and neither would they. Now this is urgent, come."

They stood where they were. "We did it, Mabbs, you said we should make friends with him. So we did, and we know everything now."

"No, whatever he's told you, he's lying," Dorma said. "I can't talk about it here, as you know. Look, this has gone from childish to sophomoric." They didn't know what sophomoric meant. "It's worse. Just come."

"Can Callo come?"

"For dogs' sake, why?" Dorma said.

"Because he knows the truth."

"Says who?"

"Cal knows everything, how to take Bolly down and all that. He said so himself. We need him. Mabby doesn't have to do all of this if we can take Bolly out at the roots. Get it?"

"If you're right. If *he's* right."

"We're right, Mr. Dorma."

"You're going to take the word of someone who is potentially on the enemy's side, instead of the ones who have always been on your side? Can't you see? Just come with me and you'll know."

"But you won't tell us here because it's a secret?" Tufa interjected.

"No, and anyway he'll just deny it. Look, you don't understand how special Mabby is to B—"

"It's not always about being special!" Syriss yelled. "The special ones aren't the only ones who can do anything!"

"And it's not always about sides."

"Yes, I know except, of course, for when they are, and when it is, isn't it?"

They turned away, even Bo, and just walked off.

"I don't understand," Mabby said.

"(Sigh) Mabby, they're trying to be good. You have to remember that."

"But why does this have to be what's good?"

Dorma knelt down. "This is the problem with being special, son. Special squirrels have to do things that others don't or don't understand, so they grow up next to everyone else but in a different world. And because of that, sometimes the special ones don't see who their real friends are. You have to do what most won't, just to survive. When you need to go do something most aren't willing to do, you can't allow yourself the luxury of picking your friends, and it will always surprise you who will abandon you. It's just life."

"Well, how do I know who is my friend then? How do I trust anyone?" Mabby sobbed.

"By the ones that remain." Deela put her paw on Mabby's shoulder.

"I know what you are trying to do is hard—"

But Dorma did not get to finish his life lesson for just then there was an explosion, and the lot of them nearly lost balance as the deck boards shook themselves to bits from the shockwave alone.

When the three of them recovered, along with the others down the boughway, they all stopped and looked on as their higher vantage point allowed them to see the Mellivern business district vanish into a cloud of fire and smoke.

Chapter 17: A Needle in a Hatestack.

They all took off as one, forgetting the established walking etiquette.

"Now do you think I'm still involved in this? I wasn't even there!" Cal said to Dorma as they pulled ahead of the rest.

"Fool of a childish mind," Dorma thought as he shot Cal a look that shut him up, for the little one had mistakenly given up his cards altogether. No one had said anything about the explosion being connected to a conspiracy, but he needed Cal to admit that in front of everyone.

When they all arrived several minutes later, out of breath, there was already a crowd. A gaggle of folks were throwing pots and buckets while others yelled directions. Parties were organizing to move timbers to rescue the women and children from under the rubble. They all set to work immediately. Helping others to safety, sometimes before putting out the flame, was the chief concern. It was several hours, on into the dark, before the commotion began to die down, leaving weeping bystanders waiting to see their loved ones or finding them again. Dusk had passed, and nearly half of the burned district had been deemed safe. The debris had been jettisoned on the forest floor before anyone asked, "Who did this?" It was Bolly Beeley, in his dusty mayor's jacket, all covered in soot like the rest. "I demand to know!" he said as he wiped his brow with his sleeve, despite the kerchief that sat haphazardly in his pocket.

Deela picked something up and walked over to Dorma with it, and put it in his paw. "I will help you rebuild your store." She smiled. Dorma smiled back. "Thank you Deela."

"Daddy? Daddy, Daddy?! Daddy! No!" Tufa screamed as her father was pulled from the destruction, and she knelt crying where he had been laid down. She took no more part in the story that day.

But as everyone looked at Tufa, Bolly had apparently found something, and he made a little pip. A few heads turned and he stood up, turned around, and dusted off some scraps. "Whose is this?" He looked mightily confused as he read aloud the text that he held in his kerchief. "Dearest, I do not know what has happened to you or who brought this about, but I will find them, and I will make them pay...My sweet, I will do away with this...Bolly Beeley...and everything he stands for." Dorma Dabby, what is the meaning of this? This is your pawwriting, is it not? This is addressed to Debby." He looked at Dorma with the most sincere hurt in his eyes. "Did you honestly believe I had something to do with that?"

Dorma looked at him silently, suddenly remembering to his own self-loathing that the strange journal he had found, along with the manifesto of Bolly's confession, had seemed so familiar because it was, quite possibly, the journal he had "lost" in the fire. He hadn't written anything like what Bolly had read, at least not all in the same place or in that order. But he could say nothing as Bolly, with tears in his eyes, held up the scrap to Dorma's face.

The writing was his, but not like his at the same time.

"I... I don't know," Dorma stammered.

"Did you do this?" He motioned to the rubble. "To get back at me for this, this thing in your past I didn't do? Is this not your diary, with your name written on it?" He flipped to the inside cover, and there it was, with an address to his lost love, and all. Dorma could clearly remember feeling that way, but not necessarily having written it down.

Everyone was silent.

"Dad?" Mabby looked at him for some confirmation that it wasn't true.

They could both feel the looks of the crowd burn into their skulls, and their cheeks turned red with fear and confusion.

"Where were you this morning, Dorma Dabby?"

"I, I can't. I..." Dorma was all but shut down. "You all don't understand. Y-You don't understand." He pointed at Bolly with a shaking finger. "He stole my diary!" That was all he could muster the intelligence to say.

"You mean the 'diary' where this came from, do you? Isn't that where it came from?" Bolly asked. "Make your words clear, Dorma Dabby, for by them you shall be acquitted or condemned!"

"Please, let me explain..." Dorma begged the crowd, but the growls became louder, their beady eyes squinted, and red shone in their eyes like embers in the dark. He tried to think of something, but there was nothing he could say that would not incite a riot at the mention of the Protectoracy, nor could he speak of anything he had found at Bolly's without incriminating himself as a trespasser. And Bolly knew it. Tufa rose from her father's side, where he was prostrate on the ground, staring silently at Dorma and Mabby. The gang receded from behind Dorma to behind Bolly. The disdain in their eyes grew when Cal Ballo said, just loudly enough for all to hear, "Now do you believe me?"

"Your personal problem with me, whatever you think I did to you, was not something to make everyone here suffer for," he said slowly.

"Wait! I seen you!" said a certain Mr. Hopp, who had turned the crowd against Dorma after the fire. "You were here. You were wearing a dark robe, but you were stackin' stuff here and there about the time I came in, in the early morning, to take care of my little mice problem...he he..." Mr. Hopp trailed off at that, for he was a baker. Not many were happy about that.

"That's it then," Bolly said. "That explains everything. You're in cahoots with the vigilantes."

"Nonsense," Dorma said, but the crowd had none of it.

"Get those infirms! Get them!" old Mr. Hopp shouted.

One of them picked up a stick, still glowing from the fire, and others picked up various makeshift weapons.

"I hereby declare, by the power vested in me by these Hesperians, that you, Dorma Dabby, are banished from this city, to join your ilk in the wild. Be gone, or suffer execution for trespassing and... murder." He let the last word hang from his lips.

"Let's go, Mabby," Dorma said. "Let's go! Run!" He took Mabby by the shoulder, and they took off running with the mob just behind. "Fly Mabby!"

"Banished!" Bolly repeated to himself. He made no move, but let the crowd do the work. When Dorma and Mabby started to run, the crowd followed suit, and only Bolly and the kids stayed behind.

"You don't want to get in on the action, hm?" Bolly said to Syriss, turning toward the gang.

"No, sir," Syriss said. "We want justice, and none of these things are it."

"Oh. Hm. Well," Bolly said,"Well, you'll *see justice.* That you will."

Syriss only looked at him, and the others seemed even less interested in whatever that meant. Syriss said, "You know, Dorma's guilt doesn't alleviate yours."

"I'm not concerned with alleviation. We are all beyond alleviation. I'm concerned with transposition. We are in the midst of a breakdown, and I intend to end it, and…with enough time and some firm moral authority, perhaps we can all be a little better."

They stared at him, open mouthed, as he walked away. "With just a little bit more time…" He trailed off, musing to himself.

"Let's go home," Syriss said. "We're done."

There, frightened and all alone with noone to talk to, Deela sobbed and held her elbows as she left. "No," she said to herself as she quickened her pace. "*You're done.* But I'm not.*"* And just as she was out of view, she turned into the shadows and was gone.

However, the mob was not done. They had chased Mabby and Dorma clear to the edge of town. "Get out of here. Get out! We never want to see you or your infirmarous kin or kind ever again. Infirm! Infirm!" They shouted. "You don't deserve to be here!" They quickly realized the crowd was composed predominantly of business-squirrels who for the economic advantage of being associated with the mayor's in-crowd had given up their wings. So Dorma and Mabby quickly took to the air, easily leaving them all behind. "You see now what kind of advantage this gives?! Only the privilege of escaping the truth! Face us, Dabbys! Face us or not, we shall find you and make your just end!" Bolly rallied the crowd into a frenzy. The dreadful irony rang through Mabby's heart, for the memory of being called an infirm between his first days at Rammerie's and now had warped into referring to anyone having wings at all.

"This is pandemonium," Dorma said, as they backed against the wall at the far reach of Promise's End. The crowd pressed in on them, and Mabby and Dorma fell through the Tanglewall. Forced to take flight, they glided to the nearest tree. "And you'll be forced out just like that if you ever come in here again."

"That's the end of them," said another. "Let the owls have them."

"Or better, the Protectors!" They laughed. Dorma simply held his son and they watched as the crowd lost interest and dispersed.

When the last of them had gone, and the two of them were alone, they heard a voice above them.

"Hey-o!" It must have been Wally. "Up here! Come!" They scrambled up the tree and met the Reverend. "Do you see any more of them? Good, let's be off."

"Where are we going?" Mabby asked.

"You know where." The Reverend smiled and, with a gesture, they followed him to the training ground. "Rather a good idea they've had there, I think."

Once they had safely arrived, Dorma and Mabby conveyed all that they had seen and heard.

"So as you can see, Bolly will stop at nothing." Dorma handed over the book, cursing himself once more for missing his chance to get his own diary of letters back from the Quarles house. "He will kill, he has killed, and he can make anything look like anything with the ability to forge and the stamp of the mayor's office. That's how he took over the bank and funneled all the money in town toward his own private ventures, including the ability to mass produce the drilling job he had done in order to kill my wife way back then, so as to get about anywhere without being seen. I could be mistaken, but I believe this book will show you it is much worse than we had all thought. He plans not only to get revenge on the Protectoracy, but to upend our whole existence. He plans to use the cat as his perfect enforcer to establish total moral and financial rule over Hesperia, and he is arrogant enough to think the cat will listen."

"This is gravely serious. And yet... really stupid all at the same time." said Wally.

"He is killing anyone that gets in his way and writing up their property as willed to him, I'll wager. I think whatever he has planned is going to happen soon, since he is getting bolder. This incident today, he blew up the entire business district just to blame it on me, I think as punishment for my...acts of opposition."

"Well, how very democratic."

"I know! The one thing I can't figure out is my wife. What's her involvement? I feel like once I figure out what she had to do with all of this, then it will be the missing link to Bolly's final master plan and bring everything else together."

"Either way, you can't go back there. It's too dangerous, so we may just have to work with what we've got. You can both stay here, and we will take you under. This is perfect, actually, because Mabby needs to continue with his training. He is almost there."

"Really? Because I don't feel like I have progressed at all," Mabby said.

"That's fine, but look, I was in the house of the Quarleses. That's his evil secret headquarters. Anyway, I came upon something. Well, I fell on it. There was a switch in the floor that opened up to the outside of the city, and it was quite a big opening at that."

"Oh? Indeed. How big?"

"Like big enough for a cat."

"Yeah?"

"Yeah. I think he plans to stage a coup. That's the only reason he would have to involve the cat; to establish total rule. "

"A coup?"

"A kitty coup."

"But a coup d'état is a violent overthrow of government. Why would he overthrow himself?"

"No, I said he plans to *stage* a coup."

"A faux coup."

"A faux feline overthrow.

"My, that's awfully low, faux show."

Dorma snapped his fingers lightly in front of them. "Focus, focus." Wally shook it off.

"I think his plan is to make himself out to be the legendary hero he thinks of himself as, while finishing what he started in the beginning. He is going to bring in the cat, after having roused all of this hatred against the Protectoracy. This time he plans to end the Protectoracy at the paws of the squirrels of Hesperia. This is just my theory, but he will pretend to defeat the cat and, after he has lured you all in, the town will take care of what he and the cat could not do. The illusion will cause everyone to do for him what he could not do himself all those seasons ago, and set everyone up to willingly give over complete control of all the realm. The cat can't do anything he won't be aware of, and by the time this goes down, if the cat does misbehave he'll have the whole city to deal with. Or the other way around."

"And when will this happen?"

"The only time the whole city is gathered in one place is on Rammerie's Race Day. And they will all be too distracted to pay attention if a cat gets into the city. My guess is, he will let Morgart in then."

"That's a big guess."

"Well, it's also because he has this big plot with strings and everything up on a wall, and the grandstands are in the middle of it."

"Hm. And just, pray tell, how does he plan to get the cat to go along with all of this?"

"I was wondering that myself. Then it occurred to me, where do you think all of the disappearing squirrels that have tried to speak out against Bolly have been going?"

"This is all so far-fetched, yet somehow believable at the same time if one knows Bolly Beeley."

"Yes."

"Y'em hm, and it's definitely worst-case scenario."

"Uh huh."

"Sounds about right then. What do you propose we do, if our presence shall only make matters worse?"

"You know the problem with evil is it doesn't play well with others. I think Bolly doesn't understand that evil lying cats are evil and lying. So no matter what the cat says she will go along with, it's only so she can perform her own little takeover, once he allows her inside the city, the one thing she can't do on her own. When that happens, then you come in. The townfolk will be confused and I will reason with them. Then we will all stop both of them."

"You think you can reason with a mob of ornery and cantankerous squirrels? That sound like the real hard part."

"I know, but it's all we've got...and…I have to believe in them. We have to believe that even those who hate us will see the truth. It's what good squirrels must do. And it wouldn't be the first time someone turned on Bolly once they learned of his plan."

"Oh? Oh."

"Yes, Hal. That was why he killed Hal. He tried to stop Bolly but failed, and I know how Bolly has been getting around. He uses tunnels he's dug. I know, but it's true, and I can imagine only one explanation for why Hal would have served him in his campaign. Bolly threatened to kill his boy."

Things began to click for Mabby.

"But when Hal realized this was much bigger than the two of them, he put himself in harm's way to save his boy and stop Bolly, but

Beeley just rewrote Hal's will after giving himself an alibi and took Cal in as his personal slave. It also gave him an opportunity to make everyone think of Hal as a martyr for his cause."

"But Callo can fly. He's strong enough to stop Bolly."

"But he's young, and he doesn't know that. He has a strong body but a feeble mind, probably because it's being poisoned by Bolly's abuses. And when he realizes that, Bolly will just kill him too. Cal is just trying to stay alive long enough to win back his father's land and legacy."

"How do you propose we take out the cat?"

"Well, I'd tell you, but I think I had better show you, really. But I need to get back to my shop somehow, if there's anything left of it." Said Dorma as he played with the needle Deela had given him back at the scene of the crime.

"Think I might have the solution for you there," Reverend Ferroule said. "Just tell me you don't plan to sew your way to victory."

"Right, then. Let's get to work." said Dorma.

"Mabby," Bumbleroot said. "Let's you and I go and train."

"Aw, can't I stay and help?"

"Your part in this will be in becoming the best Guardian you can, by completing your training. You are on the verge of breakthrough, my boy. You will only miss out on the action, if all this is right, if you don't make it over. And we only have three days. Understand?"

"Okay." Mabby sighed and they left.

So the group dispersed to go their own way and prepare for the fight of their lives. All this was on the very shaky bet that the folks of Hesperia would put down their pitchforks and fight for a hard truth. This went, of course, against history we know from books upon books, and pages upon pages that, like most societies and times, our gullible Hesperians would abandon reason for that which merely makes the most sense.

Chapter 18: The Shadow Before the Storm

The town was quiet for the next couple of days.

Dabby's Clothiery had been sold in Dorma's absence. "Good doing business with you. I am sure I can be of more service to you, good mayor, and to the community than the last owner. Swindler, that one. You know, I once asked him to make my pup a jacket and he proceeded to stab him, right in the shoulder. Out of sheer, unprovoked malice, I tell you."

"Oh? Oh my," Bolly said.

"Yeah. And he never even finished the job, just left off and my little pup came home just about blue from sitting in a corset all morning, and a needle in his arm. You believe that?" Little did the two shaking paws know that a pair of beady eyes watched the transaction from the shadows.

"Deplorable. Squirrels these days but, sir, I assure you, you are now doing business with someone who prides himself on finishing the job. We've got to get this place back up on its feet, and that'll be done or my name's not Bolly Beeley."

"Right."

"Have a good one. I wouldn't wish cleaning up all this on a dog. Hah! Get it?"

"Um. I think so. Say, will you join us for a drink in celebration tonight? My wife makes the spiciest apple wine in town and, as you know, my pastries are to *live* for." He patted his belly as evidence exhibit A.

"No, I must do plenty of work tonight, can't wait."

"Are you sure? It will be a snotty good time."

"Absolutely sure."

"Very well. Good day to you, Mister Beeley. Pleasure."

"Indeed, as always."

The two parted ways and the latter, whose name was not known to the watcher in the shadows, went inside.

Several hours later, the gentlesquirrel who had purchased Dorma's shop from Bolly emerged through the back door muttering, "Ow, ow, ow," among other expletives, and deposited several loads into the dumpster. He was covered in fresh little red dots. He went back in the shop and didn't come back.

Having presumed the owner was not about to return, the shadow emerged, stole into the dumpster, lifted the contents of one of the burlaps, and disappeared again unseen. This happened, without anyone knowing, throughout the day.

So, no one met the little creature on its journey, but for a single instance which, for the other party, was no fun at all. It was nearly dark when the little shadow emerged with the final contents of the dumpster, which held the last needle in Dorma's decimated business. The baker's son emerged, cramming a bear claw into his face absentmindedly, and saw the figure stealing out of the dumpster.

"Hey, just what are you doing?" The pup had a prominent lateral lisp. The hooded figure stopped and looked at him.

"Say, you're kinda cute! He he." The dark-robed figure silently reached up and gently began to pet him on the chin and caress his cheek. They moved closer at his gratuitous chuckling of approval. It began to tickle his chin. He looked straight up in the air and began to thump his foot in delight. Then, having offered up a clear shot, he immediately received twenty-seven punches to the throat, a large needle in each arm, and a judo chop to the diaphragm, levelling him out proper and rendering him unable to speak, touch, or swallow.

The figure ventured fearlessly under cloak of night until she arrived before the door of the control tower at the training deck of the Protectoracy. She knocked hard, looking around, and Dorma opened.

"Here's the last of it."

"A fine lady you are. Thank you."

She squealed in delight once inside. "Ohh! I get it, spikes!" She ran over to where Dorma had been preparing gadgets of some sort. "Can I help? I have an idea!" Before Dorma could issue a word of caution, she had already begun tearing into the tools and contraptions on the table and parts went a flying.

The cavernous hollow, underneath the top deck where Mabby had been training, extended several stories down for it had once housed an entire army. It had served as the headquarters and barracks hall of the Army of Elorus, named after the legendary squirrel warrior. But these seasons it rarely served and housed more than a scant five or six bodies, and hungry ones. Dorma had been working in the main hall, and most of the others had gone to sleep down in the lower levels. "Did you bring anything else?" Bumbleroot said, coming into the room with a firefly lamp and rubbing his eyes.

"Of course! I wouldn't forget the numpets." She halted her project and held up another bag, which she had secured from the bakery without anyone noticing. The others came in sleepily and, without a word, took their fair share and helped themselves liberally to what was left.

Bumbleroot yawned, patting his tummy. "A fine poppet, that girl. A fine kit altogether." She batted her eyes and tugged at her sweater while the others chuckled in agreement.

"So what have you got going on over there, Mr. Dabby?" Master Bone said.

"Oh, you know, just defensive measures, a few ideas. You'll see...Hm, I like this tinkering thing. It's like stitches, only fun."

"Right, right," they said.

Master Bang sat against the wall polishing his armor. When he thought no one was watching, he licked it. Deela, however, saw him. "Almond oil, great for the joints!"

"But not for the brain," said Bone.

"Ya know why they call me Bang?" He chuckled. "Cuz when I drop these…" He held up a sack of walnuts. "It's like, POW! Over." There was a pause, and everyone just smiled and shook their heads.

"They call you Bang 'cause you were dropped on your head," Master Bone said.

"That's Master Bang to you, Bonehead!"

"Your mom's got a bone," Mabby said, having come in unnoticed while everyone was distracted, and they all snickered. Master Bang turned indignantly towards Mabby and said, "Well, that just made no sense," and crossed his arms. Everyone lost it. Dorma came in wiping his brow while everyone was still chuckling, sat down, and took the last numpet. He dawdled at it, still thinking about a great deal of complications with the plan. He excused himself, even though he didn't need to, got up, and went outside.

"What's the matter, Dad?" Mabby had followed him. Dorma sat outside with his feet hanging off of the ledge, holding his box. "What's that?"

"Oh, just…" He hadn't meant for Mabby to see. "Memories…" He sighed.

"Of Mom?"

"Yes. Well, what I managed to salvage from the fire."

"Can I see?" Mabby asked.

"Sure." He had never expected to feel such reluctance. He had known he would do this one day, but perhaps not so soon. Mabby sat down.

"This here is a portrait I had made of your mother not long after we were married."

"She's crying."

"Well, she had been crying, but they were tears of happiness. This was only moments after she realized she was pregnant with you."

"She's so beautiful."

"She was. She was the most beautiful, most extraordinarily understanding creature that ever lived, and you'd have been a proud son if you'd known her."

"I am proud. Dad...are you okay?" Mabby said.

Dorma just looked down at the box for a moment.

"Say, what's that?" Mabby pointed at the picture of Bolly Beeley before Dorma could say anything. Dorma was arranging his words to tell Mabby that he had regretted not having known which side to take, in the beginning, and for not believing in him. He had gone back on a promise when he did that. He also wanted to say that he felt torn at the moment, for in order to keep his promise, he must let someone else be put in harm's way. And he didn't know if Debby wanted that. He couldn't figure it out.

He wanted to say all that, but instead his attention was drawn to the picture of Bolly Beeley. "What? Oh, that's just...I don't know why that's in there."

"No, but look," Mabby said. "When was this taken?"

"It was right after you were born, by a couple days."

"Oh. It's just weird. I've never seen Bolly with his wings."

"Yeah. He lost them in the figh…wait." Dorma finally did the math. "He said the cat took his wings, but here he is, days later, completely whole."

"So why would he say the cat did it?"

"I don't know. But…" He stood up quickly. "But whatever that means, this proves his campaign was a sham. A lie! The cat never got a scratch on him, and he didn't want anyone to know it! It's evidence! Evidence! He's.. in cahoots"

"Yay!" Mabby exclaimed, not knowing what a cahoot was.

Dorma ran back to tell the others.

Chapter 19: Delayed Grad-ification.

The seating was unusually comfortable that year. Probably for the best.

Dorma sat in the stands, having been there far longer than anyone else. “Wow, you’re really early,” the second patron said to him an hour after he sat down. The squirrel didn’t seem to recognize him. “Perhaps things have blown over,” he thought optimistically.

“Have to get a good seat, my friend,” Dorma said, chuckling to himself, with a “haw” and a “hoohoo,” between bites of pankeybread. He realized that he was more excited than he had been at his own graduation. Never mind that he had been there far longer than anyone had imagined and doing what, only he knew.

Then came up, it seemed from another way, about a pawful of strangers. They had appeared just as everyone else was beginning to settle in. They had split up, without a word, and chosen different places to sit. One of them, an elderly one with an extremely hunched back, bespectacled and dressed in raggedy clothes, sat down with another disheveled old thing. He glanced over at Dorma and winked. Dorma winked back.

A good thing too, what with all of the incredibly large baggy-bags full of unidentified *non*-flying objects, hidden underneath the stadium seating. They had been smuggled in with the help of some strange figures that had disappeared the moment it was done.

Meanwhile, at the First Practicum, Mabby poised, breath still, praying paws, ears cocking toward the wind, billowing through the light slats, and his tail still. The sunspears grew and shimmied around him like bottlereeds. That besides, only a joyous hale penetrated his thoughts, of a faraway gathering of voices' 'waiting,' he said to himself, awaiting they were; him. In that moment he felt a soundless groaning, up and down, such as he had never felt the crosshatch brown shack do. Perhaps a nail was loose somewhere and the wind was making it angry. It had never been this quiet before, after all; it was like even the boards were waiting.

Waiting…

Callo, Tufa, Deela, Bo, Syriss, and the few remaining in the class had all made their way to the starting platform. Deela could tell they were talking about Mabby since most of them had betrayed him and Dorma. She had made no effort to involve herself in their conversations since the breakup of their circle of friends. Syriss went over to the line and the others followed. She took it as a signal to ignore them as well, and then the others joined him. Deela gritted her teeth and whispered to herself, "Come on, Mabby, it's your time. But if you can't, I will love you anyway. Always."

Announcements were made, and the wingliers all took their places in the seeding. Ms. Padduck stood to the side, and everyone looked to her.

"Aren't you going to give us a speech or something?" Syriss said. She had been looking out toward the horizon till Syriss distracted her train of thought and she remembered where she was. When she saw they were all looking at her, she simply said, "Uh, yes. Um…This…" She waved to the course. "Will be your final exam...er...Good luck, everyone." And she went back to thinking and watching.

The class looked a little confused, but they all assumed start off position.

The remainder of the army waited, watching from outside the city, in the highest tree, close to the summit of the mountain.

"So, what do you think now, ole farthead?" said Shin.

"Aw, he ain't gunna make it," Nock said, chewing on something, as usual, and not looking up.

Pop. The shot sounded suddenly and everyone took off with Callo in the lead.

The race was considerably long, and the participants were already halfway done when Ms. Padduck arrived, for she needed to pass him. Mabby breathed a deep breath. Ms Padduck stuck her head in and said, "You've got to complete the entire course to qualify to graduate, no doubt you can do it. Go, Mabby, it's now or never! Go, and get your place in this world!"

Will not. Fail.

And he leapt…

As Mabby soared off, Ms. Padduck went down the mountain the other way, shouting, "Guardians! It is time!" And there was the slightest of ruffling of the trees some ways off from town as she called out the signal to mobilize,

"Inimical Umbra!"

The Masters were the first to see Mabby rocket out of the shack, careening toward the second course.

"He he. Hoo! There, you said he would never make it. Now I'm right and you're wrong, so pay up."

Nock didn't move. "That ain't him."

"What do you mean that ain't him?! What is it then?"

"That's a…flyin'...furry, lil' dummy ball. S'what that is," Nock said.

"*You're* a dummy ball."

Chapter 20: The Battle for Hesperia

They say the Big Race Day is the day of discovery for a squirrel or squirrelette. For all the preparation in the world does not make up for when one must simply believe in oneself. The typical course a kit or pup must take to reach the finish line took about eight months of practice. Mabby completed the courses in one pass and headed for the Raceway.

Dorma's heart leapt in his chest as Mabby came into view as a blur, spiraling and rocketing down the boughway. All eyes turned to the projectile emerging from the flying wreckage.

"Well," a rather large voice said in an annoyingly cocky yet relaxed manner, and Dorma looked to see who it was, to give them a look that would surely correct their thinking, and he doubled back. Someone in the crowd fainted, the whole audience turned, and not a soul dared to breathe their next breath for, of all the hellish sights of hounds and fiends, this was the most frightening and unexpected. For above the shaking ears of a perfectly normal-sized bloke by the name of Raxton Neebles, who worked as the Raceway announcer, perched up on her front paws over the top rail of the grandstand, was the great body of a black cat bigger than anyone had imagined. "Isn't that a sight for-rrr *dead* eyes?" she seemed to chuckle to herself, though only she found it funny. She sauntered down, baring her teeth at anyone who didn't clear out of the way fast enough. "No, no, it's alr-rrrright, I don't want anyone going anywherrrrre, we'-rre just all going to watch this fun unfold togetherrrr-rrr." Her voice vibrated the boards they sat on, which creaked under her stupendous weight. Not a tail was still. "What's the matter-rrr?" she said with a flirty grin. "I bet you were expecting me to show up a little later, when everyone gets their, oh what's the worrr-rd, numpets, huh?" Her face became a mocking pout. Dorma was moving toward the makeshift switch when she saw him. "Well, sowwy. Planned it all out and everything, I bet. Twitch an ear and I slit your thrrr-*oat!*" She jumped in front of him with her hair up straight.

He held his breath and did not move. Her glimmering yellow eyes had a searching look. He could not allow her to know there was a plan. He needed to appear to be just an innocent bystander trying to get away, so he decided to act much more afraid than he was. If you ever need someone to think nothing of you, he had once said, give them what they want. So he doubled over and fell to the ground, sobbing and wailing. "Oh, please don't kill me!" he screamed. "Please! I only want to go home! I'll give you anything, please!"

She glowed. It had worked. "Ha! In a moment, my little delicious nubby-nubblet." Her tail swayed back and forth as she turned away, searching the audience. "Oh, have I waited for this day, my own personal Thanksgiving. But you all wouldn't know about that. Hm. Let's get on with this, oh Beeley? Bolly, little Bolly Ball, my scrumptious Ball-y-of-chicken, where are you? You bore me… Oh, there you are. Are you *ready*?" she shouted out off into the north from the grandstands. Everyone followed her gaze to a figure, in the high sun, emerging nervously from the trees.

His silhouette swayed for a moment, as if looking around to figure out what to do next. "Oh, no, it's all right, I'm ready any time you are," she taunted him and sat down with her tail patiently flopping. Everyone behind her looked solidly at the silhouette. While they all seemed to wonder if she had come looking for revenge, Dorma knew she had not gone by the plan and was threatening to expose him with every mocking word. But why? he wondered. She licked a paw in boredom and cocked her head at him with a "don't test me" posture. He slowly came forward from his unwittingly exposed hiding place and disappeared again. Everyone looked at one another. “Oh, that’s right. You can’t.” She laughed. “I suppose I’ll have to start...with…”

Dorma had been inching toward the switch, hidden from sight and suspicion, and had stopped about halfway when Morgart turned around again.

“Ah, yes!” she said and, as quick as the wind blows a lamp out and darkness takes the evening for its own, she snatched him up. She pinched him between her claws, and raised him to her face, which was the size of his entire body. “You.” The crowd swooned, but no one moved or did anything but tremble and cry. He wanted to cover his head, but he was hanging by his skin with his arms stuck out. Her mouth opened, baring her fangs. They were big enough to pierce him through and through.

“This is it, I suppose. Here I come, my sweet love,” he said under his breath.

Then she stopped and looked him over again. “You look familiar.”

While she was busy preparing to fangifully eat Dorma’s head, Bolly re-emerged and waved to the now completely forgotten group of racers. They had all stopped for fear of finishing, literally. Callo looked up, and Beeley stopped waving abjectly and motioned for him to come.

Callo glanced back to Tufa, who saw him, and then he looked down, pretending he hadn’t. In that moment, her face fell, and the tears of one wronged, wronging, and having been wrong all at once began to well up in her eyes. Her tabby fur rose up in anger and fear, knowing. She had told him all that had allowed this to happen, when she could have instead believed her friends and stopped it all. Callo said out into the air, “I’m sorry.” and flew off up to Bolly’s aid. above. She watched him go and take Bolly’s paws, to glide him to the grandstands, and all the while she cursed him, clawing at the bark she clung to and crying helplessly. They all did.

Deela, without a word, raced to the top of the tree they had all stopped to take a shortcut to Munger’s Grandstand by abandoning the prescribed track. Syriss immediately followed; then he motioned to Tufa and Bo. “Come on, guys.”

“But the race?!” she said.

"Oh for the Great Nut, would you just stop being contrarian for once in your life. The race is over. And we were wrong. Now Mabby's going to need help, so we need to just not be wrong anymore. Come on!"

Tufa said nothing more and hurried after him with Bo close behind, only because he cared more for her than anything at all.

Meanwhile Mabby was nearly through the intermediate course when he took a break to breathe. "Gotta make it onto the track before it's over," he repeated to himself, not knowing a thing. It was then, in that moment, that the rush of air was not in his ears. Thank the Great Nut for, if it had been any other moment, when Morgart snatched up Mabby's dad and eyed him for dinner, the screams of the audience wouldn't have reached his ears. Well, reach his ears they did, and he happened to look down the mountainslope, where the grandstand was just in view from his vantage point. There was nothing to see at that level but the blur of a great black mass. "Oh my! Oh no!" He entirely forgot about the race and headed like an arrow for the dark target. "Inimical Umbra," he thought, realizing the dark and sinister shadow was that of the Great Morgart Wingless and all of his training had been toward this goal.

"You're going down," he thought and cocked his paws to pick up all the momentum he could muster. "All right, you demon, this is going to hurt you a lot...and that's going to be about it."

A whoosh went overhead, and everyone looked about.

"I've thought of a poem!" Mabby's voice seemed to come from all directions.

"Morgart Schmorgart, big fatty Bore-gart
The Shadow doth *loom!* Don't make me Snore-gart!"

At this an unstoppable chuckle rippled through the crowd, and Morgart looked simply annoyed. More whooshing went overhead, and she looked more and more frustrated, till...*wham!* She was caught totally off guard as Mabby's shoulder collided with her cheek, and she reeled back on her haunches. He continued whooshing by and hitting her until she had nearly dropped Dorma entirely, and all the while Mabby shouted, while being lauded by the bystanders,

"She rocked and rolled, but now she's old (*wham*)
Ate up on (*wham*) fattyrats till her tummy went white
And now her fart is much worse than her fight!
Then took a (*wham!*) trip to the squirrelton hall,
And there we shall learn (*wham!)*
When you reach in the churn
The kittycat loses its claw!"

The whole scene was in an uproar as Mabby rounded his turn and went in for the killshot.

But that was when she got eyes on him. Morgart, teeth gritted, caught his trajectory and, in the last moment before the final blow, she turned and held Dorma up in front of him. This forced Mabby to brake and hover helplessly almost in midair. For a moment they looked one another dead in the eye, and she batted Mabby down with a flick. "Hohum. You little turd-faces are all so predictable," she said, and preened herself in a moment of self-indulgence. "And if there's one thing I can't stand it's poetry. Ugh" She shuddered.

Dorma saw his son go down into the shadows and heard the crashing below. "He can't get any lift," he thought, and he instinctively began to fight like he never had before. He bit her finger hard. She meowed and threw him over the side toward Mabby.

"Stop!" Bolly had arrived, and the cat and the audience looked at Cal and Bolly. The latter hopped down deftly onto the deck of the grandstand. He immediately began rolling up his sleeves and motioning Morgart over to him. "I've had enough! I've taught you a lesson before these great comrades once before, and I intend to do so again. What ho! Let's have it!" He strode right up to Morgart, who hadn't budged and only smiled at him, and he began to push and prod her provokingly. "Let's be on with this then, you old *bore...um,* gart. He he..."

"Oh, that's just too rich. Imitating the kid now? Are you that insecure?" she said as she toyed with him. He jumped to one side, grabbed her claw, and twisted it. She gasped. "Oh! Oh no, you have my claw, you're twisting my little finger, however shall I defend myself?" Then she looked at him with a blank stare. "Quick, say something witty!"

Bolly let go and took a defensive stance, putting up his dukes. "Uh, uh, you! You ignorant, uh, cretin!" He waggled his tail and his fists, but she made no expression or movement.

"That wasn't an invitation to redeem yourself," she said. "It was just sarcasm."

Bolly paused his bit and looked at her sideways. He said in a tone no one was meant to hear. "What are you doing? Come on."

"No. I'm certain I've actually had enough of you. I have waited so long for this day. I mean you had one job, and you took just *forever."* She swatted him with the back of her paw, and he crashed into several bystanders. "Do you know how hard it was to act like I care about your stupid little overthrow idea all this time?"

The crowd gasped.

"No, no, we had a deal. I brought you here and got you inside to help me set things right. We had a deal!"

"No, you got me inside so I could do my *thang*!" She brought a paw down on him. His head protruded from between her index and foreclaw, trembling and completely helpless. "You stupid little fool. Did you really think your little sacrifices to me were all I wanted?" She threw her head back in laughter. "I serve no one. I haven't been serving you, doing away with all your little obstacles. You've been serving me. I let you think this was your plan. It was mine. Now, plans change. Play along, trust me, right?" She winked.

"No. No! You told me what you wanted and I gave it to you."

"You really think you're the only one capable of lying."

"No, you're lying, she's lying!" He said to the crowd. He winced as she raised her paw once more to end Bolly's life.

“Going down!” shouted Mabby and, in a surprise attack, rammed her in the plexus. The impact sent her flailing over the edge. Seconds later, Mabby landed nicely on the ledge and

Dorma landed right after he did and looked over the edge to make sure Morgart hadn’t landed. There was only the rustling of leaves and silence. “She’s below, we’ll let the Protectors take care of her.” Dorma turned to the crowd.

“You’re not supposed to be here,” one of them said

“We don’t understand what’s going on,” another said. Half of them were looking confused and afraid, and the others looked angry. Dorma could see he hadn’t won just yet. He turned to the crowd. “This squirrel is guilty of the crimes of murder, conspiracy, extortion of the fine citizens of Hesperia and, last but not least, terribly, terribly bad style!”

The crowd gasped and then hesitated, somewhat confused by the latter charge.

“I suppose that’s not really a crime, but it matters. And I’ll show you all why when this criminal is brought to justice. Now, let’s take him away.”

The crowd was perplexed by what was transpiring. Bolly Beeley was the town hero. If it weren’t for him, they would all have been dead. Right? Wasn’t it Bolly who had stopped Morgart the first time, when the Guardians could do nothing, so long ago? They watched in confusion, too stunned to pass judgment on what was going on, as Bolly Beeley looked afraid, an uncommon countenance for him. “Why should we believe anything you say?” they asked Dorma. “How do we know you’re not lying and Bolly’s not telling the truth?”

“You heard the cat!”

“We heard her say she was deceptive, that she played him for the fool. Who are we to judge his intentions?”

Bolly saw his chance. “That’s right. All this time, I was just trying to do what is best for you all. The cat made promises to me that she wanted to help.”

“Help do what? What exactly did she say?” Dorma had been waiting for Bolly to play his card. “Because I have, on myself, proof that you are a fraud and your entire campaign is a sham. A lie." He produced his trump card, the picture. "Here is a picture of you receiving the key to the city one week after you helped Morgart into the city to take out the Protectoracy's watchpoints and secret members inside of town. When you stopped her at the hospital, the two of you had a conversation. Now I know what you said to her: 'Change of plans. Trust me, play along.' But you were thinking on your feet because you thought she had gone too far, weren't you?"

Bolly was silent. "For sham and for shame," the crowd murmured.

"That's right, you didn't come to my shop to get that pocket fixed like a proper mayor because you're ashamed. And you didn't lose your wings in that fight. She took them from you in payment for thwarting the plan to take everything over the first time. This time you waited and played everything right to get the job done properly and, what, you were going to just trap her and feed anyone that opposed your supreme highness to her forever? Hm? Well, whatever your plan was, you're not going to get away with it anymore. You can all see here, this is Bolly Beeley, post cat-fight, with wings and not a scratch to show for his troubles. You lost your wings another way, and your story is an invention, isn't it? Isn't it?"

Bolly had no chance to make a clean confession for, just then, Morgart's paw swiped the three of them to the deck. Dorma and Beeley rolled together, but Morgart grabbed Mabby and lost her grip over the side again.

Dorma wasted no time. It was plain they were too few in number to hold her themselves. He had been right on that hunch after all. He rushed over to Deela. "Another change of plans. Get the reinforcements to ground level. You can probably use the nearest of Bolly's shafts. I'm going to go help my son. The Masters have gone, I presume, to tell the others there won't be a signal to come fight and to meet us below. We'll just have to hope. See you down there."

"Got it," Deela said. "We'll figure it out, sir. But, how are we going to catch her in the bag if we're on the ground?" She saluted, "I don't know, but we'll use everything we have." Dorma said, and he left without another word.

Deela turned to the gang. "It's on us. Are you with me, or against me?" She gave Syriss a stern look, and he simply looked down for a moment and then crossed over to Deela's side and looked back at the others. Tufa looked at Callo, who quietly dusted himself off after carrying Bolly, and left without a word. She, and subsequently Bo, joined Deela, and they huddled to hear her plan.

After a moment, they broke and went over to the ledge, while Bo went to the part of the bleachers containing the hidden plan A, extracted the giant baggy-bag at least four or five times his already unnatural size, and slung it over his shoulder with ease.

"Just what are you kids doing?" one of the bewildered audience members said as they all debated the sky away.

Syriss piped up, "We're going to go do what we're best at: cleaning up after you adults, always waiting till it's too late and then doing the wrong thing."

"Watch your tone, youngrel! Where is your father?"

"I'm tired of your little adult games. My father is the great, no, the legendary Ekkhorn Beethorn, the greatest commander of the Army of Elorus history has known, and I'll never fill his shoes. But I'll tell you what he would do right now. He would tell us all there's a life in danger down there, who is trying to save us all, but he can't do it alone."

"You'll get yourselves killed."

"No, actually, you will. Because we are only going to lose or, should I say, die if we don't stand together on the truth, no matter what it is. That's the only way to really survive. And right now, you're either with us or against us. And if we die, it won't be the fault of those who fight for it. It will be the fault of those who hold on to lies and games, because it's those lies and those games that brought on all this oppression, and now death. And fight amongst yourselves about whether or not when that cat is done, how soon she'll come up for you. See you at the floor." And with that, they jumped, making their way to the shaft in the fallen tree.

"Well, how do we know what the truth is?" one of them asked. "Is he suggesting we examine facts and evaluate beliefs for ourselves? Like, take responsibility for what we say and believe, and… think, and stuff?"

“I read an article about that once, they said it causes the gout. Wouldn’t recommend it.”

“Yeah. Jerk,” said another.

Chapter 21: The Guardian

They set to work getting the baggy-bag down. The giant sack was simply too full to fit. Deela and Tufa worked the ties as Bo began to tire, trying to hold the giant bag with one paw and himself up with the other. "Let's just drop it down." said Tufa. Deela shook her head. "It will break open and kill more of us, while only slowing her down. Same as if we just dump them. We'll have to pour it down the channel."

"But the bag will be useless." said Tufa.

Deela agreed. "But it's the only way."

Mabby had wrenched loose as Morgart fell down below the Tanglefloor, Morgart had been knocked out from the fall, but was just beginning to wake as Mabby got to the floor. Dorma landed, and, joined Mabby's side. "Leave her down here. Let's just go, son." Said Dorma.

Mabby shook his head. "She'll just get back in. The city is too compromised. It has to end here, and it has to be us." Dorma resigned to the fact.

Mabby and Dorma circled the cat, making sure to stay far enough apart to keep her from attacking, trying to stall. "Aren't you cats supposed to be graceful and, like, land on your feet and stuff?" Mabby taunted Morgart as she shook off her thud onto the ground floor.

Morgart eyed him unceremoniously. "What are you doing here? Better yet, how is it that you even exist? I must say, I don't think it could be too easy to quite understand the conundrum. I am here, I could kill all of you with a flick of my paw, and you are there, a pathetic outcast, a loser, threatening me when nature has only allowed you to exist because it apparently wasn't paying attention." With those last words, Morgart leaned in closer, ruffling her fur, readying for attack, and searching Mabby's eyes for the slightest sliver of fear anticipating shredding him into a delicious high-protein dinner.

"Ok, you're in my verbal touch bubble," Mabby said. His nonchalant, matter-of-fact tone was infuriating to Morgart, who didn't just want to kill but to strike fear, to terrorize, and make her supreme dominance known to all. So Morgart swept Mabby into the nearest tree with her open claw, making good on her claim. Mabby struggled to his feet, trying to catch his breath, as Morgart sauntered closer, appearing to relax at the prospect of an easy victory. That was exactly what Mabby had been waiting for.

"What is he going to do?" one of the school kits asked out loud.

"I'm not sure," answered an adult. "No one has ever dared to take on Morgart alone. Not even the other Guardians."

"Mabby…" Deela said to herself. "the Guardian."

"Come on guys," Mabby thought. "Get here already."

Mabby coughed, straightened, dusted himself, and cocked his head at Morgart. "So you think you can fight? I've been hit harder by toddlers. You can do better than that." Morgart's head popped back in surprised respect at Mabby's unrelenting defiance, and she began to smile. Mabby calmed and sobered his tone and looked her square in the eye. She met him knowingly. "You've terrorized this town long enough. It's time to end this once and for all. It's over, Morgart," Mabby said. The cat's jollity at the painfully easy battle she had anticipated was overcome by the graveness in Mabby's tone.

"All right," Morgart said in an almost defensive tone, as his condescension peaked, "you want to get nuts, boy? Let's get nuts."

"We don't talk about nuts like that."

Morgart screamed and sprinted at Mabby. He ran at her but, just as she was about to waylay him with a hard left swipe, he ducked and slid underneath her. He planned to make a figure eight to get the momentum to take off and get some good hits. "Oh no you don't." Morgart reached out just in time to grab Mabby's tail. She sank her claws in, hauled him up above her, and slammed him to the ground.

"Mabby!" Deela screamed and hurried with thc ropes. Syriss broke away to throw some sticks and rocks at Morgart, but it created no distraction, and Morgart put her paw on Mabby's chest as he was still reeling. Then she drew out his arm and began to cut away at his wings.

Mabby screamed in bitter protest, begged, and pleaded with Morgart uselessly as Morgart continued to cut slowly, making the removal of Mabby's wings, his special gift, as long and painful as possible.

Morgart was just about to finish Mabby for good, brandishing her massive paw one claw at a time. Mabby winced, and Morgart's eyes glazed over for an instant as she noticed a small bit of dirt in one of her claws. Then she hesitated and began uncontrollably licking. "Hold on, just…" Mabby looked confused and briefly relieved that Morgart's annoying fastidiousness had permitted him another moment of life. Morgart finished. "Ahh, nowwww…" she drifted into a low, carnal *groan*. She eyed Mabby hungrily and drew back again, ready this time. Her jet black arms rippled in the moonlight, shivering with power, with malice, with the anticipation of blood, and with pure hate, totally and deliciously gratified. Then suddenly there was a very distracting distraction in the form of a walnut or two hitting a tree somewhere-abouts. Then Morgart let out a yelp. "Ohhhh, mmmmMMMM! Oh, that's getting really soft!" Then a whistle from behind, and Morgart looked back, still choking the life out of poor young Mabby, who was, at this point, slipping into a desperate unconsciousness. He was barely able to make out the words of Ekkhorn's slow drawl.

"Thought I'd find you here, ol' boah." Ekkhorn was almost too late. Almost. "Do you remember me." He said as if it were a declarative statement, rather than a question.

Morgart looked about, as annoyed as ever, but tried to hide it in his hatred of his old enemy. "Well, little Ekky-BooBoo. You're here to die too.

Very good. Tell me. How is that crossed eye I gave you?" Morgart's somewhat forgotten grip on Mabby's chest permitted him a long-awaited draw of sweet air. "Didn't think you could hit anything with that. You must be seeing double."

"I have two nuts. One for the both of yuh." Ekkhorn brandished the two walnuts remaining in his pouch and stopped, eyeing Morgart from a distance where he would still be effective. "Now, if you let the boah go and pick o-n someone yuh own size," Ekkhorn raised his paws innocently in the air, "ah promise Ah'll go easy o-n yuh." He leaned toward Mabby. "Good boah, son, we can handle the rest, take it easy now—" He was cut off by a hard swipe from Morgart straight in the gut. He toppled, rolled, and lay still. Mabby winced.

"You arrogant rat-faced twerp!"

Morgart forgot entirely about Mabby, perturbed by Ekkhorn's deliberate arrogance. "I'm gonna finish that job like I should have all those years ago! I hate you! I'm gonna eat you alive!" Ekkhorn rose to his feet again, and as Morgart ran at him, he leapt, spun, bounded off a tree trunk to get the lift he needed, and did a sideways 540 spin, catching her directly on the jaw, and he clapped her on the ear on his next turn, dazing her. Then he ducked below one swipe and went through her legs, catching the air and drawing her away and out into the open.

"Wow," thought Mabby, as he watched the master work. His part was done. He crawled away and slumped to the ground, in tears of pain and loss, and shivering. Lathered in his own blood, he reached for the useless piles of flesh that were once his precious wings. He had despised them when they made him special, and now they were gone and his life was meaningless. As Morgart and Ekkhorn fought the battle they had both ached for all their years, Mabby slipped in and out of consciousness and tears rolled down his face. Deela broke away from the trunk containing their attempt at a secret weapon and knelt by him, oblivious to the raucous surrounding them.

Morgart had Ekkhorn pinned against a tree almost immediately, but Ekkhorn was still smiling. "You're dead! You're all dead! ...Why are you smiling?!"

"He he. Uh uh. Heh. There's more of u-s than yah think, ol' boah."

"I'm not a boy!!!" she screamed at the top of her lungs.

Konk. Morgart reeled back, blinded by a painful, nutty cloud of rage. A blind swipe had left Ekkhorn on the ground, bleeding but still laughing. The laughter of crazy old fools could be heard approaching from high above. Then another pelt, and another. And Morgart found herself facing a whole crew of Guardians. Ekkhorn got back to his feet, joined by the unlikely Nock and Shin, parachuting down, then Mr. Hopp the baker, and another townsperson. Five, six, seven. "Who are all of them? They're not in your little club." Then out of the shadows, the whole town emerged slowly and stopped just behind Syriss and Bo.

"Don't have to be," Syriss said leading the crowd. Bo and Tufa turned to face her, with the contents of the transport shaft spilling out of the door in front of them.

"Oh, my dear sweet mommy," Morgart muttered in resigned terror. "They figured out spikes. Who figured out spikes?!" Then she yelled out to them, "Who makes the laws here that you unorganized simps don't obey, you who disregard your rightful masters? Give up your leaders to me, and I will show you order once and for all!" Morgart said. But her bluff didn't work.

"The grandmaster is not here," Masters Bang and Bone said together.

"Yes! She is!" Then Ms. Padduck, whom no one had expected, walked to the forefront of the approaching crowd. Then she stepped over the line of jacknuts, kicking them aside with her armored boots, and shed her teacher's robe to reveal the garb of the Protectoracy. The crowd went into a fury, divided over the new hope in the presence of the Grandmaster and the Protectoracy and the fact that they had succeeded in infiltrating the deepest workings of their society. "What are you doing here?!" some simpleton shouted. "This is our fight, here on the ground! Your kind ain't supposed to exist!"

"Silence!" Everyone hushed. "Class is now in session!" she said in her shrill, deafening voice, as the Guardians, their identities now known to all, drew together. Then she let out a yell that could put an ox at unease, and the Guardians, all in perfect formation, threw their front paws in the air, robes and cloaks flying off, to reveal their brilliant Guardian's armor and their massive wings, one and all. Miss Padduck seemed a little self-conscious about the nipple armor, but no one said anything.

Then the Guardians all let out a battle whoop, threw their arms down, and catapulted into the air, spinning like kamikaze death straight toward Morgart's terrified person. Every one of them was screaming in blinding rage. Morgart tried to fight, but the constant barrage of Nock and Shin's deadly aim and the bone breaking air-strikes from all directions completely inhibited any ability to block, and all she could do was stumble about. Victory was imminent.

"Mabby!" Someone's weeping brought a hush over the battle. Mabby had gone limp.

"Mabby, you're my hero." Hero. He could no longer keep his head up. He let his head fall to the side, looking back for Tufa, as the townsquirrels made their way around him. They had listened after all. To his surprise, it wasn't Tufa, whom he'd had such a crush on because he thought her being a bit different would make her understand him. It was Deela, a perfectly normal kit, running to his side, tears streaming down her face, with no regard for her own safety.

"Mabby, no!" she cried. "Have I been such a fool as this?" he thought. The Guardians looked back when Deela screamed and then continued fighting with a renewed fervor, holding the cat off a little while longer. But the distraction caused a gap in their assault, and Morgart exacted it, catching one of them, Mr. Ferroule, and swiping him into a tree, and turning the tide of the fight. Deela looked about desperately.

The fight was beginning to wane back to Morgart's advantage as the aged knights began to tire. She knew she had to do something. "I'm sorry, I know I said I would never leave you, but I have to right now. I'll be right back." She gave him a kiss on the cheek, and laid his head down, filled with rage. She went to the jacknuts and found what she had been looking for, for in the pile was a set of perfectly normal looking nuts that she had built as her own project. All the townsfolk watched as she went over to the barrier and found her three special jacknuts tied together.

She untied them and, with a flick, one converted to a helmet. She put on the others, which served as fighting gloves, and began to walk. The other Guardians were briefly subdued, pulling themselves up breathlessly for another round, and Morgart took the chance to survey her work. In doing so, she went from looking about triumphantly for a moment to seeing tiny Deela, standing alone halfway between the population of Hesperia and the fight.

She just cocked her head at Morgart for a moment. Then she said, "You know what I don't understand..." She flicked her wrists and the jacknut shells in her paws suddenly projected several rows of needle-sharp spikes like the ones on the helmet she wore. "Is why everyone thinks they can just mess with my *boyfriend!"*

Mabby's head popped up. "Wait, boyfriend?!" he squeaked.

"Yes! You...*YOU ARE MY BOYFRIEND!"* she shouted back at Mabby, and at that he simply plopped his head back on the ground.

Deela's eyes twinkled and twitched once, twice, and then she screamed bloody murder and charged into Morgart head on. Wally screamed, "Deela, NO!" The others were renewed in the fight, encouraged by the new member in their ranks.

Deela's battle scream had another interesting effect for her tiny, high-pitched voice stirred something deep in Bo's memory banks of when the wall came down and made all the colors come on. He remembered the last thing he had seen was the cat. His eyes got wide, and he slowly, silently moved in. Then he began to gallop, and a wild smile showed up on his face. Soon he was charging full speed into Morgart, and hair, spit, blood, and cat-teeth started flying. In the cloud of dirt and rage, Bo started to giggle. Morgart sent a normally deathbringing blow to Bo's head, which just made him angrier. Then he really started to have fun. Bones popping in and out of place were heard as Bo began tying Morgart up in various knots and shapes, squealing in delight at each new accomplishment.

Morgart flurried her claws, finally batted him and Deela off and escaped his arms, like treeroots. Deela backed off knowing she could not take the cat alone, and she stood resolutely next to Bo, breathing hard.

There was a pause in the action at that point. The knights and gang took the chance to regroup while Morgart caught her breath, cursing at them all the while. And there the band was, all standing there, minus one, the last standoff, between the line of spike-nuts protecting the townsfolk. Syriss had not engaged the fight. He was still standing in the great pile of hundreds of weaponized jacknuts, trying to figure out how Deela had made instruments of hell out of them. “How did she do that…oh, whatever.” Then he gave up and just grabbed a big stick, weighed it for a moment, and he stood in front of the whole crowd. He had a thought, and reached the stick down and picked up one of the jacknuts, using its ends as prongs, and he hurled it with deadly accuracy at a nearby tree. To everyone’s surprise it slammed with such force that it exploded, leaving only a patch of needles embedded to the eye in the trunk. Then Dorma saw, and picked up a stick to test out just the same. “That’s it, that’s the ticket!” Then the whole town started gathering sticks.

“Oh mommy.” were the last words of the great cat Morgart Wingless to be recorded in the annals of the Hesperiana.

He gave the signal to charge, sending the town into a flying rage behind Syriss, who threw the first nut with his throwing stick which landed dead in the Cat’s soft tummy parts and she let out a howl. Then they ran at her all together. Morgart fled, pelted with spiky balls of doom the whole way off Nearly Mountain. Rabbits, hedgehogs, turtles, and so on, hid the eyes of their children as Morgart the cat was chased by the whole town of Hesperia from the last reaches of Nockshin Wood.

Only Dorma stayed behind, attending to Mabby and Ekkhorn. When the triumphant congregation returned Deela threw off her helmet and gloves, and sat down with Mabby. Bo picked up the body of Ekkhorn,

“Careful, Bobo. I think he is paralyzed.” Said Dorma. But Ekkhorn hung still in Bo’s arms, but on his face there was a look of peace, and his elusive smile. That was when Syriss arrived and emerged from the crowd, panting. They were all talkative, but fell silent one by one as they took notice of the scene of Mabby, bloody and fading, and Ekkhorn, motionless.

“Dad?” said Syriss. His smile faded.

Mabby could only now feel the hurt of his foolishness. His body would no longer work, but his mind remained active. "Is this dying?" he thought. "All this time I've been chasing someone because I wanted to feel better about myself. She likes me for who I am, and I never noticed. Fool. You bloody, dying fool." He felt the caress of her tiny paw as it lifted his big stupid head and pressed his bloody face against her heart, and she kissed him. "Mabby you can't, you can't leave me." He felt himself slip away, and the cries and sobs grew more distant as the shadows took hold.

"Mabby, come back, come back, please..." Deela said, but her words fell to no response.

"I love you…"

"Please…"

The crowd stood quietly, helpless to comfort the young kit in her grief. Perhaps future battles had been won but, they slowly realized, not this one. A great light was going out, and they gathered round. Dorma, Reverend Ferroule, Ms. Padduck, and all the town bowed their heads.

Love, she had said. Mabby closed his eyes.

"Mabby saved the town," someone said just before it all went black.

"Mabby the Guardian brought the cat down! Mabby the hero."

Chapter 22: The Trial of Bolly Beeley.

"All rise."

"The honorable Judge Padduck presiding."

"Oh, come on!" shouted Beeley, in chains.

"The 'held for' shall in velleity and vagary bide SOUNDLESS!" Ms. Padduck said at a volume that left everyone's ears ringing. Someone (achem)ed. "Oh! What of it? I have labored *selectly* and. And, ...oh stuff it I can yell if I want to with whatever language I like!" Then she calmed herself promptly and sat down, somewhat embarrassed. "What is the charge?" As if she didn't know.

The back doors of the courtroom swung open. Since Bolly's deposement as mayor, Dorma had been voluntold to serve as acting mayor, and he had done such a fine job that everyone had voted for him. He strode to the front in the dapper jacket of a proper gubernatorial official, and a top hat because, because. Everyone oohed and aahed. He looked neither to the right nor the left as he gave her the pamphlet containing the charges, despite the murderous look Bolly had on his face. It was the first he had known of it, being in jail and all.

"Oh, look at you, Mister Perfect! You can't do what I can do! You don't have what it takes. Nobody does!" Bolly grimaced, straining at the shoulders as the guards held him back.

"You're right," Dorma said, finally casting a glance Bolly's way. "I would have to correct you only to say most of us don't have what it takes, because, unlike you, most of us are morally good." Dorma got a few snickers out of the crowd, and he puffed his chest, extracting some confidence. "Furthermore I don't plan to do what you've done. I plan to *undo* it."

A cheer went up, and Bolly shook his head, looking about furiously for some semblance of support.

"For the high crimes against our city, resulting in the death and/or disfigurement of the following—

"The great and honorable Ekkhorn Beethorn,"

Syriss' eyes closed, and many shook their heads, and bowed their heads to wipe their tears.

"Dolly Tadwick Ferroule," Mabby's eyes went wide at the mention of that maiden name. Deela sat behind the prosecutor's bench with him.

"Bobo Neebles,"

"Tufa Tankery,"

"Mabby Dabby,"

"Debby Quarles Dabby,"

The list went on.

Deela squeezed his paw. "We have the same birthday," she said with tears in her eyes, and Mabby finally understood. "I tried to tell you when we met. Dolly Tadwick was my mother." Mabby remembered something suddenly. "So, Riffa…" He started, and Deela nodded and finished his sentence. "She's my cousin. She wasn't born with wings. I'm alive because my father rescued me, but in doing so he didn't have the time to save our family…She has never been the same, and she blames me. She might be right…" He shook his head and hugged her and they wept together, her in her sweater and him in his suit of bandages. The audience section of the courtroom in the hall of the Great Commons was astir until the list was ended and all were silent. Mabby's breath hung in the air, having for the first time realized how she could possibly have understood him so well. She was not born with the right wings, but that did not stop her from living all the pain of a Guardian's life. Yet she still dreamed of protecting others. And she didn't just resort to living that life through him either; for she herself fought, as others joked to this day, with the fearsomeness of a rabid mongoose.

As he sat there and watched, Bolly's face contorted and sneered at each name, justifying everything to himself as he condemned his fate with each prideful confession on the stand. He realized the power of being a Guardian didn't reside in the structure of one's bones and skin, as he realized Syriss, Cal, Bo, Deela, Bolly, Ekkhorn, Ms. Padduck, Hal Ballo, and the list went on, were all just as capable as he was as they had all shown from time to time. Those who became great, did so because they were powered by great love.

The cross-examination revealed, as Dorma expected for he did it himself, that Bolly was either a savant or a savage. And yet, at the same time, he didn't expect Bolly's answer at all.

"Mister Beeley, I have shown the court that not only did this plot of yours prove against the values of our great city, but that you had done so without the sanction of your own conspirators. They tried to stop you from letting the Cat into the city to kill off the Guardians, so you killed them yourself. I submit this to the court as evidence." He produced the journal and explained the location of the bones of Debby's parents. "You see, your honor, here are the receipts and forged signatures of the various businesses that Bolly now 'owns,'" Dorma made quotation marks with his fingers, "or should I say simply collects from. And you will find that every date corresponds to the dates of the disappearances of those who signed. This is how he became so wealthy so fast." He turned to Bolly. "You killed them so you could kill my wife to get at me, didn't you?"

"No! I wanted to free her, not kill her! They got in my way just like you, and screwed everything up." The crowd gasped at Bolly's emotional admission, and he realized his mistake.

"Tell me, Bolly, I must know, and since you have been so forthcoming up to this point. How did you know where the cat would be when you showed up at our hospital room?"

"I wanted to hurt you the way you hurt me," Bolly said.

That didn't answer his question, but he went on. "But why, Bolly, why my wife? Why would you try to hurt me by killing my wife?"

"You're an idiot! Why in the blue blazes would anyone care about you?"

"But you wanted to hurt me, yes?"

"Of course, and I still do."

"Well, does not even spite imply caring in a sense?" Dorma was simply trying to get a rise out of him, and the poor bright-eyed savage went directly for it as the audience snickered at a good show.

"Rrr... Didn't anyone ever tell you that Dorma is a girl's name, and a terrible one!"

"Why does that matter?"

"I told the cat to go after you, as a favor, and told her 'Dorma Dabby at the hospital in the birthing ward.' She thought you were a girl because of your stupid name. You were supposed to be the one to die. Don't you all see? This is your entire fault. Your fault! That's the truth! I loved her and you stole her from me by being…Stupid!"

Everyone simply sat in silence. Dorma shook his head.

"So the deaths all of those lovely persons whose names were just read aloud to us happened because of my semi-androgynous moniker?"

Bolly picked up on his indignation, and Dorma regretted having opened himself up to it, for Bolly dug right in. "Yes, I say! Yes, and not just that, but your sappy pants, and your stupid weak chin, and everything about you that is stupid that got her to feel so sorry for you that she got all your attention, instead of that of a real squirrel. She was the only person in the world that ever mattered to me, and you got to her first! That's all! She should have been with me! I would have protected her, like you *couldn't!"*

Dorma looked down for a moment. "She didn't need you to do that. You and I both loved her, yes. But you see, you just said it yourself. You don't care about anything. She cared about everything. Everything and everyone. You had feelings for her, but that is a far cry from loving someone. It does not matter how much one feels if the quality is poor. I loved her, so I sought to understand her. Feelings want. Love gives. Feelings seek sympathy. Love seeks understanding--"

Bolly shrieked, "Shut up! I'll kill you! You don't know *anything about anyone!*"

Dorma's face became dark. "Case in point, judge. When you refuse to try to understand others, you have no choice but to live a selfish life, no matter where you come from." The audience cheered, and Dorma went on. "Judge, as for the next matter, I have reason to suspect the location of the cat's entry into the city, and as I promised the Bolly's sorely unprofessional dress."

"I think you're going to have to go slowly on this one." said Judge Padduck.

"I present evidence that Bolly Beeley has used the funds he coercively gathered from forging ownership first from Ballo's farm, on up to Rammerie's School and half the business district to stage a legal appearing takeover. Not so that he could serve the poor, mind you, but so that he could gain control of everything within these Tanglewalls for himself. Bolly killed Hallo Ballo because Hal tried to stop him. He killed my wife's parents for the same reason. He never intended to serve the populace, but to rule them by way of the strong against the weak."

"Ha! What other way is there to rule?!" Beeley interrupted. He thought he had Dorma, but the audience did not seem to agree.

Dorma went on. "You see, your honor. This journal outlines Beeley's entire plan, but what I want to show the court for now is that there is a purpose for all madness. Bolly's coat is disgusting. So dirty all the time, and always fraught with tears and fringes, that one would wonder why he wouldn't just take it to the tailor. His pants are all but falling off, and stained right through, but he would never get them taken in. Why, you may ask? Well, it's because I, your honor, am the tailor. I'm the best, so good at what I do that there isn't anyone in this town who would bother to compete with my business."

"You're lucky!"

"Quiet!" Yelled the judge. Bolly quieted.

"No, you're lucky Bolly. Lucky you didn't get caught before now. My point is, your honor, Bolly won't come to me because deep down he knows he killed my wife; that he is guilty."

"I'm dirty because I have a dirty job! I'm nothing but a poor farmer who got what I've got from hard work and honest determination!"

"Wrong! Again, your honor, I submit samples of the dust from the secret escape tunnels under the abandoned Quarles' house." He handed over a little phial, which Ms. Padduck turned over and over in her paw. "You will find it matches with the dust embedded in Bolly's clothing, and here is a sample of the dirt from the forest floor which does not. That dust, on his jacket, is from a saw. He is a hard worker, all right, but he works feverishly only to seek power, not to have integrity. At that, he has never worked a day in his life. He wouldn't have time for both. I think we all remember the late shipments from Ballo's roastery since Beeley took over after Hal's death. And I can only imagine the hardship he put the youngrel Cal through, forcing him to slave away while Beeley plotted to steal from other innocent squirrels, twisting his mind." Bolly bowed his head and spoke no reply.

Ms. Padduck's face was skeptical. "All these conclusions from dust?" she said. But Bolly's face told all as his defenses slowly began to crack and he fell silent.

The remainder of the trial went quickly and was rather boring, save plenty of outbursts from the defendant's bench. Suffice to say, Bolly Beeley received a unanimous guilty verdict and a lifetime for each he had stolen, which was no justice at all, but it was all that could be done. By the end, Bolly had remained quiet and resigned to his fate, a most peculiar thing altogether. For in the end he realized it simply would not bring back his only love that he in all his anger could never let go enough to see who she had really been. After he was taken from the room to await sentence, no one could say for certain since what had happened to him. Some say he had broken out of his cell and escaped; others subscribed to much darker prognoses. But one thing was sure; he was never seen in Hesperia again.

As everyone quietly got up to leave, Tufa finally saw Callo again. He had remained in the back of the courtroom, trying not to attract attention.

She caught his arm as he was trying to head out.

She gave him a hug, to even his surprise. "How have you been?" she asked.

"I'm fine. They couldn't...pin anything on me…"

"So I suppose you'll be getting your inheritance back."

"Yeah." He was his usual quiet self. "It was all I wanted, just to keep my father's memory alive."

"It must have been hard…" she said, distantly.

"Well...But all of it is okay since I've been with you," Callo said, and Mabby rolled his eyes in disbelief that Tufa could be falling for his load of crap.

Then Tufa began to cry.

"What's the matter? Are you okay?" Callo said.

"I feel like I don't even know who you are anymore." She sobbed great heaving, rolling sobs. "I just can't think of how you could possibly do such a thing to my friends…and at the same time…lie to me." She looked at him with her big blue eyes. "How could you not have told me? You didn't have to go through it alone."

"You don't understand, I—"

"No. Your father had to do what he had to do because he loved you and he couldn't have known what would happen. He wouldn't compromise. You think you are in his shoes because you have to make hard choices, but thinking you have to serve this evil person instead of be our friend, that's not a choice any of us would have made over you."

"I... I'm sorry." Callo looked down. "I'm so sorry. Will you forgive me?"

"Perhaps." She wiped a tear away and gathered herself. "Someday. But…(sob) I don't think I could ever be with you." And at that she burst out crying full force and, despite Callo's dejected pleas, she walked away. She joined Mabby and the others.

"Are you alright?" Mabby said.

"He he. Got something in your eye?" Syriss said.

She laughed. "Yes, I think so, but it's out now."

But of course Bo Neebles had been paying attention, and quite so. "Marrb?" He said and put a gentle paw on her shoulders.

Her tail perked somewhat.

"Marr-b, Marr—"

At the sight of Bo comforting Tufa, with her head on his broad shoulder, Callo simply bowed his head, said, “I’m sorry, I’m so sorry…” one last time, and turned to go.

“No. *sniff* I’m sorry. I’m sorry I was confused by love.” She turned to the lot of them. “Or what I thought was love, anyway. I loved, but I didn’t understand. I was so wrong. I had no idea I had something better than hiding and being skeptical of everyone. I thought no one understood him. But there are those who are truly misunderstood, and to give the ones who only want to be the attention they don’t deserve, it hurts the ones in real pain. He should never have come this far. I-I understand now.” She lifted her head. “I have something better than…a boyfriend.” She laughed at how silly it suddenly sounded.

“Yeah, y’know….” Mabby and Deela both said, toeing the ground.

“Marr-rr-bee!” Bo exclaimed, throwing his paws in the air with his tail waving excitedly.

Tufa laughed, feeling relieved. “Yes, Mabby is a great friend. I think so, too.”

Mabby looked down knowingly, and Syriss shook his head.

Syriss looked about a bit before he leaned in to whisper in her ear, “Tufa, he’s not saying ‘Mabby,’ he’s saying…” He looked about again and whispered “He’s saying, ‘Marry.’” in her ear. Mabby chuckled, for everyone else had known all along. Tufa squeaked in a way squirrels aren’t supposed to admit to doing and scurried off, embarrassed beyond all belief.

Syriss gave Bo a reassuring pat, quite satisfied with himself. “Oh. (Sigh) How am I the only one that puts these things together?” he said, shaking his head and grinning from ear to ear.

Chapter 22: Another Wedding Day.

Mabby looked out at the silent, seated congregation and cleared his throat. "I call this one, 'A Squirrel's Vow.'"

"Stupid name," he thought. He steeled his paws as he held up the shaking paper and began to read;

The billybubs' baby buttums still a greeney glow, a month or two from gold, and the sky still bright from the winter's very cold.

The speeders were still spilderings, and the billybubs still bleeps, the skylarks' eggs still cracking and the chatterings not yet cheeps.

And not all was usual in that time of year, when all is by necessity, young and new, and rushed and clear.

For on the morning of the fifth of May, a bustling chapel was heard near'n away, for there were three weddings on the very same day!

(The crowd cheered.)

Newly grad'iated, four, and two old teachers, one, of sensibleness and good, and the other, well, just actually thinks it's fun!

And became I a writer, dear, do suffer no duress, Dorma Dabby, the town's greatest… tinker… He built a press!
(The crowd groaned.)

Forever and for ever would be thine, till our faces no more glow, to have you have me, someone as *normal* as you, the honor of honoring you mine.

And one of these days I'll figure out how to give my stanzas time,
And you shall know me then, like you never knew me when, on this day I swore and swear, 'till the sky runs out of air….

To lovey-dove you, have and hug you, to wave our tails in happiness, and to pick up all my mess, and understand you for all…Rhyme?

Mabby finished his poem and went back over to where Deela was waiting. The clapping began slowly at first and soon subsided, and attention shifted to the one standing at the center of the three circles. They were all about to rise. Dorma Dabby, the town's newly elected mayor, was the only one with municipal authority to officiate. The three couples being married were: Mabby and Deela-soon-Dabby, Bo and Tufa-dying-to-be-Neebles and, last but indeed greatest, Reverend Wally Ferroule and the trembling former Grandmaster Alfreda Elena Gersteinbach, "Cloudsparrow," Padduck , and imminently Ferroule… "All six of you at once now…Do you?" They very much did. "Well! Unless there is any disagreement, may I pronounce you all respectively, husband, and wife!" Dorma was advised to finish quickly, and the procession began and their platforms raised up to the sky.

Two of the three platforms would have probably been fine, but Bobo was simply too heavy, and little Tufa was no counterbalance. The top began to wobble, and then two squirrels started to lose their grip in the undulation. The whole top suddenly went end up, and they all drifted apart to keep from too many getting dragged down. Bobo, however, was afraid of heights, and Tufa held onto him, knowing he was afraid. They went down together, and he broke her fall.

Tufa shuddered at the nasty gurgling sound, but it was a moment before her nerves would let her unflinch, realizing that she was okay. Her eyes went wide. This felt so familiar. Horrifically, sickeningly familiar. She heard a groan, a groan that she had also heard once before, and she whirled around. Bo was there, underneath a pile of tent poles meant for her, and he was not moving. She could feel the tears welling up as she and several others furiously cleared away the riffraff, and she fell upon him weeping and fearing the worst. His eyes lay closed,

"Not again. Not again, my sweet, sweet, dear husband. Please. Why couldn't you let it be me… why…" And she wept there a while to the dismay of the ceremony guests.

As she wept in silence, a comforting paw came to rest on her back.

"I'm sorry, deary dearest, this seems like a bad time," someone said to Tufa in a voice she barely recognized. "But could anyone tell me where the food is?" She rose on Bo's chest, eyes wide, for it was Bo, come back from the dead and speaking whole sentences!

"I am just terribly, terribly famished."

"Oh, *Snap*dragons!" Syriss said.

Chapter 23: On the Need for not Needing to Feel Too Important.

"So that is the story of why I am here, my little ones.

"As you may be able to tell, it took a long time to write this story out so even I could understand it. What's the moral of it? Well, I don't really tell it to give you a moral. Really, I tell it to give you an *idea."*

"*Teach! Teach!"* A little kit with a shock of red in her otherwise blond tail raised her paw.

"Yes, little Miss Ferroule?"

"So did you and Deela get all kissy-kissy like everyone said in school? Ha Ha!" She laughed, Mabby laughed, they all laughed.

"Well, as a matter of fact, we did!" Mabby said.

"Ewww," the class said. "And you know what else? So did *your* parents, whom I know, and that is why *you* are *my* sister in law! Isn't that crazy? Me, and you? Ha! I mean, how's that for embarrassing!" The whole class laughed hard. Beela sat down, hard.

"But Teacher!"

"Yes?"

"You never said in the story what your secret was!"

He pretended to gasp in shock at this revelation. "You know what, I didn't! Would you like to know the secret of how I finally passed that platform test that, I may mention, you yourselves are about to take soon?"

"Yeah!"

"Nah. I don't think you wanna know…" Mabby shrugged.

"No! Tell us! Tell us! Please, please, pleeeeeee—"

Then Mabby threw up his paws in a maestro's pinch. "You know what you just did?" he asked the class.

"What?"

"It. The thing itself. The secret!"

"Huh? What do you mean?"

"You cared! The secret is…that there is no secret. There is no talent, no special factors, no tricks, no magic. There is only passion. Caring or not caring. That is all. You all, not at the beginning when I was literally begging for your attention, but at the end of the matter when all is known, is that not when you thirst for yet more knowledge?"

They sat looking at him, and one caught himself snoring and snapped awake in his seat, and his eyes popped up while others giggled a little. "Mister Dabby, this is boring, can we go flying?"

"Ah but boredom is the product of an impoverished mind, someone wise once told me." He winked, and the little one groaned and went back to sleep. "Like I was saying. The trick is not in the technical doing of anything but in the process. Tricks just get you to avoid what matters. Tricks are for the foolish, but passion comes to those who endure to understand. It is not that differences don't exist."

They sat motionless.

"The secret is nothing more than the same thing all must do when faced with an impossible task of any kind. When you are tired, nervous, scared, or you just plain think you don't have it in you, you think of the platform at the end. The finish line, and of how much it will matter to you then. There, in that vision, that moment, you will always find the strength you need, no matter how long it takes. The 'trick' is simply to care."

"So if I just care enough, then it will make me fly, like better than everyone?"

"No, that's stupid."

The children gasped.

"I'm saying that…" Mabby was distracted for, at that moment, his father and his wife both showed up outside the classroom door, waving to him with balloons and some large present with a big blue bow.

"I'm, uh, I'm saying that...being able to fly, much less being able to fly better than others is nowhere nearly as important as being good."

They looked confused, rightfully. "So being good at flying is better than being the best?"

"No, I mean being a good squirrel. Flying is fun, don't get me wrong, and it helps us get around, but it's not everything. I said before that we are all here for a reason. Well, everything that you learn here is not just to get you all graduated and moved on. It's for you all to be best equipped to be good. That is truly what it takes to be a hero. It is a trademark of an evil squirrel to think that it is unrealistic to be good. But a good squirrel will hold himself accountable to truth, even if it means losing…his or her wings. Now, sometimes we forget that, indeed, often the whole world forgets that. But it always comes back. It has to."

"What do you mean?"

"I mean that one day, after all this, most of you will go on and start your lives, find occupations, get families and, believe it or not, when that day comes you will deeply value every day you spent here, and you will go and work all day long most days, not just till the afternoon, and you will choose to do it. Why, you may ask? Because of the things you *will* care about. For everything you learn here to make a real difference, is not up to me. It doesn't matter by itself. It's up to you. To keep caring, and keep learning."

"About flying? How much can there be to know?" Said another of the children.

"Oh, loads. Loads about everything! Everything you can.

"My dad said you've got so much knowledge about flying because you had to work so hard at it...because you're an infirm. Is that true Mister Dabby?" Mabby swallowed, for he knew the little one must not have meant it like it was said. "We're all infirms." He said simply. "Knowledge builds to heights without measure, but passion keeps to depths without bottom. And I know one day, win or lose, you'll all make me proud, if with knowledge I have given you that."

Several of them had begun to doze off completely. Then the school's new bell began to ring, whereupon they dashed immediately to the door, nearly dashing each other.

"Anyhow, that's our lesson for today. Now I believe I have a meeting." Mabby stood up, and the children got their bookbags and began to leave. "Goodbye, children. See you tomorrow," Mabby said to each of them at the door, as they took off to their parents and homes.

"Happy birthday!" Dorma and Deela said at the same time.

"You two!" Mabby, with his arms akimbo, pretended to be mad. "What kind of mischief are you up to now?"

"We think you're going to like your present."

Epilogue

"Mabby-babby!" yelled Deela from the kitchen. "Are you ready for dinner?"

"Oh, I was going to try out the present."

"No! Wait, I want to see."

Then Deela came in, laboring over the prominent bump on her belly. Mabby looked at her and said nothing for a moment. "Hey hero." She said.

"Let's be real. I may have brought the cat down, but that was only one action. They say I saved the town, but you saved me. And they saved themselves, really."

"But they needed someone to show them how." Deela said.

"By show of strength? That strength they which they insisted was weakness, and now only accept because it's strength they still value, not truth. I didn't accomplish anything; if I had, they would have seen it wasn't me at all. They only accepted the truth insofar as it helps them win."

"And it helped them win because truth is stronger than the strongest tree." and to that Mabby had no reply.

She hugged him. "I love the way you are. Always."

"I love you too, my dear. Always." Mabby gave his legs a good warm-up stretch. "Are you ready?"

"Do you think it's too soon? Will the stitches hold?"

"They seem a little tight, and kinda sore, maybe," he said somewhat uncomfortably, adjusting himself from inside his robe, "but Dad's the best. He said it ought to hold better with this new thing he's got going. He called it a… zippo. No. Zip-zip, zippy…Zip, something," he said as he played at the attachments a little. Zip, zip, it went smoothly up and down, and he almost winced at the sight of his (now artificial) wing separating from his body. True, they took a lot of the complication out, what with but a tiny strip covering the whole prosthesis. He flared them out, and they felt lighter than air and yet even wider than the old ones. "He always did believe in me," Mabby said. "I shouldn't have given him such a hard time. "

Deela looked at him and hugged him even tighter.

"Thanks, Dad," he said to the air and thought of old Dorma, probably in his shop making some type of spinny whatchamazappit.

Mabby stood up fully and walked out the the balcony of their new house, rebuilt on top of the old one on 16 Tadwick Way, Tankery Bough, that now boasted a landing pad and a library, what with all of the new school materials coming out all the time thanks to Dorma's handy new invention. He looked around to make sure no prying eyes were about and creeping. Then he opened his arms a little at first, hesitantly, and then all the way, and he let out his new prosthetic wings, finely stitched from the finest black feline leather around, shining even in the dawn light courtesy of the best tinker in town. They flowed to the ground, both bigger and lighter than before. "Now, I'm not sure if I'm going to need more lift or not to get started."

"Honey, I'm sure you'll be fine. Stop acting all nervous," Deela said teasingly. She went back to get her robe as the winter months were setting in. Time for the Guardians to go to work, making sure all the stores were safe from pesky outsiders for the duration of the winter for that was all there had been to do for some time.

With that Mabby the Guardian, the champion of his age, stepped off the ledge and into the unbendable, uncontainable wind. And soon the whole of the mountain was below him. There, in the treetops, on the way to the 176th tree from town, emerged two, three, four, then twenty of Syriss

Beethorn's new regiment of youngrels, and Syriss himself with his manner of calling from the flank all squirrels of all ability who could but keep up, by whatever means necessary. The school had been massively expanded what with the aid of its new and most prominent benefactor, Mr. Cal Ballo, who was these days known for saying, "We are given work to make a difference, and money to be kind." Syriss was an excellent leader, and Mabby was glad he had given up the job of pushing squirrels around to someone so more capable. Someone had to take over, after all, and it seemed only right that Syriss should follow in his father's footsteps. Ekkhorn had given his life honorably and without complaint, even when he had succumbed to the battle wounds days after that fight, that already seemed so long ago. Mabby did his best not to think about the pain Old Dog must have been in. Ekkhorn had said Syriss didn't have what was needed. He was wrong. In being totally and completely normal and without deficiency, he in a world of brokenness knew best of all their fate. "Fair winds and following clouds, Syriss Secret-Keeper."

He tightened his wings up and soared off above the trees of Nockshin Wood, vaulting to the clouds and out into the breaking night.

The End.

Other works by M. G. Claybrook:

The Clarity of Fire
Psychocide

...and coming soon, from the world of Mabby the Squirrel's Guide to Flying:

The Voyage of Gethsarade.

I love my readers! If you like my work, you can follow me at:

facebook.com/mgclaybrook

twitter.com/mgclaybrook

matthewclaybrook.com

Or please give my book an honest review on amazon.com. It would be the most tremendous help to me since we writers live and die by our customers' reviews. If you do so, let me know so I can send you a copy of my next book for free! You like my work, I like you, so win, win! Thank you very much.

CPSIA information can be obtained
at www.ICGtesting.com
Printed in the USA
BVHW051214220719
554057BV00025B/1756/P